B E S T
LESBIAN
EROTICA
2003

BEST LESBIAN EROTICA 2003

Series Editor

Tristan Taormino

Selected and Introduced by

Cheryl Clarke

CLEIS
PRESS

Published in the United States by Cleis Press Inc.,
P.O. Box 14684, San Francisco, California 94114.
Printed in the United States.
Cover design: Scott Idleman
Cover photograph: Laurence Jaugey-Paget
Text design: Frank Wiedemann
Cleis logo art: Juana Alicia
First Edition.
10 9 8 7 6 5 4 3 2 1

"LIVE: By Request" © 2002 by Samiya A. Bashir, was originally published on www.kuma2.net. "Venus in Therapy" © 2002 by Betty Blue, was originally published in *Tough Girls: Down and Dirty Dyke Erotica,* edited by Lori Selke (Black Books, 2002). "Wide White Sky" © 2002 by Cheyenne Blue, was originally published on www.mindcaviar.com (Summer/Fall 2002). "Bull Rider" © 2002 by Sacchi Green, was originally published in *Body Check: Erotic Lesbian Sports Stories,* edited by Nicole Foster (Alyson, 2002). "Cop-Out" © 2002 by Rosalind Christine Lloyd, was originally published in *Bedroom Eyes: Stories of Lesbians in the Boudoir,* edited by Lesléa Newman (Alyson, 2002). "How It Started" © 2002 by Mary Anne Mohanraj, was originally published in *Wet: More Aqua Erotica,* edited by Mary Anne Mohanraj (Three Rivers Press, 2002).

TABLE OF CONTENTS

Foreword
Tristan Taormino

Thanks to the Internet, people, places, and things are easier than ever to find. You can locate your high school English teacher, the perfect apartment, or a personalized T-shirt with your pet's picture on it. Type a few words into a search engine, and you're almost there. It's like having access to your own private detective who combs the virtual universe to find what you're looking for.

Each year, I search for unique, surprising, and really hot stories for *Best Lesbian Erotica*. Although erotic writing has become plentiful (thanks in part to the Web), it hasn't necessarily made my job any easier. I'm hunting for new voices, intriguing scenarios, and works of fiction that make my panties wet. I don't want the ordinary, I want the best. I find what the guest judge and I think is the best in handmade chapbooks, at open mike nights, or waiting for me in my post office box. These tales may come from familiar names or unpublished writers, but they are all waiting to be discovered. They want to be found. It's not exactly a hunt for buried treasure, but there are similarities between the process of reading and selecting submissions for this anthology and tracking down a pot of gold. I sift through common, everyday gems, seeking the magic and the heat of an erotic bond captured in words. I feel so lucky when I've found them!

The people who inhabit the tales in this year's collection are engaged in their own compelling searches—for a new lover, a sexy trick, a Daddy, or a secret tryst. Often they seek treasures less tangible: understanding, affirmation, comfort, redemption, revenge. Their private (or sometimes public) erotic reconnaissance missions take them to unexpected places, where unrequited crushes turn into real-life romance and erotic triangles are explored from new angles. They may find a forbidden love, an unlikely connection, or raunchy, uninhibited affection.

Not surprisingly, sex is central to the stories, but it's also a metaphor for what people want, what they need, what they'll risk to get it. Whether it's authentic intimacy, an elusive orgasm, or the adrenaline rush of capturing prey, these characters will put their careers and reputations, their identities and relationships, and their safety and sanity on the line to get it. What fuels both the search and the discovery is longing, attraction, love, lust, and fantasy. Or it may be a darker muse: the smell of fear, a taste for danger, the satisfaction of payback. Not all of them find what they're after. Some discover something entirely different along the way, and the genuine surprise is a turn-on. Others are still looking, left empty-handed and hungry in the end. Dogged pursuit, the glow of gratification, or a lingering, unfulfilled wish are what make these stories so titillating and satisfying. Reading them is like having really good sex. So turn the page, and have at it!

Tristan Taormino
New York City
October 2002

Introduction
Cheryl Clarke

August 14

Amber Hollibaugh, last year's *Best Lesbian Erotica* judge, is a hard dyke to follow. I will try, because I'm proud that Amber and I are still doing the work we were born to do—writing. And here I sit in this almost one year anniversary of 9/11 funk/spunk with a lap full of this year's erotic prose from lesbians. "Erotic Prose"—sounds like a toy company. Yet, as a poet who's often written about the erotic and the sexual, it gives me great pleasure and trepidation to be holding these hard copies, leafing through them, choosing exemplary passages, and laughing out loud at a writer's construction of erotic moments and the way that can change forever the construction of erotic writing and its theorizing. Yes, lesbians always lead in that respect—no respecters of anyone's traditions. Sex is there. Because sex (and gender) are why we are so greatly and perpetually embattled. (In our literature and on the streets.) We homosexuals, transsexuals, bisexuals, bulldaggers, butches, sissies, queers.

August 17

Sex/Gender—whether we practice them or not. Race too.

Plenty of sex, gender, and race here, dear reader. Sacchi Green's "Bull Rider" is exemplary for its interface with all three:

> *I should have tried harder to figure Anneke out. A damned fine rider, in total control of herself and her mount, she was all blonde and pink and white with cool, butter-wouldn't-melt-in-her-mouth self-possession. But a certain Preppy Princess with a long chestnut ponytail and a cute round ass—and delusions of being a world-class equestrienne—had been using up too much of my energy at the time.*

And class—the loud secret in all of our lives.

August 20

I make no other diversity claims about the writers featured on these pages, yet the array of writing styles offered readers of this year's *Best Lesbian Erotica* is indicative of the vitality of both the genre, "lesbian erotica," and those who write it (and want it).

In choosing the stories for this book, I became ever more convinced that place—physical place, cultural place, emotional place—are crucial to lesbian erotica: whether a character is hauling "a collapsible tripod over a hillside in Gilgamesh" in Catherine Miller's "Along a Rocky Hillside"; or serving in the "English court" of Elizabeth I in Julie Levin Russo's "Elizabeth"; or "alternating between galleries of naked women and the lurid, gruesome or bizarre" at the Metropolitan Museum of Art in New York City in Carol Rosenfeld's "Art History 101." Or, again, in the "Amster-god-fucking-*damn*," of Green's hilarious "Bull Rider." Perhaps, we (lesbian writers and readers) want our stories to enunciate place—in the same way we once demanded writers' identities be made transparent so that the experience of our lives is authenticated.

September 10

I am purposely not writing any post-9/11 anniversary poems this week like Billy Collins' poem read before Congress on Wall Street today. A skinny, bald-headed and funny-looking little man. Why aren't we listening to a Guatemalan survivor who got out just before the second tower collapsed? And not Billy Collins, though the poem sounds halfway sincere. But back to the best o' lesbian erotica for 2003. I'm looking ahead and trying to look up—(somebody's skirt).

"'Oh God,' I gasped later, when she plunged three fingers into me. 'Oh God.'" Only the second line of Sharon Wachsler's "The Pitcher," but it kept me reading as the two dyke characters—one a "New York Jew" and the other "an Alabama Baptist"—alternate between the diamond and the bedroom (or rather, the floor of an equipment storage room!) pitching and catching. "I was the catcher, she was the pitcher, the way God intended."

"...we get our drinks and the almost relieved kinda jealousy washes over the face of the b-girl bartender who was trying not to cruise you before i got here. i stand behind your stool, my polished hands hide inside your jacket, between your thighs is just you tonight. good..." Poet Samiya A. Bashir in her lyrical lowercase experimentalese, "LIVE: By Request"— 1,637 words of clit-orality and compression. I want to hear more about "the b-girl bartender" and "those other b-girls." Write on, sister.

In 1977 Adrienne Rich gave the speech, "The Meaning of Our Love for Women Is What We Have Constantly to Expand," to a small group of women who had chosen to separate from the Gay Pride demonstration against Anita Bryant in Central Park. Rich was speaking to the issue of coalitions and alliances, but these erotic narratives take that mandate seriously as well. The writers let us know that lesbianism is more fluid during this wave of feminism, as is the sexual imaginary of lesbian writers (and readers) more fluid—as fluid as the voyeur/actor in a ménage à trois.

Peggy Munson in the "The Edge of Day and Night" evokes "Daddy" as certainly as Sylvia Plath does in her famous poem of the same name and far less stridently. "'Now strip,'" says Daddy, pushing me away. "'Your Daddy wants to come.'"

Yeah, the dance—whether it occurs in the bar, the house party, the club—is still a crucial part of the lesbian lore of the erotic. I was taken with how sexily one or the other figures into many of the stories and must still figure in our lives as lesbians. It's not the alcohol. It's the dance and the possibility of sex. The club—still a site of the erotic. That gives me hope. These writers keep the politics and the art of writing as lesbians vital and sexual. Hey, hey. In "How It Started," set in Berkeley, Mary Anne Mohanraj bears this out:

> *I let my body move to the music, let it carry me over to her. We were dancing alone, a foot or so apart, and then a little closer, a little closer still. That's when her eyes opened—dark green... She smiled at me, slow and lazy, and I slid closer, just an inch or two away from those glorious breasts. Dancing hard, sweat flicking off me as I shook my ass, arms up in the air, arching my back and hoping my breasts looked bigger than they were.*

In Elspeth Potter's "Free-Falling," the triple action occurs in a utopian "Grrltown," the most famous—well, the only—dyke resort in the solar system, where Trixie and Dixie fuck the brains out of the newly "come out" heroine.

September 15
Forty years ago today, the Sixteenth Street Church was bombed in Birmingham, Alabama. Four young black girls attending Sunday school were killed in the blast and two teenage black boys were shot and killed in the ensuing mêlée. And R. Gay's story, "Of Ghosts and Shadows," haunts me today. Set in Haiti, where "the moon burns just as hot as the sun," it is the story of Amèlie, the loved, and Marie Françoise, the lover/narrator, whose mothers "are best friends," whose fathers were "taken away for supporting free elections," and who live in defiance of the proscriptions against love between women. Defiance exacts a high price—in truth and in fiction.

Passing women and trannys people the erotic terrain, like "Troi," in Rosalind Christine Lloyd's "Cop-Out." An ex-Marine, former college hoop all-star, a New York City detective, and black, Troi likes to pass as a man and pick up straight women in hip-hop bars:

Hip-hop clubs were perfect venues for her obsession because the social element was fiercely dark, wild, uninhibited and crowded enough for her to move around freely without inciting any suspicion... The only problem she ever encountered were the down-low, bisexual switch-hitter boys prowling around who correctly detected her on their 'gay-dar', but incorrectly assumed she was a gay man or something even more ambiguous...

And let us never forget what a site of sex is the academy, where the lines are never straight and are sometimes very thin between the sexual and the intellectual. The narrator of "Keeping Up Appearances," Norma, researching, of all things, "lesbian erotica," falls under the tutelage of Professor

Katherine Carlyle, who advises: "Try and develop a mouth fetish. It will make poetry much more fun to read."

Plenty of domination among the best of lesbian erotica, in Kate Dominic's "Cinderella's Shoes," and Tamai Kobayashi's "Egg," for instance.'" In fact, in most of the pieces, the dimension of domination is explored in some way. Strong women love to be told what to do and be made to do it, and lesbians no less so.

These stories are in the world, but also full of visions of how the world can be, might be, will be. They are historical, political, and cultural analogues awaiting the possibilities of future. The best erotic writing by lesbians awaits you. Tune in.

Cheryl Clarke
New York City
September 30, 2002

Cop-Out
Rosalind Christine Lloyd

Troi was into picking up girls at straight clubs. Tonight, her destination was Butter, a hip-hop club in Tribeca.

An ex-Marine and former college hoop all-star, Troi was now a New York City police detective. Her preoccupation with combat and competition defined a quiet but powerfully aggressive demeanor. She kept her 5'10", 160 pound body buffed to masculine perfection with rigorous daily workouts that involved pumping iron with the muscle queens at a gay gym in Chelsea where she matched their workout regimen to achieve similar macho results. Every inch of her was solid, sinuous, rippling muscle.

Her skin was like dark fudge, as rich and even in tone as a sinfully delicious chocolate cake. When she laughed, a mouth full of perfectly spaced teeth framed by thin, silky lips accentuated a smile that ignited the light in her unusually light brown eyes. Her hands were massive: hands designed to palm basketballs, handle heavy artillery and apprehend suspects, among other useful things.

Tonight she opted for a pair of soft brown leather pants

and a suede camel-colored shirt. She had a knack for choosing loose-fitting clothes that enabled her to neutralize any semblance of femininity. Her breasts were almost always held hostage, bound tightly beneath her clothing. She selected one of her larger dildos, the one she'd named Shaft, along with her new leather travel harness. Shaft was handmade, designed precisely to her specifications to include, among other things, a skin tone that matched her complexion. The startling replica even came equipped with a fake foreskin that made it feel that much more authentic. It served its purpose. It set her back quite a lot of money but she quickly discovered it was worth every cent and more. She finished her outfit with her favorite designer square-toe boots (for men, of course), splashed on a men's designer cologne and dared to accessorize with a fat ruby in her left ear and a matching pinky ring for that hint of gangsta.

To throw people off her trail, she would often flash her police badge on her way into the clubs she cruised. Besides being allowed admission at no charge, she avoided being carded. This particular evening, it was obvious that Butter was seriously implementing its ID policy because of the excess crowd of underage kids hanging out behind the ropes, trying to get in.

Hip-hop clubs were perfect venues for her obsession because the social element was fiercely dark, wild, uninhibited and crowded enough for her to move around freely without inciting any suspicion. The carnival feeling reminded Troi of her freaknik college days. Most of the men were typical in their badass attitudes, adhering to the typical negative stereotypes of male posturing, and taking the pessimistic connotations of the music way too seriously. Talk about game—all of this worked in Troi's favor because she offered an *alternative*. Her meticulous, classy, cash-money look attracted the girls' attention every time. The only problem she ever encountered were the down-low, bisexual switch-hitter boys prowling around who correctly detected her on their gaydar, but incorrectly assumed she was a gay man or something even more ambiguous. Troi found these occasions amusing but off-putting. For this reason, using the restrooms, any restroom, was strictly out of the question.

Scanning the club, she easily found her mark; a tall, red bone with the face of an angel dipped in honey, with two long French braids that went down her back tickling a fat, juicy ass squeezed into a cheap, tight, lycra hoochie dress. The slinky fabric stretched and strained against the milk-fed curves of her breeder hips. Her calves, sprung from svelte, golden thighs, were incredibly sculpted in a pair of chic platform ankle boots that had a sci-fi affect: the entire boot, including the heel, was encased in stretched black leather. Troi liked the way they made her calves look. Long and wispy eyelashes like the fringe on a gypsy's shawl draped huge, sensuous eyes. Wearing too much jewelry, she was definitely into "bling-bling". Her nail tips were long, decorated in startling designs and colors; but her tits, piled into a push-up bra, were voluminously for real. Ms. Thing was ghetto fabulous in all its glory.

Troi watched the girl closely, studied her standing at the bar as if waiting for a bus. At least three men asked Braids to dance, but she declined them all. Braids was waiting for Mr. Right. She was waiting for Troi.

Troi sent her a glass of champagne with a shot of Hennessey poured on top (commonly known as thug's gold) and waited for the young lady's reaction. Initially, Braids hesitated with suspicion, refusing the cocktail. But when the bartender pointed at Troi, Braids stared for a moment with those eyes, assessing her admirer before smiling seductively and mouthing the words *thank you* with lusciously burgundy-coated lips. She then proceeded to sip slowly from her glass as if digesting something very precious. Troi would not allow her much time to think, knowing she would have to crank up the charm to get Braids where she wanted her.

Their eyes locked and remained so while Troi slowly walked to the end of the bar, as if she was a pimp strolling along a catwalk. Unable to read anything from the girl's eyes, Troi relied on her feminine intuition, and she felt the adrenaline surge through her. It was the same feeling she got before taking the winning layup shot or the feeling she had during a stakeout—the feeling of victory in enemy territory. Flexing her muscles, she walked right up to Braids, suddenly feeling the aura of heat emitting from the girl's body. This startled Troi for a moment. As if reading Troi's mind, Braids took another sip of champagne. Taking a deep breath, Troi leaned in toward the girl, telling herself not to inhale her whole.

"I can see you appreciate the finer things in life." Troi whispered in her ear, letting her nose brush against the length of her neck for a trace of her scent.

"Is that your best line? Now I know you can come better than that especially when you sending over champagne and everything. What's your name, Mr. Got-all-the-Right-Moves?" The dark pools turned into magnets, drawing Troi in.

"I'm Troi—and what do they call you, Ms. Got-all-the-Right-Moves?"

"If you're nasty."

"Oh, I'm plenty nasty."

"I bet you are. I'm Staci." She sipped from her glass again, her eyes lowering, her comfort level improving.

The dance floor was a virtual free-for-all. No respect was given and every liberty was taken with the feminine gender. The brothers practically mauled the girls alive and the girls appeared to enjoy the attention, but whether this was really the case was another matter altogether. But this kind of atmosphere played in Troi's favor as she gently removed the glass from Staci's hands and led her onto the crowded dance floor.

It was so hot it seemed like everyone was simulating sex.

Staci wrapped her arms around Troi's neck, rubbing herself against Troi's thigh like a puppy in heat. Something was on this girl's mind.

Troi was enamored by the overture and didn't waste any time stroking Staci's back very provocatively and grabbing her ass, positioning Staci so that she was gyrating on the head of Troi's dildo.

"You a big boy, Troi. You could hurt a girl," She purred in Troi's ear.

When Staci stuck her hot, wet tongue into that same ear, Troi wanted to sink her cock right in the ass she held, but she settled for plunging her fingers through Staci's lacy thong and in between her meaty lips.

Staci felt so good riding Troi's dong and fingers, her soft breasts crushed against Troi's bound, puckered nipples. Troi could feel Staci's muscles clench in the palm of her hands. Staci found Troi's lips with her own, forcing them into a kiss so provocative it made Troi's head spin. Sucking tongues, lips, mouths like they were sucking on the world's best-tasting treat, each of them settled into some serious dry-humping, riding the crest of their quivering horniness. Before Troi realized it, the front of Staci's dress was hiked up against her hips and Staci began stroking Shaft through Troi's leather pants: a great big no-no.

Troi reached behind her belt for her handcuffs, and placed them on Staci.

"Am I under arrest, officer?" Staci was unfazed.

"Yeah, I'm taking you into custody." Troi made only a small spectacle leading Staci out of the club in handcuffs. Security and other patrons looked on suspiciously as Troi flashed the badge attached to her belt. Staci loved every minute of the crude public display.

Troi's truck was strategically parked on a secluded side street. Listening to the sounds of their heels clicking against the slick cobblestone street, Troi continued to steer her "assailant" by the cuffs. Her eyes were locked on Staci from behind, while Staci enhanced the view by shifting her ever-ripening ass with every step she took, her calves casting a spell over Troi's mind. They stopped once they reached Troi's jet-black Lincoln Navigator.

"I like your big, black truck." Staci whispered over her shoulder.

"Oh, we'll see just how much you like it." Troi whispered back, gently pressing Staci up against the hood of the truck, the girl's hips and thighs shivering as they met the cold fiberglass.

Staci giggled nervously but obediently spread her legs apart. Troi pushed herself against the her; the girl was built like a gazelle, tall and graceful, with limbs so delicate and fine they seemed breakable. If only Troi could feel those long, thin hands wrapped around her Shaft, it would be a sensual nirvana. If only Troi could watch those burgundy lips wrapped tightly around her Shaft, her strong hips pumping into that burgundy mouth like a piston, she knew she could fall in love. Instead, she would have to settle for the ass, which she exposed to the cool November air, super-tight, lacy, tiger-print thongs encasing two fleshy mounds of delight.

"Cool air couldn't cool this ass off." Troi was kneeling now, her eyes taking in the vision before her.

"But I bet *you* can." Staci's tiny voice grew up in a second, morphing into a mature growl.

Troi sank her teeth gently into the flesh of Staci's right cheek, pretending to gnaw while allowing her hand to reach in between Staci's moist bush— to find that her pussy felt like a hot piece of fruit left out in the sun too long, mushy and sticky, oozing sweet nectar along her fingertips. Staci wiggled around, her breathing getting heavier as she whispered, "Come on, baby. Come on. Tear my shit up. I'm ready for you. You better take this pussy now!"

If this girl said anything else to Troi, she knew it was entirely possible that she could come right there, just by the sound of Staci's voice and her scent, sticky on Troi's fingers and thick in the air. Troi reluctantly refrained from any more finger and oral play. Safe sex between two women felt so unnatural to her, but she could not have sex any other way with any woman, straight, gay or otherwise.

Standing back up, she held Staci down firmly with one hand while the other reached for a condom from her back pocket, ripping the packet open with her teeth.

"What you got for me, Big Daddy?" Staci was writhing now, the handcuffs both restricting and exciting her. As Troi readied herself for the ceremony, steadying them both by shoving a leathered thigh along the slick backside of this hot young thing, Staci began breathing and moaning, as if she had watched one too many porn videos.

Young, "straight" girls really dug Troi's handcuffs. Anything considered freaky and kinky was fashionable. But the handcuffs served a much more important purpose. Troi slid the rubber along the length of Shaft, lubricating the tip with a little of her own saliva before ramming into Staci's hot pussy with a sharp thrust of her hips. Staci went flailing against the hood of the truck while Troi skillfully guided herself deep into Staci's center. They moved together, Troi going in deeper with every forceful thrust, while Staci gyrated against every push, ensuring an easy, slippery fit, full of friction. Her hips swayed and bounced, pushed and pulled, bumped and ground to some mad truncated rhythm in her head and in Troi's pelvis. Troi could have pumped inside of her until the break of dawn, but after the third set of multiple orgasms rocked Troi's body with dizzying episodes of heart-stopping mini-seizures, sweat popping from what felt like everywhere, she had to disengage herself from the girl who had resigned herself to Troi in total submission. Troi had to ignore the girl's desperate pleas for more (they *always* wanted more)—a precautionary measure, as she was always in danger of giving too much away.

The drive to Staci's home in Brooklyn was quiet. These were awkward moments for Troi because nothing would ever come from these encounters. This was just how she liked it, just how she planned things. There was always the mystery of whether any of these women knew the real deal. That was part of the allure. Sometimes in the heat of passion, Troi could testify that it didn't really matter, because she knew she had skills, mad skills. She drove the girls insane with her shit.

With Staci, she had half a mind to leave the handcuffs on until they got to Staci's place, because Staci was all over her.

"I can't believe you're still hard!" Staci kept squealing whenever Troi failed to keep the girl's hand out of her lap.

Troi had half a mind to bend her over the back seat and slip her another heavy dose of Shaft, but Staci was too much into it.

In front of her brownstone, Staci wrote her phone number down.

"Can I get yours?" she inquired.

"Nah, that's not a good idea," Troi replied deliberately, not looking at her. It was all part of the routine.

"Why not?"

"It's not important. Maybe I'll see you again at Butter."

"Damn, it's like that?"

"Girl, if you knew, you couldn't handle it."

"Don't be so sure." Staci smirked, crumpling up her phone number and tossing it into Troi's lap before climbing out of the truck. Troi followed those long sculpted legs up the brownstone stairs with her own pretty, seductive, huntress eyes, before pulling away in her beautiful black truck into the cool November night.

Elizabeth

Julie Levin Russo

I am irresistible. I go where I want and I do what I please because I taught myself early to know my own desire and to live it without apology. I dress like a man. I fuck like a woman. No one confronts me in my sin because everyone finds themselves wanting to burn with me in damnation. Lovers come to me because they know I can teach them the secrets of their own cunts and cocks. But it is rare that I meet someone who understands, like me, how to rule others by *not* fucking them.

This thought occurs to me as I stand poised to enter Elizabeth, the end of my cock slick where it rubs in the juices of her wide-open cunt.

When I first arrived at the English court, Elizabeth was deep in conversation with a lord or advisor I could not identify. Her eyes flicked up once as they registered the unfamiliar grace of my stride, but she showed no other reaction to the presence of another unremarkable foreign nobleman. When I approached her and knelt in front of the throne, she turned, when she was ready, and brooked the ritualized exchange of formal greetings and ring kissing. I don't know when Elizabeth realized I am a woman. And whatever idle, salacious, or bitter talk took place between allies in the maze of back corridors, no one dared to openly defy the Queen's tacit approval. Not for something so little as one more perversion to add to the already well-filled ranks of court intrigue.

I imagine I know what these minions see when they look at me. A young man, dark-skinned and handsome, with black hair that curls around his shoulders, delicate, boyish features, and a slender, broad-shouldered frame. Perhaps they evaluate a bit, and judge me a charming recluse who laughs easily and speaks little. Perhaps instead they listen to my voice, which can silence a room, or pool in the hearer's stomach like the heat of desire. Quiet, deep, touched with a rich accent and the hint of a threatening purr, it is unmistakably a woman's voice. Whatever they saw or heard, the ladies at court flirted with me only slightly more than they did with any appealing newcomer, and I flirted back slightly less than a man would have. I was commanding and inscrutable, and a few of them started trailing in my wake, a sort of coy, feminine flotsam. I followed Elizabeth.

Seduction is more demanding than sex, but I didn't choose this life because I appreciate things that are easy. I could spend into any cultivated lady-in-waiting who thinks she's found a clever way to give up her maidenhead and keep her purity, but that is a shallow, dishonest pleasure. As dishonest as the life I was born into. And a dangerous extravagance, since my pleasure is always a transgression. I've learned to recognize the women who want what I am and not what I am not. I know a woman who wears a cock under her skirts when I see one, who rules the men around her by the set of her hips and not by the flutter of her eyelashes, but I've never seen anyone do this as breathtakingly as the Queen. She shuts her body into a shroud and then uses the mystery of it as a snare to capture those around her. Elizabeth has learned the secret of her own power, and there are only two kinds of people she would let inside her: a man more woman than she is, or a woman more man than she is. I was smitten.

I know Elizabeth's mind, or I tell myself I do. I frighten her, and that is why she tolerates my presence. There are precious few things that inspire terror in her now—she's already excised that part of herself. She's as precise as a surgeon too in the way she keeps her house, and she watches her retinue operate. I know when to cut across the room to put my hand on the back of her chair as she rises, which garden she'll be walking in at noon, and how to defer with my words while I challenge with my eyes. All this is conventional. But I am more than a lord (or less than a lady), and from me obsequiousness is less than respectful and solicitude is more than flattery.

When I passed her in the hall one morning and bowed irreproachably low, without taking my eyes from hers, she no longer knew the anatomy of the gesture. The anxiety of the undissected knotted itself into her stomach, and she finds this anxiety a rare and cherished source of amusement. So she stopped, stifling her rising laugher at my subtle audacity, and held out her ring to be kissed. I turned her hand and pressed my lips to the exposed sliver of skin at the inside of her wrist.

It is a remote stretch of corridor where the Queen often walks at the same time of day, in the same solitude, toward her customary visit to the chapel. Suitors have surprised her here—she encourages it. But my surprises are of a different character. She rounded the corner to see the tailored lines of my back curved into the shadow of an alcove. Curved, in fact, against the milky bosom of one of her high-ranking ladies-in-waiting. The wanton was pinned to the marble at her center by my dark thigh, and my hand caught both of hers above her head. Waves of red-gold hair fell loose around her shoulders. I sank my teeth into the sweet flesh below her ear, and she stretched out her throat and moaned voluptuously. Elizabeth saw her face. It was the perfect image of her own desire. She looks like that now, her skin flushed and glowing with a sweaty sheen, her hair fanned about her head like a crown of flame. But Elizabeth stares me down with her eyes wide open.

Making love and keeping your virginity is primarily an act of will. Elizabeth's pleasure is no part of her power, and she need only divide herself to free it. She has two bodies, and one is an illusion. Soon after her coronation, she had a portrait of herself painted, and prominently hung. It is all surface: the rich brocade of her extravagant gown fills the panel, glittering with jewels and gold filigree. Her white face and hands are tiny islands in the splendor, remote and pure. In life, the Queen plays the portrait. Its sacred surface is her maidenhead, and it will be eternally unbreached. When her subjects look at her, they see what she wants them to see—even her lovers. Elizabeth knows that everyone thinks about undressing her; she arranges it that way. Every excess of embroidery, every elaborate wig and enormous farthingale, tells the story of how she withholds her body like she defends England: strategically. But the body the masquerade invites them to imagine is not the body I'm about to slide my cock into.

When the Queen came upon my seduction in the hall, she swept by as if impervious. But that afternoon, I was summoned to her presence by one of her pinch-lipped sycophants. She is always direct.

"What were you doing with our lady?"

"With all respect, your Majesty, I believe that was perfectly clear."

"On the contrary, the immodest nature of your assignation was apparent. However, what you were doing, or rather what you were going to do, is not at all clear to me." Her back was to her functionaries, and she glanced speculatively at my codpiece.

"My Queen, I meant no harm or discourtesy to the lady or to your illustrious self."

"You are too bold."

"Yes, your Majesty."

"What do you think Constance wanted from you so desperately that she would openly risk my displeasure?"

I coughed demurely. "What any woman wants, I suppose, who is not chaste. Will you punish her?"

"And what do you want, then?"

"I want what any man wants."

"But you, your Grace, are not any man."

"You do too much honor to one who vexes you."

"You vex me and you intrigue me. How do you intend to make amends for your appalling behavior?"

"I do not flatter myself to think that my humble person is worthy to attend so magnificent a Queen. But if there is any service I can perform that would be acceptable to your Highness, it would be my most ardent desire to render it."

The underlings had the grace to hide their distress.

After dusk, there was a faint knock at the outer door of my modest chambers. It was my little wanton, who threw her arms around me and peppered my cheeks with kisses as soon as I had secured the entrance.

"You have found favor with the Queen?" I asked her, amused by the display. I found her lips, and tried to snake my hand through an opening in her skirts. She danced away from me, smiled coyly, and fished a folded leaf of paper out of her bodice.

"I can't stay," she purred, and slipped out with a lewd caress.

The note was from Elizabeth.

The guards and servants were conspicuously absent from the Queen's apartments and the castle still, apart from the midnight sputtering of torches, when I showed myself in as instructed. Elizabeth was seated regally in a monstrous chair, her gown billowed around her. She watched impassively as I approached and, in a carnal parody of our first decorous meeting, knelt to kiss her ring. I held her hand against my breath for a moment, and then she turned it, and ran her fingertips along the arc of my jaw to my hairline. She pulled on the knot at the nape of my neck, and my black curls fell soft into her palm. Tracing her way along the skin of my throat to the fastenings of my tunic, she slackened the ties until I could shrug it off my shoulders. Her eyes were dark against mine as her touch discovered the slight rise of my breast through the linen shirt, as her fingertips pressed roughly into the resilient flesh, and then found the peaked punctuation of a nipple to tug at. She smiled savagely and watched me struggle not to press myself into the contact. Then she dropped her gaze as she undid the buttons to reveal the chest of a woman, studying my swarthy, pointed breast, and laying her hand over it so that it filled her palm. She traced the outline of my lips, and I opened my mouth to lick at her fingers. Sliding them in deep so I was sucking, she spoke: "Show me."

I stepped back, my shirt still hanging open, and posed for her with my hips cocked arrogantly. Then I unfastened the front of my breeches and let the firm, cylindrical leather phallus spring out. It is ingenious and lovely, nearly seamless and worn buttery smooth, and Elizabeth stood up to appreciate it with genuine curiosity. She wrapped her hand around it and stroked it, and then slid her palms down my hips so that my breeches fell, and the straps that attach my cock to me were revealed. She laughed at me a little, when she saw the harness, and I snarled and pulled her hard against my body, clawing into the exposed swell of her breast, and kissing her bruisingly. She opened her mouth to the assault, biting at my tongue as it filled her. I gentled and licked over the inside of her lips, and then shifted my attentions to her ear, so I could rasp my words into it:

"You want the secret of my body? Then let me show you the secret of yours. If I'm a woman under my clothes, then so are you."

She shoved me away with her forearms, leaving only my fingers hooked under her bodice, and we stared at each other, panting. I took another step back, giving her space to strip for me. She removed her wig first, and set it on a dressing table, and then she pulled pins from her hair until a thick coppery coil fell free. I stood behind her and hefted its weight, burying my face in it. It smelled of oil and sweat. "The laces," she directed me, and I helped her begin the laborious process of extricating herself from her gown, corsets, farthingales, petticoats, and collars. It was more ritual than seduction, but with each vestment draped heavily over a chair, I could feel more of the heat of her skin slipping under the harness to swell me. I fondled the arcane and alien under things like she'd stroked my cock, letting her watch me rub them against my lips, my nipples, my crotch. With each layer she peeled away, her jaw clenched tighter with desire. Last was a modest shift, which she pulled over her head in one graceful and lascivious gesture. Elizabeth was naked.

I know how to give it to a woman, but I can't say I've ever fucked a Queen. I spread her out on her back at the edge of the bed, and she held her own knees to open herself. Her skin is freckled, and the russet marks dust the curves of her breasts down to her nipples, which are long and slightly off-center. She is too thin, and her ribs and hipbones cast dark shadows. A line of long hairs trails up the inside of each thigh to a thick auburn bush, now split and showing its slick red center. She is all flesh, all sweaty and pale and bruiseable, and the transformation arrests me. I am standing and leaning over her, the end of my cock our only point of contact. Looking at her, in a dizzy spiral of contemplation, I realize I'm afraid that if I touch her the impossible beauty of my triumph will vanish.

Impatient with my reverence, Elizabeth stares straight at me, arches her back, and says, "Fuck me" in a tone that makes it an order and not a request.

My cock throbs, overriding my meditation, and I use the sudden weakness in my knees to thrust forward, half burying myself in her. Both of us gasp. I can feel her muscles sucking me. Then I'm talking to her.

"You want me to fuck you, open you up so wide my cock will show on your face, get in you so deep you'll always feel me there...."

She fists my hair and yanks me onto her, mauling my mouth. My cock goes in hard and I grab a handful of flesh at her hip, digging in my fingernails, and start pounding. I try to bite her everywhere, leaving brutal marks along her shoulder and around her nipple. She bites me back, levering herself to meet my thrusts with her heels on my ass. Both of us are so wet our thighs slide against each other, and I slap harder against her cunt to make up for the lack of friction. It's too soon to come, so I slow down, feeling her close and open around me by excruciating inches, and watch her grit her teeth and ball her fists on my shoulders. Pushing in as deep as I can, I make small fast movements that shine my clit, and she keens and reaches between us to rub herself. I hold myself up with my arms so I can see her fingers in her cunt, circling as she swells, my cock splitting her just below. My hips start slamming in time to her strokes, and then I hit a spot that makes her scream. I punch it over and over; her brow furrows, every muscle goes taunt, she yells curses and comes exquisitely. When I feel her clamp down on me, I shove in violently, bracing my clit against her bucking hips, and spend into Elizabeth.

We end up sprawled in the middle of the bed, my breath cooling her throat. She hums quietly against my temple. Then she rolls me over and crouches between my legs.

"Can you take it off?" she asks impishly, fondling my

cock. I grin and loosen the straps so I can remove my legs from the harness. She leans close to examine my cunt, parting its folds and playing in the juices still trickling out. Then she plucks the cock from my hands, studies it for a moment, and starts putting it on. She kneels over me, her hair cascading down onto my stomach, cock resting between my breasts, and tells me imperiously "I will fuck you, milord." I would laugh, but desire is too heavy in my gut.

She puts her face beside mine, pets my sides, and speaks low and exactingly.

"I imagine you are many things to many lovers, like a snake who sheds its skin for each new season. Tell me, have you ever been a sodomite?" She reaches for my sex, but slides her fingertips down through the wetness to my asshole. I groan, and turn under her so I'm face down. She keeps stroking the sensitive pucker delicately until I'm rubbing against the bed in a delicious torment.

"Well, what do you answer? Have you seduced young boys, fresh-faced and tender as women, and penetrated them? Have you given in to one of my noblemen who look at you so darkly?"

Now, one of her hands holds my cheeks apart as her fingers push into me, slick with cunt-juices. I'm breathless. "I've fucked boys, but this sin I have never tasted."

"You're my boy tonight, and I will have you."

My legs are spread around her knees. Her cock feels immense as it opens my ass, and I try to shift away from it. She holds me down with kisses on the back of my neck. I burn, and then, as she moves minutely, I ignite, my skin and muscles finding the pleasure. I bend my head and arch into her, and she growls and grabs a handful of curls, riding deeper along the stretched and secret flesh with each clinging thrust. Finally, the tip stabs some interior joint nucleus of my clit and my spine, and my cunt clenches on the bliss as if I were filled everywhere. The Queen's cock is inside me.

Much later, Elizabeth and I lie together under the coverlet in a tangle of limbs. "I want to have your portrait painted," she says, scratching along my collarbone with her fingernails. "I want you painted in a doublet the color of blood, looking like a handsome mystery, with the fold of a dark cloak obscuring your nether parts. I want to hang you in my gallery."

I roll onto her, letting her feel my weight, and answer her. "I want to take you in your gallery, your Majesty. I want to fuck you naked on the cold marble, while we watch ourselves from the walls, and smile."

Luck of the Irish
Kyle Walker

"Thanks for coming," Alan told Mari. "I *have* to go, but I'm *not* looking forward to it, and you're better at saying something nice than I am."

He picked up their tickets at the box office of the Off-Broadway theater, and an usher guided them to excellent seats. When Mari commented on that, Alan shook his head: "Good seats to see a bad show." His boyfriend was doing the costumes for *Star of Delight*.

Mari thumbed through her playbill and spotted a name that gave her heart an odd twist.

"Brigid Flanagan? Is that the one who was on tv…?

"Some old show before I was born," Alan said. "Back in the '60s or something…"

" 'Cowboys and Girls,' " Mari finished. "I *loved* that show. Well, I loved Brigid Flanagan…."

"I think I saw it on 'Nick at Nite,' " Alan said.

Mari had seen Brigid Flanagan in her dreams. From the time she was eight until she was twelve, her Friday nights were reserved for "Cowboys and Girls," a drama set in post-Civil

War Wyoming, following the stories of a strong, beautiful matriarch (played by '40s movie star Molly Webster), her brood of daughters, and the cowboys on her ranch. Brigid Flanagan played Maeve, the Irish cousin.

Each week, Mari waited for Cousin Maeve's scenes, fascinated with the way her auburn ringlets spilled down her back, how she clung to the horse and rode like the wind for Doc when someone broke his leg, or got bit by a snake.

In hindsight, Mari realized it wasn't a very good show, though Molly Webster had brought a level of dignity to her part, and Mari's fascination with Brigid Flanagan had taken her on quite a journey. She began to write stories about herself and Cousin Maeve in a secret notebook, adventures in which they got lost in the mountains together, or left the ranch and went to San Francisco (even at that age, Mari knew she was destined for the big city).

She rehearsed the stories each night as she fell asleep, and woke one morning from a dream in which Brigid Flanagan had smiled at her, and they had begun to kiss. In the dream they'd kissed until Mari felt herself beginning to throb. She woke from the dream and reached down to touch herself, and found her fingers were wet.

At her all-girl school, the general opinion was that boys could masturbate, but not girls (if anyone had discovered otherwise by the sixth grade, they hadn't shared it). Mari wondered if a girl could turn into a boy. She wished she could be one, so she could kiss Brigid Flanagan. The dream disturbed her for weeks, and she watched the show with a strange feeling of guilt.

She became fascinated with all things Irish, not a bad thing at a Catholic school. Her knowledge of saints, poets and playwrights drew her toward Irish Studies in college, and her senior thesis on Boadicea, the warrior queen, got her high honors and a fellowship from a Hibernian society to graduate school.

Nearly two decades into her life as an editor, she wondered what career she might have had if she'd sublimated a crush on one of the Brady girls instead.

The lights dimmed and the play began. As soon as Brigid Flanagan walked onstage, Mari's critical faculties ceased to operate. She was twelve again, sitting too close to the tv, enthralled by the Irish beauty. Brigid's voice was lower than it had been in 1968, but still clear and lilting; she appeared to have aged gracefully. Her still-excellent figure was shown off by the beautiful costumes.

She played an Irish mother whose adult daughter was visiting from the United States. The mother wanted the daughter to move back, an old beau of the daughter's tried to start things up again, and there were other events about as predictable and interesting as a fairly good television movie.

According to Alan, the playwright wrote for a popular tv series. Mari was touched by her heartfelt but misplaced desire to write for the stage. She thought up some nice things to say if they went backstage, which she desperately hoped they would.

In the second act, Brigid had one excellent scene that almost transcended the work. Mari was glad to find out that her first love had been someone with real talent; she'd briefly worried that the flesh-and-blood actress might not measure up to the memories. Mari found herself swamped again by all the powerful feelings that had swept over her each week.

She leapt to her feet and applauded at the curtain call as Brigid bowed. "Do you want to go back?" Alan asked.

"It would be polite," Mari said.

Backstage, Mari told Alan's boyfriend his costumes were fabulous, and met the playwright; she commented favorably on the production, and how much she'd liked Brigid's performance. Zoey put her hand to her heart:

"She's my guardian angel! I met her a couple years ago when she did a guest spot on our show. I'd always loved her...you remember, from 'Cowboys and Girls'...." Mari gave the playwright a sharp look. "I was obsessed with that show; it turned me into a writer, I swear! When I finally met her, she was just as gracious as she could be; she encouraged me to write this play."

It hadn't occurred to Mari that Brigid might have had that effect on anyone else. Perhaps they were all picking up on a little something?

"She and her husband were so good to me," Zoey went on, derailing that train of thought. "They were devoted to each other until he died. When I got married, I told my husband I wanted us to be like them."

Finally, Brigid emerged from her dressing room, tying the ribbons of a broad-brimmed hat.

"Would anyone like to grab a bite?" Zoey asked. "Brigid?" She took the actress's hand and led her over. "This is Mari Myers, an editor at a publishing house here. She saw the play and said *very* nice things about you."

"An editor, is it?" Brigid replied, putting her hand on Mari's arm. "Well then, you must publish something this girl writes. She's very talented, my Zoey."

Mari had had the experience of meeting people she'd admired, and had learned how not to frighten them. Still, it took all her discipline not to leap on Brigid, sobbing *I LOVE YOU I LOVE YOU.*

"I was just telling Zoey how much I liked your work in that last scene, Ms. Flanagan," she said. "I was one of your many fans from 'Cowboys and Girls,' and it was gratifying to see you again."

"Please, call me Brigid," the actress said with an inviting smile. "I always tried to do my best, even though the show wasn't a *critical* favorite."

"I can't imagine you doing any less," Mari replied.

"That's grand to hear at this stage of the game," Brigid said.

"Have you ever thought of writing a memoir?" Mari asked, happy she had a profession that made it appropriate to ask such questions.

"I'll take my secrets to the grave!" Brigid swore with a wink.

"Well, I've got to run," Zoey said. "Do you want to come to dinner? Or can I drop you?"

"No, dear, thanks for the offer," Brigid demurred. "And you're on the West Side and I'm on the East...."

"I'm on the East Side, too," Mari said. Alan had already disappeared with his costume designer and she'd have to find her own way home. "Perhaps we can share a cab?"

It was a glorious spring day, and when they emerged from the theater, Brigid asked Mari if she minded walking. "It's hard to find people in Los Angeles who've heard of such a thing. They'll run for miles on treadmills, but here, you can actually get from place to place on your own two feet."

"Walking is one of my favorite things about New York," Mari told her. "I would miss it if I lived anywhere else."

"Oh, California has its compensations," said Brigid. "Beautiful weather, beautiful scenery, beautiful boys and girls." She put her arm through Mari's in the European manner. Mari saw herself bending Brigid back into a passionate kiss, and focused on saying something that wasn't: *YOU! ME! HERE! NOW!*

"I lived in New York when I first came over," Brigid continued. "So exciting: you'd do stage, and television and radio all in the same week. But I went out to Hollywood for a screen test, and never came back."

"It's good to have you here now," Mari told her.

"Especially in the spring, when everything is coming back to life."

"Like me," Brigid said. "I needed to get away for a bit...I haven't been myself since Max died...my husband. I can't believe it was almost three years ago. Heart attack."

"I lost my...soul mate about then," Mari told her. "We learn to live with it, but I don't know that we ever get over it." Presumably Brigid knew plenty of gay people, but Mari wasn't sure how out she could be to a woman of her age and background.

"We were lucky to have loved, and been loved, weren't we?" Brigid said.

Mari invited Brigid up for a cup of tea, and Brigid seemed happy to accept.

"I don't really know anyone here anymore," she said as they entered Mari's building. "We had a wide circle of friends, and traveled quite a bit, but my husband was my favorite companion. I still know a lot of people in the business," she added. "But they seem to speak a different language. And they don't talk about anything but work."

"Oh, I've got opinions on everything," Mari said lightly as they ascended. "Some are even based on fact. I'd be happy to discuss how I think the world should be run."

"Careful," Brigid said. "That's how people got black-listed."

"Now *that* was before your time..." Mari began.

"Bless you, dear," Brigid replied with a brilliant smile. "I was a slip of a girl when I got to Hollywood in 1959, but they still talked about the blacklist, and the careers it ruined; Hollywood was, and is, very much a place where you keep your mouth shut, and the smart ones keep their business as private as possible."

Mari's apartment was bathed in the late afternoon light, and Brigid went to the window that faced the river.

"Oh, what a grand view!" she said.

"It's even better from the bedroom," Mari replied, delivering another mental kick to herself.

"May I?" Brigid asked.

As long as you let me join you....

"Of course," Mari replied out loud. "I'll just start the tea...."

She busied herself boiling the water and selected some teas, then felt her face to make sure she wasn't still blushing. She found Brigid in the living room inspecting her mementos.

"Is this your departed soul mate?" she asked, gently picking up Mari and her partner Darby's reception photo.

"Yes. What kind of tea would you like?"

"What do you have?" Brigid asked, replacing the photo.

Lesbian tea! Crushed out, woman-loving tea that I would like to lick from your lips.

"Umm...green tea, Earl Grey, Constant Comment...What do you like?" Mari held out the packets.

"What do *you* like?" Brigid asked, moving closer.

Mari selected the Constant Comment and managed, "How's this?"

"I like it very much," Brigid replied, taking the bag. She inhaled deeply. "The aroma brings back memories of a love affair I once had."

"I guess that's why they call it sense memory," Mari said. "There goes the kettle. I'll get the teapot."

"Take a good deep breath!" Brigid declared, thrusting the bag under Mari's nose. Mari knew what moment the smell of Constant Comment would take her to from now on.

They shared some shortbread with the tea, licking their lips for the last sweet crumbs.

"You missed one," Brigid said. "Here..." she took the bit of cookie from Mari's lip on her fingertip. Her tongue darted out and licked it. "What an intimate ritual. Max and I made it a point to have tea at least once a week."

"Darby wasn't much for tea, but she always had a cup of coffee with me," Mari said. "I miss that, as much as the other intimacy. It's so nice when your lover is also your good friend."

"Max was my husband, and my good friend, but he wasn't my lover," Brigid said. "We *did* love each other, though, make no mistake about that."

Mari said nothing. She'd long ago learned that not asking questions was one of the best ways to keep someone talking.

"Max and I were very well matched," Brigid recalled. "Molly Webster introduced us. She taught me the rules of Hollywood."

Mari had seen some of Molly Webster's movies; she played gun molls and dames of the sort who would take a bullet for their man. She'd married at least once, though some books mentioned her as one of the "Sewing Circle" of glamorous Hollywood lesbians.

"Now *there* was a fine actress," Mari offered. "You couldn't take your eyes off her when she was on the screen."

"Or in person," Brigid said. "That one knew how to get a girl's attention. Invite you to lunch in her dressing room, offer to coach you in a difficult scene."

"Would you care for an after-tea cocktail?" Mari offered.

"How is your martini, my dear?"

"Not good," Mari confessed. "I do a better gin and tonic." "Well then, g-and-t it shall be!" Brigid giggled. " I don't often imbibe anymore," she confided. "Bad for the skin and my tongue gets loose. I never know *what* I'll say, or where I'll put my hands!" Mari poured a hefty slug of gin into a glass, and sprinkled in a drop of tonic, floating a lime on top.

They clinked their glasses, and Brigid took a long sip.

"Here's to old fans and new friends. And what's yet to come!"

"Hear, hear," Mari agreed. Brigid grew serious. Mari allowed herself to see the age that Brigid was fighting tooth and nail. There were crow's-feet by her eyes, and her jawline was not as firm as it had been. Her lip line had shrunk, and she'd filled it in, and tried to conceal the lines around her mouth. Still, her skin was fair and unblemished, and not pulled taut. Her auburn hair, several shades darker than Mari's, was full and soft and fell around still-classic cheekbones. Mari thought she was more beautiful than ever.

"There was a time, you know, when one's career could be destroyed at the whisper of a scandal. The studio could make sure you never worked again."

"It's not like that anymore, is it?" Mari asked.

"Hollywood is still the biggest closet of them all," Brigid told her. "I suppose you find that appalling."

"Who am I to judge?" Mari said. "Am I here to hurt people? Or to let them be, and maybe try and make things better?"

"Spoken like a true Catholic schoolgirl!" Brigid said.

"Bless the dear sisters..." Mari said. "Some were *so* lovely."

"Isn't that what gets us into trouble?" Brigid said, almost to herself. "A kind eye, a soft hand...a sweet voice and a spiritual nature...the next thing you know, you're sent home from school and told not to come back."

"You went far away," Mari observed.

"What else was there for it? To be a town pariah in the bog-end of Ireland? Marry some lout to prove I could drop babies like a normal girl?" Brigid took another sip of her drink. "I went to London...that's where the fallen women were supposed to go!"

"How did you survive?" Mari asked

"Quite easily, really!" Brigid said with a grin. "I was a pretty thing!"

"Beautiful, you mean," Mari said.

"Thank you, sweetheart. A pretty girl can go far, and if she keeps her wits about her, she needn't end up being taken advantage of. Dear, would you freshen my drink?" Mari did, noting that Brigid had a way of making her requests seem like she was bestowing a favor.

"I got work as a model for art classes," she said. "The pay was good, and the boys and girls wanted to take me out. The boys spent pots of money trying to get me into bed, the girls were more gentle and seductive. And once you meet artists, you start meeting writers and actors and all sorts of interesting types...."

"Sounds like a lovely time," Mari said appreciatively. If she'd had a clue about herself before she was in her `30s, she would have picked off a few young women writers, instead of just falling in love with their work.

"At first, I kept thinking of what the nuns had taught me, what my family would say, but somehow I was able to put it behind me. Why should I put any stock in anything they said when it made me so unhappy?"

"You're a wise woman," Mari said. "I bought into it for many more years."

"Then be thankful that you eventually found out what you needed," Brigid said, laying her hand on Mari's arm again. This time she left it there.

Mari wanted to kiss Brigid, but stopped herself. Brigid was someone to be wooed delicately. A sudden lunge would put her off. Mari rather liked sudden lunges, but she would have to adjust to Brigid's tempo. The charge building between them was exhilarating.

Brigid brushed a lock of hair off Mari's forehead. "You look like you were going to say something," she commented.

"Did you have some kind of plan for what you would do?"

"I'm by nature a careful girl," Brigid replied. "Not that I'm cowardly," she added. "But while I was gathering rosebuds, I knew I needed a future. One girl took me to her acting school, and I met the head, who was a dear, loving woman, and I began to learn how to live, onstage and off. I felt so good and free when I was acting...." She ran her hands through her hair, and slipped out of her shoes. "How glorious to speak the Bard or O'Neill, or find the good bits in even a bad play, and make people pay attention and think."

"I love artists," Mari said with a sigh.

"Lots of people do," Brigid replied. "My teacher had a circle of influential friends, and got me seen for things, but I got the parts myself, on talent. It worked well for us both. She took care of me, and my success enhanced her reputation."

"Did you love her?" Mari asked hesitantly.

"I was never with anyone I didn't love," Brigid said, not offended. "I couldn't do that. I would find something loveable about them. I was only ever with someone I cared for."

"I'll bet you're a very good friend," Mari observed.

"I am," Brigid agreed. "If anyone has been good to me, I don't forget it. That much of the nuns' teaching remained... though I'm not sure Sister Mary Joseph would have been able to see it without fainting dead away!"

They giggled a bit too much, and Mari realized they ought to eat something, or risk passing out. She offered to make dinner.

"I'm pining for a home-cooked meal," Brigid said. "Max did the cooking, and I'm not the least bit talented that way."

"My repertoire isn't vast, but I can whip up an omelet...."

"My dear, you could be a professional chef!" Brigid declared a few minutes later. "May I?" she reached to Mari's plate and speared a mushroom.

"Let me..." Mari said, holding out a forkful. Brigid steadied Mari's hand with her own, and licked the fork.

"Inspired..." she said.

"I'm inspired, all right," Mari replied.

"I was hoping you might be," Brigid said, folding her napkin.

Mari pulled out Brigid's chair. As she rose, Mari gently brushed her neck with a kiss. Brigid's fair skin colored prettily, her eyes sparkled.

"I thought you might...you're very...subtle," Mari said, blushing again.

"One has to be," Brigid said, looking away. "One might want something very much, but you have to think of the risk...."

Mari suddenly realized the effort it must have taken Brigid all those years to try to find love without losing everything else. Mari knew some of her friends would scorn anyone like that as a coward and a liar. *Maybe I wouldn't have done what she did*, Mari thought. *But she's the one who had to live with her choices, and it does neither of us any good for me to turn away, and anyway I don't want to.*

"You can do and say anything, and none of it will come back to hurt you," she told Brigid.

Brigid moved into Mari's embrace, and nestled between her breasts. Mari liked being tall, and loved the feel of her arms encircling a woman, holding her, kissing the top of her head, feeling lips so close to her nipples. She kissed Brigid's upturned face, her eyelids, the tip of her nose, then a gentle brush across her lips. She was rewarded with a ragged sigh.

"Again, please," Brigid whispered. Mari complied, as bits of the stories she'd written so long ago flashed into her head. She was the passionate, ignorant adolescent, and the character she'd made up for herself in the stories was having an adventure with cousin Maeve; no, she was a grownup of deeper, more informed lust kissing a beautiful woman, who happened to be an actress, who played the first woman she'd fallen in love with, who was kissing her in her apartment in New York City later in the same lifetime.

She bent Brigid back in the kiss she'd been coveting all day. Brigid twined her arms around Mari's neck and threw back her head after their lips parted, leaving Mari to suck and bite her neck.

"Careful…I have a show on Tuesday," she murmured.

"Of course," Mari replied between nibbles. "I'll only bite the parts of you that are covered!"

"You're a thoughtful girl," Brigid sighed. "I want to *feel* something…."

"Trust me, you will," Mari said, leading her to the bedroom.

Mari's hands caressed the silk of Brigid's blouse, unzipped her crisp linen skirt; she was delighted to discover Brigid wore a garter belt and stockings. Brigid unclasped her bra, turning her body away. Mari could see her steeling herself, caught a glimpse of uncertainty, could almost hear Brigid think: *Am I pretty enough? Am I too old?*

"My, what beautiful legs you have, said the Big Bad Wolf," Mari purred as she shed the last of her own clothes. She rubbed her cheek on the silk stocking over Brigid's inner thigh. She licked the exposed flesh between the top of the stockings and Brigid's panties. She laid her body along Brigid's, touching their nipples together. She felt the wetness of Brigid's pussy. Brigid clung to her and rubbed her crotch hard against Mari's thigh.

"Do you have a cock? A big one to ride me with?" she asked hopefully.

"How big?" Mari reached under the bed for her toy bag. She pulled out a large black one that barely fit into the harness.

"Ooh! That's lovely," Brigid said. "Then, if you like, I can use it on you!" Mari laughed with delight.

She pulled the harness on and the dildo bobbed jauntily at her crotch. She'd never been able to decide whether she was more turned on by seeing a woman wearing a cock, or being that woman. Brigid went down on it, and Mari swore she could feel Brigid's lips on her actual flesh; she thrust forward as Brigid's head moved faster and faster. Her nipples stood erect as Brigid's hands stole upward to squeeze them.

She pulled the cock from Brigid's mouth and said: "I need to go in you."

"I like it from behind," Brigid told her. Her pink ass rose in the air as she thrust it upward, and Mari bent down to kiss and bite her cheeks. She ran her tongue to where Brigid's pussy began, smooth and hairless. It was quite wet, and Mari heard her mutter: *Please, yes, I'm ready....*

She guided the head of the cock into Brigid's pussy and held it for a moment, until she felt Brigid relax, then thrust it in slow and deep, guiding herself by the hard, almost relieved moans she heard, until she was deep inside.

"Ah, yes...so good," Brigid murmured. "So long...oh ride me..."

Mari pushed harder, until she was slamming into Brigid, She draped herself over the other woman, squeezing her breasts, biting her neck.

"More...more...harder!" Brigid sobbed. She suddenly breathed in through clenched teeth and fell silent. Mari could feel her orgasm, like the ocean, first drawing back, then crashing to shore. She felt her own heart beating fast, as hard as Brigid's. She gently slipped out, and Brigid slumped to the bed, eyes closed, glistening.

Mari took Brigid in her arms, and kissed her, babbling words of love and comfort. She was surprised at how undone she was, how much it had meant.

"Oh, lovey, that was brilliant," Brigid said, nuzzling Mari's neck. She licked the sweat from Mari's breastbone. "I haven't come like that in...too long." Mari grasped the dripping dildo. She ran her finger along its length and brought it to her mouth, Brigid's tongue twining with hers as she tasted the come.

"What else do you have in your bag of tricks?" Brigid asked, reaching for the toy bag. She looked through the collection of dildoes, vibrators, collars, butt plugs, and other items. She selected a strand of blue silicon beads, graduated in size. "Do you enjoy a little something up the bum?"

"I'm a backdoor girl," Mari admitted.

"And here's a wee pot of lube," Brigid said. She coated the beads, and Mari grew hot watching her. Brigid knelt before her, as Mari spread her legs. With her little finger, Brigid gently began to probe Mari's anus. Mari relaxed and let the finger slide in, and soon felt the smallest of the beads entering her. Brigid crooned as she guided them in slowly, gently. She lowered her face and Mari could feel Brigid blowing on her clit, which stood hard and erect.

"What a dear pearl you have," Brigid whispered, and Mari felt Brigid's lips brushing it as the beads continued to go deeper into her.

It was slow and melting and Mari stopped thinking, let herself be swept away by the nimble, knowing lips and fingers. Brigid teased her clit and made it stand at attention and Mari growled with delight. The wave of her climax was growing, swelling and she willed it higher before it broke. She twined her fingers in Brigid's hair and pushed herself forward to take the next bead until she was holding the entire strand, bearing a delightful fullness enhanced by the ever more intense tingling in her pussy. Brigid suddenly pulled the beads out and Mari came in a wet rush with a long, loud howl. Brigid looked up, her face damp. Mari's body shook, and she felt tears on her own cheeks.

"Oh, so you're a screamer," Brigid teased. She snuggled in

next to Mari. "It's always gratifying when someone appreciates your work." Mari could tell she was proud of herself.

"Can I have your autograph, Ms. Flanagan?" she murmured. Brigid shouted with laughter. A short time later, Mari reached for the phone. She called her office and left word that she wouldn't be in the next day. Brigid looked at her hopefully. Mari rolled back into her arms.

"Now we both have tomorrow off. I'd be delighted if you'd stay."

"As long as you'll have me," Brigid said. "And I won't wear out my welcome. The show ends in a couple more weeks."

"You could stay after it closes…" Mari suggested.

"Bless you, dear," Brigid replied. "But California is my home. I would miss my house, and my garden, and my friends." Brigid squeezed her hand. "I'd ask you to come to Los Angeles, but this is *your* home."

And, Mari thought, even if she had wanted to go to L.A., she didn't want a relationship she had to hide.

"We have a few glorious weeks," Brigid told her. "And after, there're phones, and scented paper for *billet doux,* and planes that can fly you across the country in just a few hours."

"Then we'll make the most of it," Mari said. "And when you go home, I'll hope we can stay in each other's lives."

"I'll keep you in my heart," Brigid said. Mari felt herself tearing up. "You're someone who belongs there. Somehow, you've learned to love freely, when you're moved to, with everything that's in you."

"I dreamed of kissing you when I was twelve years old," she told Brigid. "And I didn't actually kiss a woman until I was thirty. That's too many years wasted worrying about the wrong things. Once I knew what I wanted, I stopped being afraid, and love became something worth everything else combined."

"You're a true romantic," Brigid smiled. "Like my friend Marlene Dietrich. I never met anyone who loved love as much as she did. She'd have liked you. She'd have wanted you."

Mari thought that was one of the finest compliments she'd ever received.

"You look quite pleased," Brigid said.

"And why not? I'm lying next to a beautiful woman who makes love like an angel—I assume angels make love—and I have the day off tomorrow."

"So am I, and so do I!" Brigid said. "What a coincidence!"

They rejoiced again over their mutual good fortune.

Venus in Therapy
Betty Blue

Honestly, I was trying to concentrate on my therapist's voice, but the fishnet stockings and the steel lockbox purse distracted me.

"I haven't seen you in months," she said. "*Why are you here?*" (My therapist has a way with words.)

It was a damn good question. She annoyed me. I had spent two years of therapy sessions explaining each week that I hated my job. "Well," I offered, "I hate my job."

"Oh my God. You're *still* at that job?"

"I'd just like to not be pissed off at work all the time. I don't think it's really the *job*. I hate people."

"Well, why is it that you get pissed off?"

"Because I hate people."

"Well, how are they making you mad?"

"They're stupid."

"Is there something else you can do when you're feeling that they're stupid instead of getting mad?"

"Like what?"

"Well, you could change your self-talk and say something

else to yourself instead of 'this person is an idiot!' Could you put a little yellow sticky note up on your computer that reminds you of something else to say?"

"Like what?" (She gave me a blank stare.) "I mean, I could put, 'this person is *not* an idiot,' but I don't think I'd really buy that."

"Well, you're creative. I'm sure you can think of something. If you drove a taxi, for instance, and it pissed you off to have to weave through traffic all day and listen to people give mixed directions on where they wanted to go, you'd be pissed off all the time."

"Uh-huh."

This woman was an idiot. Did they just give *anybody* a Ph.D.?

Furthermore, she did not have cotton-candy pink pigtails and bleached white bangs, nor did she carry a steel lockbox for a purse—which few people do, so you can hardly fault her for it—but the girl in the next office did. As I said, it wasn't my fault; I really was trying to concentrate, but when you see a girl like that in the waiting room of your local Kaiser Permanente right before you're whisked off to your session with your estranged therapist, there is little else you can think about.

I wondered what the lockbox girl was talking about in *her* therapy session. She looked pissed off. I like that in a girl.

"So," I imagine her very original therapist asking her, "why are you here today?"

"I don't have to answer you, jackass."

(I figured she'd think he was a jackass, because he looked like a jackass to me when he came out to the waiting room to call her in.)

She'd been sitting opposite me, looking at me looking at her over the top of the book I'd picked up that afternoon as a guilty-pleasure reward for something I'd done. (Which was probably "not getting pissed off at some idiot." It was one of my therapist's ideas.)

There were dark-smudged rings of liner around her eyes that made her look like she'd been in a fight—and it would have been an interesting fight in that ass-tight mini and the four-inch platforms, not to mention the fishnet stockings. I tried not to look at her looking at me look at her, but she kept arranging little things inside her lockbox on the table in front of her, and I couldn't help it.

"Excuse me?" says her therapist, the jackass, still trying to absorb the fact that he's a jackass.

"If you think I'm gonna put down my purse, jackass, you can go fuck yourself."

"...But that's what driving a taxi is all about," interrupts an annoying voice, "so it wouldn't make sense for him to get pissed off. It's only going to make him angrier."

I'm sorry; *what*?? Is she still *talking* to me?

"Yeah?" I say, "Well, why is he driving a taxi? Maybe he shouldn't be driving a taxi."

She gives me another blank look. "*Okay.*"

It *has* to be more fun in the other room.

"I'm not telling you to put down the, uh...purse," he says—clearly having issues with the lockbox. "Why do you think I want you to put down the purse?"

"Listen, you motherfucker, I see you lookin' up my skirt."

"I'm not looking up your skirt."

"Yes you are, you a-hole!"

I figure she's got father-figure issues. She's clearly acting out by wearing those platform boots with the fishnet stockings and an ass-tight mini. (And he probably *is* looking up her skirt, because *I* was looking up her skirt...and I wasn't even trying. Very hard.)

"But that's your job," says Doc Annoying. "You're a taxi driver."

Okay, *where* was she going with this one?

"I am not a taxi driver. I'm a word processor."

And what I really should be doing right now, I think, *is getting up out of this puke-pink chair and walking across the hall to liberate the lockbox girl, so the two of us can make a break for it.... Of course, then we'd be stuck outside waiting for the stupid crosstown bus, which is* always *late, and usually jam-packed with a bunch of* idiots *who don't know to move to the back when they get on a damn bus.*

...Say, maybe she's a taxi driver.

"Where to?" A pair of pink pigtails swings around as she turns to look over her shoulder. Jade-green eyes are looking me over, one blacked-in eyebrow raising with interest. "Why don't you sit up front?"

I drop my bag in the back and close the rear door, opening the passenger side door instead. I look down at the seat. It's occupied by a small, steel lockbox with a black Bakelite handle.

"You can just put that on the floor," she says.

"What's in it?" I ask as I slide in and shut the door. She doesn't answer.

She's picked me up at the New Orleans Amtrak station. It's midnight and my train has just gotten in, five hours behind schedule. It's the middle of June, and it's hot and sticky outside even at midnight. It's a heat like I haven't felt since I left my childhood home in Tucson, only this heat has texture, moving over the body, seeping into the crevices, quickening the breath.

I wipe my brow and lean back in the seat, little tributaries of sweat trickling down between my white cotton tank and my breasts. The dampening cotton feels good against my warm nipples, like a welcoming hug.

"Where to?" she asks again.

I give her the name of my hotel, and she shakes her head, setting the pink tails bobbing. "You don't want to go there," she says. "I know a great little B&B in the Quarter. You'll love it." She props one elbow out the open window and leans her head out, blasting the horn as she swerves around someone. "Watch it, you idiot! Get the fuck off the road 'til you learn how to drive!"

My cunt jumps.

She cuts in and out of lanes, taking the corners at forty miles an hour. I watch her fishnets and boots as they pump the gas and slam on the brakes. She jams her foot into the pedal when she's pissed, but her legs are spread wide and relaxed. On her right forearm is tattooed a black cross, sharply cut and filigreed like ironwork. On her biceps, nicely displayed by the ripped off sleeves of her black T-shirt (which reads "Life Sucks, & So Do I"), perches a Vargas girl with flaming red hair and a pale blue bikini, knees together and hands holding them there as if that's the only thing keeping them shut.

She pulls up in front of a Spanish-style manor house in an outer block of the Quarter, where the drunken crowds are muted by distance, and hops out to open my door before I can reach for the handle. I throw my small duffel bag over my shoulder and she picks up the little steel lockbox.

"Come on. They know me here. I'm sure I can get you a room."

A sweet Southern gay gent is at the desk, open all night, and he smiles when he sees the lockbox girl. "Hey, honeybunch, where ya been?"

"Oh, here and there."

"I saved your room for you," he says, taking a key off the wall. "You're lucky you got here when you did; everything else is all booked up, and yours would have been next."

"You're totally booked?" I say, and he looks from her to me and back again.

"It's a big bed," she says. "You can bunk with me."

I hesitate. "I can probably still get my room at the Marriott—"

"At one in the morning? Baby, you lost that room hours ago. Trust me. Fuckin' Amtrak." She's already out the door and crossing the courtyard, and this time she's taken my bag. Trust her? Not at all; but every time she's says "fuckin'," I, well, want to. I look back at the desk clerk. He winks at me.

The room is Victorian, the bed, as promised, huge—an antique. She sets the little steel lockbox on the bed and flops down beside it, candy-pink pigtails spread out beside her as she hooks her hands behind her head.

"So what's in the box?" I say again.

She smirks, dark eyebrows twitching beneath the white-bleached bangs. "You wanna know what's in the box? I'll show you what's in the box...but you have to come here."

It's ridiculously warm in here, even with the ceiling fan turning overhead, casting flickering shadows over the fishnets, pink hair, and the box. I drop my bag and venture onto the bed, sitting on my knees in front of the little steel lockbox. She takes a key from a chain around her neck, nestled between her breasts beneath the cotton T that has begun to stick to her skin. She puts the key in the lock and turns it, but doesn't open it, looking at me instead.

"First you gotta kiss me," she says, and grabs the back of my neck, rings and leather wristband pressing into my skin as she yanks my head toward her mouth.

I resist for an instant, protesting meaningless sound into her mouth, but her steel-studded tongue is sweet and her lips salty and she's soft, goddammit, and I don't care if she's got plastic explosives in the little fucking lockbox.

She pulls my hair, jerking me away from her mouth, and leaps on top of me, knocking me onto my back as she bites at my throat. I briefly recall The Vampire Lestat; apparently, N'awlins is just crawling with the undead. The sting of her teeth against my skin is drawing moans from me; she has found my wildest erogenous zone, the side of my neck below the temple.

I hear the catch on the lockbox opening, but that doesn't interest me anymore. I'm running my hands down the back of the stretch-cotton mini, arms hugging the rough fishnets and feeling the damp diamonds of her thighs where they press through the net as she crouches over me. Her hot breath against my neck distracts me and then something cool and hard slaps against my left wrist.

"Hey!" I try to jerk away, but she's cuffed me swiftly to the post of the tall antique bed.

"Now don't be bad," she says reprovingly as she wiggles out of her underwear. She was wearing something beneath that skirt; it's a pink thong and she stuffs it into my mouth. The scent and the taste of sweet pussy engulf me.

She secures me neatly to the other post, and then rips off my jeans (and thank god, 'cause they were suffocating me), slowing down to savor the removal of my underwear—white cotton bikinis in case anyone's writing this down. My pussy is bared and she nips at it briefly, eliciting an actual squeak from me from within the folds of her wadded up thong.

Then something alarming emerges from the little steel lockbox. She licks the curved tip of a knife and then drops her naked cunt onto my lap (and it is entirely naked; shaven), pressing her knees into my sides like she's holding on to a horse. My lungs heave anxiously, watching the blade flicker with the ceiling fan's motion. She points it close to my throat and then moves down to my shirt, slipping it under the spaghetti straps and cutting them in two.

My shirt is yanked down roughly, but my breasts are grateful to be free, and then hers is yanked up to reveal a very full, very round, very sweet pair of tits, tipped in a perfect pink. She flips the top over her head and tosses it across the room, and then those breasts are pressing against mine, crushing and slipping delightfully in our mutual sweat. She thrusts her wet pussy against my thigh and lets out a little sigh and a moan, lifting her head to briefly flick her tongue across my nipples before she does a sudden about-face on top of me, straddling me on hands and knees. As her tongue dives into my cunt, I can only stare up her skirt, past her garters and into the glistening cleft beneath her ass.

Her tongue stud kneads my clit as she licks, and I try to moan around the nylon in my mouth. She's teasing and biting and then letting the steel ball rest tormentingly beneath the hood. Then she's sucking the shaft, sending rapid shudders of building anticipation through me. I try to spit the panties out of my mouth so I can reach her, but she plants herself firmly against them and begins to rock, rubbing her pussy as rapidly against my stuffed mouth as she is her tongue against my clit.

A rocket of pleasure arcs through me and I squeal against her fucking as my hips shake and buck up into her. She presses her tongue stud against the hood once more while the orgasm jolts through me, and then she begins to quiver and moan. She's making a soft, high panting noise like a child, a long drawn out "ooooooooooh," and then she cries out, a loud almost-giggle, and all of her sweetness collapses on top of me.

We lie there for a moment, panting, glowing, and then she climbs up on her knees and unlocks me, pulls the thong out of my mouth, and tosses the cuffs back into the box. As the cuffs clatter against the steel, she pulls something else out, a lipstick, and repaints her lips cherry red. I peer over the edge *of the box and see a jumbled mess of tubes and pencils and little pots.*

"My makeup bag," she murmurs, curling up beside me. She draws her net-stockinged legs up, curling into a ball, and presses against my damp side, her bangs brushing my breast. She is already breathing deeply, halfway to sleep. I wrap my arms around her despite the damp and the heat, and we—

"...that's when I just try to say to myself, 'okay, this person isn't an idiot; he's just trying to do a job' and I change my self-talk."

Oh, yeah. This person *is* an idiot. And that's what I'm putting on my little yellow sticky note.

LIVE: By Request
Samiya A. Bashir

platform heels so high on these boots i bent down to see you
thru the sky. the brown suede snaked to the tops of my thighs
and grabbed your eyes as soon as i walked in the place. textures always aroused you.

where did my terra firma brownness end and the smooth suede
begin? my skirt wasn't as short as you like me to wear on my
sluttier days, but it flared and reached heights too dangerous,
for tonight, when i turned. i'd forgotten to think of that.

you sitting at the bar.

i remember it darker than it was perhaps. the beer in your
hand almost empty. the glass the bartender gave you abandoned. your other hand poised as if just about to check your
pocket

for something. i sway over to your end of the bar, try not to
notice all the other butches who try not to watch me sashay

my way down to you. i know that's your job. it's part of our
thing   tonight i come to play   baby. i bend forward slightly
when i reach you so the ass you grab is just ass. you think
it's to show you the deep valley of barely contained cleavage
my tight top presents so you let your tongue linger a moment
there after we kiss. you forget to slide your hand up the warm
brown suede to the top, forget how bad you wanna know if i
wore panties tonight   'cuz i want a drink. now.
please, baby.

we get our drinks and the almost relieved kinda jealousy
washes over the face of the b-girl bartender who was trying
not to cruise you before i got here. i stand behind your stool,
my polished hands hide inside your jacket, between your
thighs is just you tonight. good. i let you carry my drink
saying nothing 'cuz i still can't tell you how that smooth, sure
it isn't practiced, voice of yours turns me on, gets me wet. of
course i'm not wearing panties tonight——gotta be careful as
i swish not to let my backside twirl——i'm glad your hands
are full of drinks.

the big back booth i wanted sits empty. you just smile, knowing you worked it out that way before i got here. i'm always
late. you wait.

you hold the drinks while i sit down so i won't knock the
table. these boots make my knees so high up I gotta work
to keep my skirt under my ass. you sit down, take off your
jacket. you look so handsome, flash me the most irresistible
damn kid-caught-hand-in-cookie-jar grin that i wanna just eat
you alive.   soon come.

so we talk. i haven't seen you in a week. you missed me. i want
you. damn. i wanna talk, catch up, giggle with my drink, cross

my legs under this too-short table. but just your voice gets me moist and i ain't got on no panties——tonight is for you. and you don't even know it yet.

it's perfect. you're feelin' yourself tonight in black jeans so tight you give the fag boys a fright when you stroll past. hair oiled just right, new boots, even the tank under your shirt is pressed. i'm impressed. i'll let you play the flirt a little while longer. it's important that this is done right. we gotta get outta here.   finish yr beer.
please, baby. you're comin' with me tonight.

i ignore the raised eyebrow—a challenge. you ignore the twinge in your cunt—the erotic fear of being known. your eyes linger too long on the butch behind the bar on the way out—you thought neither of us noticed—but that just turns me on tonight.

i feel the cool breeze on the wetness between my legs first, then coming from the cold stares of street strangers as we walk down the avenue. you tighten your arm around my waist and i fold myself more closely into you, stare my adoration into your eyes.

we'd planned dinner, but i can't wait anymore. i've got other plans so we stop off at your place. you get that knowing, arrogant smile on your lips and try to put your hand up my skirt while you get your keys.
please, baby. look don't touch
tonight. i'll tell you when you can do what you can do.

again with the eyebrows. whatever. this time i walk behind you up the stairs it's all i can do to ask for some water.
please, baby.

i'm torn trying to get my nerve up too and restrain my blistering desire to possess you   here   now. but i knew who'd win that internal battle. in the kitchen i walk up behind you at the sink. you look so tough as you wash a glass for me with the tenderest hands i've ever seen. i feel a drop of sweat ride my spine to my ass when i reach around you to run my nails up your stomach, pull your back into my breasts and push my pelvis into your ass, push your pelvis into the countertop like i want you—like you want to need to be when you realize what i've been hiding.

all those nights of erotic imagination didn't prepare you for this stiff reality. you didn't think i had it in me. you open your lips almost as if to protest even as your legs spread wider to meet me, even as your deep soft moan betrays you. my fingers in your mouth become a simple formality.

i gotta move quick before we talk ourselves outta this. i whisper in your ear, say: *you can be mama's queer boy tonight if you like.* my fingers run up the crotch of your jeans, you stifle a scream as my nail grazes your ass.

all butches have a black leather belt somewhere. yours is at hand as i grab it and pull your ass a little higher while you reach between your legs to feel my cock. i'm still rubbing it between your thighs when i see the stubborn relief in your eyes as you realize it's not your dick you're drippin' on. it's mine.

you never knew how much you loved me before you got down on your knees on that dark kitchen floor, lifted up my skirt and slid my dick down your throat. i showed you mercy, took your hand as i led the well known route to the bed, sat you on it with that dazed, amazed look on your face to watch me strip.

off with my blouse—i left the red velvet bra on for a minute. pulled down my skirt—left the brown suede boots on for a minute. let my locks down and stroked my cock.

i let you take off my bra and play titty games for a while to get you comfortable—make you drip like i dripped all down my girlish thighs. i whispered all the ways i would fuck you tonight. you fought off your fright, felt your throat get tight, wouldn't let emotion overpower desire. you cowered into my breasts. you thought that way i wouldn't make you beg. remember?

i took your shirt off—left you the tank. pulled your pants to your ankles so fast you fell facedown, boxer-clad ass in the air—i'll let you think i practiced that move—tight-ass black jeans locked your legs. i let your black belt fall free—that time.

and yes i rubbed your back and whispered my love in your ear, ran my tongue from the nape of your neck to your rear before i made you say it.

and yes i loved you with every part of my body, every part of your body, while the last of your time-toughened defenses melted beneath my touch and you knew you were safe.

and when you finally begged—just a whisper—

fuck me

i knew i could tell you to say it louder. i made you beg for it again and again until i heard you cry *if you don't fuck me goddammit, right now, one of us is gonna die!*

alright then. i entered sacred space you opened to me, let you bury your face in the pillow, helped you fight the monsters of old humiliations, new fears that i wouldn't let you keep your swagger, the staggering dread that i wouldn't be able to see the strong, sexy woman you need to be anymore. you let me bite your back and grab your cunt and tits and whisper over and over that you're mine, tell you this time how good your pussy feels from the inside because we know this is the kinda love that reaches thru these barriers.

you scream your release. i do too—after fucking you some more.

 we had never known love like this. we lay in bed all night, took turns feeding each other whatever we had delivered. we talked a little and loved a lot more and freed ourselves for our own acceptance. by morning i had put my dick down for a little while, and you got yours up again and it was like never before. `cuz i knew you, and you were known and still loved

anyway. we've had a lot of those nights since then. i always try to surprise you. and when you sit in that bar, when those other b-girls try not to look at you, you can stare straight back and know that—in the next twenty minutes or so—the kinda soft/hard love everyone wants not to speak of gonna storm thru that door on five-inch platform boots, worn for your pleasure, and lead you by the hand back home.

Girl Ascending
Laurel Halbany

She wasn't the type you would normally expect me to pick out, even at a Lesbian Avengers party—too skinny, for one thing, and a little too obviously young and trendy. Something about the way she was put together, the way she moved, perhaps, made her stand out from the pack of twenty who surrounded her, talking about protests or the Michigan Womyn's Music Festival, or whatever the hell it is newly-out dykes talk about to show each other they really are members of the tribe.

I watched her disengage from her friends and push her way through the crowd to the washtub filled with ice and beer bottles. Her shirt was white cotton with baby-doll sleeves, the modern femme's answer to the butch's plain white T-shirt of old. She had wonderfully concise little breasts; I wished that I could see her nipples, but the heat of August and the roomful of sweaty bodies kept them soft and hidden. Her thick, curly hair was just long enough so that if you were fucking her from behind, you could wind your fingers right into it and pull her head back, keeping her back arched while you pounded into her. I couldn't see the color of her eyes, but that doesn't matter when they are as prettily shaped as hers were. They went very well with her caramel skin.

I was propping up the wall near the beer tub, keeping an icy bottle of hard lemonade as my charm against heatstroke. She leaned over to grab a Rolling Rock. As casually as possible, pretending to search the crowd for a friend, I pushed away from the wall far enough to check out her ass. It was worth the risk of getting noticed, too, even though she was wearing baggy boxer-style shorts with a paisley flower print. Beautiful, and nicely filled out, which you don't often see on skinny girls. Not too big, but if she were crouched over you while you buried your face in her cunt and lashed at her swollen clit with your tongue, and you held on to her ass to keep her from thrashing away from you, your hands would be filled with sweet woman-flesh, not bone.

Somebody started up the music—loud—making normal conversation a bit tricky unless you were within arm's reach of the person you were trying to hear. People started dancing, or what passes for dancing in a crowded old house with carpeted floors and wall-to-wall lesbians. I wasn't going to get to talk to her then, so I waited a while for the inevitable. Eventually she excused herself to her friends and headed for the bathroom, leaving her empty beer bottle on the edge of the staircase. I gave her a few minutes before I fished another Rolling Rock out of the ice and followed her up.

The line of women waiting for the bathroom wound most of the way down the hall. I hung back from the landing a bit, partly so that I could talk to her privately when she was done, and partly to avoid being asked "Are you in line?" over and over again by women who were either hopeful that I wasn't, or suspicious that I might be line-jumping. At a bar the bathroom might be a social annex, but at a party, cutting in or hogging the bathroom to do a quickie with your date is a hanging offense.

"Blue Monday" was most of the way through some extended dance mix or other by the time she emerged. Before she could mumble an "excuse me" and squeeze past, I twisted the top off the beer I was holding and handed it to her. She raised an eyebrow, but she took the beer. We were almost at eye level, since she was standing a step or two above me. I closed the distance, enough to be more intimate, not enough to push into her personal space. I took her hand and shook it briefly. Her grip was firm and her fingers were long and slim, the perfect size to twist themselves inside another woman's slippery cunt and tease all the sensitive places until she cried with pleasure. I wondered if this girl knew how popular her kind of hands were, yet.

"Alex," she said, "and you're...?"

"Jess," I said. She nodded and took a swig of her beer, still watching me. A lot of women go on to ask if it's short for something, or to make a comment about how I don't look like a Jess. Alex didn't, which got her almost as many points with me as the idea of her naked body did. "And no, I don't think you've met me before. I'm a friend of Moira and Dash's, but I don't come out here often when they throw parties."

"I know Dash, but not Moira," she said. "She comes to the Avengers meetings once in a while." That wasn't surprising. Moira was a little too old-school dyke to mess around with newfangled stuff like the Lesbian Avengers. And the house was Moira's, too, which meant that Alex probably hadn't been here before. So the plan I'd thought of while I waited—to give her an interesting little tour—was good to go.

We chatted for a while about little things, people we might both know, her graduate program in paleoanthropology, my work as a physical therapist, how we each had ended up living in the city and places we liked to go. Small talk, the kind of distracting surface things you say when you're waiting for one of you to come out and ask what you're both really thinking:

Why did you decide to talk to me? Am I attractive? Do you want me? Which of us is going to stop circling and make the first move? Between swigs of beer she cruised me as casually and subtly as she could. She was no doubt wondering why I wasn't doing the same. I was keeping my eye level above her neck, since I'd seen as much of her as I wanted from more than arm's length away. If I were going to be staring at her now, it would have to be from a place so close that if something caught my fancy, I could easily put my hand on it, stroking it and getting her warm and wet for me.

Alex's curiosity finally overcame her need to appear sophisticated and in control. "So you stopped me to ask me out on a date, right?"

I shook my head with a brief smile. "No, although I wouldn't mind that too. What I really want is to take you to a quiet part of the house and get those cute little shorts off you. I'd guess, from looking at you, that you don't scream like a banshee, but you don't come very quietly either. I'd like to see if my guess is right or not."

Alex stared at me, too well-bred to let her mouth hang open. I closed the distance between us and took the bottle out of her hand, putting it to the side of the stair. I cupped her chin gently and kissed her sweet, curvy mouth, lightly, to let her know I meant it. If she slapped me or told me to take a hike, she wouldn't be wasting my time, at least.

Instead she put a finger on my breastbone and pushed me away. "First, you give me a real kiss. If you can't kiss, I doubt you can fuck either. If you can, well...then we can talk about getting my shorts off."

We kissed again, hotter and longer this time. Alex grabbed my belt loops and pulled me in, as her little tongue flicked at my lips, like a cat lapping cream. I opened my mouth and tasted her, her tongue and lips still cold from the beer. We broke the kiss and touched lips gently again.

I glanced down to see that her nipples were still soft. She caught my gaze and grinned. "Checking out my boobs, huh?"

"Just looking at them right now. I want to check them out in private, see how sensitive your nipples are." Out of the corner of my eye, I saw that we were starting to attract attention, which meant that in another minute we would have a crowd of voyeurs. I took Alex by one elbow and gently steered her back up the staircase, past the eternal bathroom line, and down the hall to a door that looked like it might lead to a linen closet.

Moira's house is a historical structure; it was built as part of a wealthy family's estate. Because of this, it has all kinds of little quirks. One of them was an extra staircase meant for the servants to use without having to bump into the family on the stairs. I waved Alex through the door and up the stairs, shutting the door behind us and turning the old-fashioned latch lock.

She gazed up the narrow, dusty stairway. "This lead to the guest bedroom?"

"Sort of. Go on up, it's two flights and first door on your left."

The room at the top of the stairs was usually Moira's sewing room, but they let me use it as a guest room when I stayed over for parties. Inside, Alex looked at the Murphy bed in the large wall across from the French doors, the dusty stained-glass lamps with their dim yellow light, and the slanted ceiling that made it look like we could be in somebody's attic. "What's through those doors?"

I swung the French doors open and stepped out onto the balcony. Alex followed me and made a noise of surprise. We were on the highest floor of the house, on what would be a widow's walk if we were anywhere near the sea. Instead, we looked far down the wooded hillside to the city, an upside-down night sky starred with the lights of nightclubs, apartment buildings, and restaurants. To either side were the houses of Moira's neighbors, screened from us by the thick evergreens that had grown here since before anyone lived on this hillside. It was beautiful, and private, and the sounds of the party and the city were no more than a soft murmur from here.

I turned her around then, away from the view, and knelt on one knee. I kissed her right breast, brushing the front of her shirt until her nipple started to respond. I licked at it through the soft cotton, wetting it with my tongue and lips, making the white fabric translucent. Her breathing got faster as I teased the sharp point of her breast with my tongue. I moved to her other nipple, wetting the cloth over it as well, until both of her sensitive points showed. I pulled her down to me and cupped her breasts, rubbing their sweet tips between my fingers. Alex gasped and put her hands over mine, then stood back up.

"Wait," she said, and tugged her shirt over her head. I got a moment to see her beautiful little breasts before she walked past me and sat down on the Murphy bed. I sat down beside her. She took my hands and put them back where they had been before. She closed her eyes as I stroked around her aureoles, circling the base of her hard nipples, working my way to their very tips, lightly pinching them between my fingers, together and then alternately. "Harder," she whispered. "Harder, you're making me so wet, I think I'm gonna come already...."

"From me playing with you like this?" I ran one hand down her flank and caressed her hip. I played with one nipple as I stroked up and down her side, with just enough pressure to keep from really tickling her. Alex squirmed, caught between my hands. "Or do you want me to get inside your panties right now?"

Alex opened her eyes. "I don't want to come yet. I'm not a "dome" type, okay? I want to get my hands on you, too." She unbuttoned my blouse, her fingers a little clumsy from arousal, getting stuck on the second button and popping the third off my shirt. She pulled it out from my jeans. I shrugged it off my shoulders as she worked the front hook of my bra open. Larger and much softer than her own, my breasts filled her waiting hands. She stopped to touch the thin white scar that ran along my left breast from aureole to ribcage. "Jess... does it hurt?"

"No," I reassured her. "It was a long time ago." She replied with her mouth, but no words, nipping at me with her white teeth, hesitantly. I pulled her against me and sighed, and she bit harder, sending bolts of pleasure from my nipples down between my thighs. She squeezed my other breast with her long fingers before moving her mouth there. I ran both my hands down over her hips and then her rear, caressing the round curves, and lightly fingering the sweet spot where they joined the back of her thighs. I slipped my hands under the edge of her baggy shorts, stroking first the outside of her legs, then her inner thighs, keeping well clear of her delta. Even without touching her there I could feel her heat.

Alex pushed me away and undid her shorts. She stood up and awkwardly pulled her shorts and panties down, stepping out of them and kicking the crumpled pile across the room. I lay back on the bed as she climbed on top of me, grinding her hips against my jeans, panting as she rubbed herself against the denim, soaking me with her musk. I slipped a finger between us, my hand full of wetness and soft flesh; she was bare except for a small tuft of hair at the top of her mons, more a decoration than anything else. "Lie back, let me do this," I told her, and she rolled over and onto her back, her thighs apart and open for me.

I took a few deep breaths to calm myself down. I didn't want to rush, but there is nothing—nothing in this world— more intoxicating the smell and taste of an aroused woman. What I really wanted to do was bury my face in her wetness, use my mouth to make her cry out and dig her fingers into my scalp and come again and again under my tongue. It would be better for her, though, if I took my time, and I kept that thought in front of me. It was the only thing that could hold me back.

Alex's outer lips were soft and rounded, her inner lips almost paper-thin, rising to form a round pink pearl that was hard and slick with arousal. I licked carefully around it, never quite touching her there, teasing her so that she rolled her hips in a desperate attempt to get my tongue to where she needed it most. It wasn't long before I needed it as much as she did. I wrapped my arms around her upper thighs, holding her open, and slowly licked from the top of her clitoral hood to the very tip, once, then again, my tongue moving faster as her breathing grew faster and higher-pitched, her fingers tightening in my hair. When she moaned "Please, please, I need it," I stopped thinking about pace or timing, and buried my face in her, her thighs pressed against my head so that I felt her cries rather than heard them. I was running out of breath and didn't care; all that mattered was keeping my lips and tongue on the very center of her, bringing her to peak after peak, tasting and smelling and feeling her pleasure through my mouth.

Her hands moved from clawing at my neck and shoulders to the back of my head, smoothing back the long strands of straight brown hair that had escaped from their braid. I pulled myself up, breathing hard. Alex slid down the bed toward me and kissed me, smearing her own hot musk from my face across hers. She kissed my jaw, then my neck, moving down across my body. She gently parted my lower lips with her fingers. I could feel her warm breath as she hovered.

Alex eased one of her slim fingers inside of me, moving slowly, then slipping in another. With her other hand she dipped into my wetness, then took my clitoris between her thumb and fingers, stroking gently up and down, matching her movements to the rolling of my hips, caressing my most sensitive spot from both outside and in. She played me deftly as my thighs started to clench beneath her arms and I trembled each time her thumb passed over my hardest, most delicate place. She pressed a third finger inside of me and turned her hand, a key opening my lock, and I poured over her, the sounds of my pleasure matching the thrust of my mons against her patient, steady fingers.

As I slowed, Alex eased her hand out of me and scooted herself up on the bed, curling her body against mine. I turned sideways to make room for her against my body. We lay together as a warm evening breeze swirled in through the French doors, cooling the sweat from our skin. I reached for a flannel sheet from the floor, crumpled where we had shoved it aside, and pulled it up around us. In the quiet we could hear snatches of music and laughter rising and falling, like the surf on a faraway shore.

Alex gently shifted her weight so that her head was tucked comfortably into my shoulder. "Sleepy?" I asked her.

"Nope, just resting. Don't want you to tire me out right away."

I lowered my mouth to her nipples and brushed my tongue over their very tips. She breathed a soft moan and arched up to meet me. "But I want to tire you out," I murmured, in between taking sweet, hard tastes of her. "I want to exhaust myself in you."

She pulled the clasp from my braid and fanned out my hair so that it fell around me, a soft curtain that brushed across her breasts as she pulled me up to kiss her mouth. Her thigh pressed up between mine, and she broke the kiss to smile up at me. "No hurry," she whispered, as our hips moved in rhythm. "No hurry at all."

How It Started
Mary Anne Mohanraj

When a hot new dyke moves to Berkeley, you've only got a tiny window of time in which to make your move. If you don't move quickly, she'll be snapped up by someone else, and you'll be left alone in your bed—wet fingers for company, waxing the saddle and wishing for love.

It was late at the Calyx, past midnight, and the floor was packed with couples, hip to hip, breast to breast. But she was dancing alone, shimmying to the beat with a circle of space around her, head thrown back and sweat dripping off her body. She was so fine—skin like toasted coconut, lips dark and lush. A tight white tank over huge breasts; god, each one looked bigger than my head. Curving belly. Hips that moved in deep, wide circles, like she was fucking the air. I'd never seen her before. I didn't know why no one was making a move on her, but I wasn't going to wait to find out.

I let my body move to the music, let it carry me over to her. We were dancing alone, a foot or so apart, and then a little closer, a little closer still. That's when her eyes opened—dark green. Yum—I've got a thing for green eyes. She smiled at me, slow and lazy, and I slid closer, just an inch or two away from those glorious breasts. Dancing hard, sweat flicking off me as I shook my ass, arms up in the air, arching my back and hoping my breasts looked bigger than they were. Our sweat was mingling in the air, falling to the floor; the whole place was hot and damp with horny cunts writhing to the music. She opened her mouth a little then, and I almost just went for it, almost dove in for the kind of hot wet kiss that could convince a girl that she wanted to go home with *me* tonight, that I could show her the best time she'd ever seen. And that's when she said it.

"I have a girlfriend. She just doesn't dance. Sorry."

Fuck. I kept dancing; there wasn't much else to do.

"I'm Janna," she said.

"Susan. You been in town long?" I knew the answer to that one, but I had to try, had to keep the conversation going. I was still hoping it wasn't serious, that I had a chance. Not that I was the sort of girl who tried to break up relationships...but if a couple was already on the rocks and you just came along at the right time, that wasn't really your fault. You might even be doing them a favor.

"Just moved out. I'm teaching at the U." She paused there; I hoped that she was going to say something about having just met her girlfriend, or that it wasn't working out, or that the woman was mean or just plain nuts. Instead, she said, "Carla came with me. We've been together eight years."

Goddamnit. That was it, then.

She disappeared into the crowd after the song ended; I figured she was out of my life. But over the next few weeks, I kept running into her. At the co-op, buying groceries, we'd be picking out cucumbers and carrots side by side. At the bookstore—not one of the regular bookstores, but the scifi one, we reached for the same copy of Delany's latest. Across the counter at Sushi-A-Float, I watched her slide sea urchin into her mouth, watched it move down her throat. By the third encounter, I was dying of unsatisfied lust. The worst time was Saturday night at the hot tubs; she left just as I was walking in—we stopped and exchanged a few words. And even though I was with a cute redhead, a girl with sweet thick nipples and a fat ass just right for grabbing, I fantasized about Janna the whole time I was fucking the girl in the tub. I had three fingers in the redhead's pussy and my mouth on her nipple; I was dizzy with the heat and every curl of steam rising from the water reminded me of the black curls of Janna's hair, made me wonder if it was just as curly down below.

I got the redhead off, but only just, and she never spoke to me again. Guess she could tell my mind wasn't really on her. That was when I lost it. I'd never tried to break a couple up before, and I wasn't going to try now, not really. I didn't need to date Janna—I just had to have her, had to fuck her. Just once.

I signed up for one of her classes at the U. She was teaching some feminist theory crap; I never went for that stuff, but I read up on it now, just in case she called on me. Not that I talked much in class. It was summer term, as hot as Berkeley ever got—70s or 80s most days; cool crisp mornings followed by brief heat. I wore the skimpiest clothes I had, and when I ran out of those, I raided the used clothing stores, looking for more. Pale mesh tops with dark push-up bras; short tight skirts and tall black boots; thin white T-shirts with no bra at all; cut-offs and ankle bracelets and bare feet with the toenails done in red…every sexy look I could think of. I sat in the front row for weeks and alternated crossing and uncrossing and recrossing my legs. No panties, red silk bikinis, black lace thongs, damp white cotton. I leaned forward in my chair, rested my elbows and breasts on the table. I didn't try to catch her eye; that would have made it just that little bit too obvious. She would have had to confront the fact that I was deliberately fucking with the teacher, and that the teacher was enjoying it. Janna *was* enjoying it. I could tell. I watched out of the corner of my eye, in quick glances. Her face got flushed when I uncrossed my legs; she called on the others, but she kept looking at me.

The day it climbed up to 90 degrees, I had a Coke with ice in front of me. I kept fishing ice cubes out of the cup, sucking them slowly until they were half gone, then chewing the rest. I wondered if she had heard what I had heard—that girls who chewed ice were sexually frustrated. God knew it was true. Janna was wearing a thin white dress that day—opaque, but thin enough that it clung to her curving body, moving as she moved, damp with her sweat. Little trickles of sweat slid from behind her ears, down her neck and collarbone, into the *V* of her dress, disappearing between those breasts. I was so thirsty, and hot enough that I couldn't think straight. So I pushed it further than I ever had before—I fished out another ice cube and used it to trace the same path on my own body, right there in class. Anyone could have seen me. Started behind an ear, down my neck, across the collarbone, shivering with pleasure. I was carefully looking at the chalkboard, but I could feel her eyes on me—and then I dropped the ice down the front of my shirt. It slid down between my breasts, coming to rest for a moment in my belly button. It was fucking cold—too cold to leave it there. So I shimmied a little and it slid down further, coming to rest where my thighs met, melting against my clit, creating a little wet puddle on the wooden seat underneath me. Janna watched everything.

When the class ended, she waited until the other students had filed out. I sat in my chair, looking at nothing, hot and wet and a little scared. She had a right to be mad. She walked up to me, stopping in front of my desk.

"Drop the class," she said. "You're distracting my students."

I nodded.

Then she reached out and picked up another piece of ice. She placed it on my shirt and held it there, just above the nipple. Let it melt a second, dripping Coke-sticky cold water down onto my nipple, which popped straight up. She watched me, watched my breath catch, watched me swallow. Then she dropped the ice back in the cup, smiled sweetly, and spoke again.

"Just one rule. Carla gets to watch."

Oh shit.

I'd done some group stuff in college; everyone did, right? When dyke club meetings got late; when everyone got drunk and giddy. You ended up sprawled over some girl's couch, feeling up someone's breasts by candlelight while someone else felt up yours. But none of those had ever gone all that far; clothes had mostly stayed on—they just got pushed out of the way. All the real screwing I'd done had been one-on-one. Still, it didn't sound like Carla would be doing anything—just watching. Watching would be okay, right? I could just ignore her, and it would be worth it—it would *so* be worth it to get my hands on Janna's breasts, on her belly and hips and ass. I wanted to grind my pubic bone against her clit; I wanted my fingers fucking her, in and out, fast and hard and sweet. I wanted her screaming, and I wanted it bad. So I said yes.

We walked back to their house, not touching, a foot of space between us, my body humming with desire.

Carla worked at home; she was there when we walked in, leaning over a computer, long brown hair falling in front of her face. She turned around when we walked in the door, and I could tell right away that she knew; she knew exactly why we were there, in the middle of the afternoon, when Janna should have been holding office hours. Carla looked at us and knew. I was ready for her to get mad, or to get weepy, but instead she smiled. It was a wicked grin, stretching her mouth wide and showing teeth. That grin took her plain pale face—a face I wouldn't have looked at twice in a club—and turned it into something else again. Something maybe a little dangerous.

Janna said, "This is Susan. She wants to play."

"You two go ahead and get started. I'll be there in a minute." And she turned back to the computer and started typing again.

Shit. I couldn't believe she was so fucking casual about the whole thing. Did Janna bring women home like this all the time? What was going on with these two anyway? But then Janna was taking my hand, leading me through the house to the bedroom, pulling me onto the bed, and I didn't give a damn anymore. So Carla didn't mind if Janna fucked other women—this was my problem? Hell, no. Janna's mouth was on mine, moving hot and wet, and her fingers were unbuttoning my cutoffs, pulling them off. I lifted my ass to help, and in a couple of minutes I was naked and she was too, and we were writhing together like two fish on a wet dock. Fuck Carla!

I finally got my mouth on one of Janna's breasts—just as gorgeous naked as I'd hoped they would be, and even bigger than I'd thought—and sucked hard, pressing my face against it, smothering myself eagerly in all that soft flesh. I couldn't breathe, and didn't want to; she was on top of me, her body crushing me into the bed. I liked it; I wanted more. I tried to reach down to her cunt, but her hands grabbed my wrists and pulled them up over my head, pinning me down. Her thigh pushed my legs apart and pressed against my crotch; then her hip was grinding into me, shoving me down hard against the mattress. She was pushing me, pushing me up and over, and I was moaning. Usually it was me making the other girl come, *me* making *her* scream, but Janna had me down and begging for it, and when she bit my nipple I came hard. I came once, then again, and it was when I was gearing up to come for a third time that I noticed my wrists had somehow gotten tied to a bedpost. Fuck.

I tugged against the rope—it was tight. I opened my eyes, and there was Carla, comfortable in a rocking chair, snuggled up in an afghan, of all the weird-ass things, a fucking orange afghan. She was wearing granny glasses, and if she'd been a couple of decades older, she could have *been* someone's granny. But I knew that *she* was the one who had tied me up while Janna was busy distracting me, and she was definitely the one grinning now, watching us. And when Janna paused for breath, Carla was the one who reached out to the bedside table, picked up a giant economy-sized tube of Wet lube, and said, "I think she could use a good fisting, honey," as she handed it to Janna. Then she sat back in the chair and started it rocking, her eyes fixed on mine.

I could have said something. But instead, I closed my eyes. I bit my lip and lay back; I wrapped my hands around the ropes and let Janna drizzle lube into my snatch. A little to start—then she was swirling her fingers around the mouth of it, getting every millimeter of skin wet. It had been pretty wet already, but for fisting, it was going to need to be a lot wetter. Or so I'd heard.

She rubbed my clit until I started squirming on the sheets again. Then she slid a finger into my hole—two. Three. No problem. Four was easy. I had taken four plenty of times. And when she slid her thumb in there, I spread my thighs wider, inviting her in. That part, I knew how to do. She fucked me silently—she hadn't said a word this entire time—had hardly spoken since we'd left her class. But I could hear her breathing, could feel one of her hands pressing down on my open thigh and the other sliding into me, in and out. More lube. She was doing something with her hand—spiraling it as she slid in and out of me. Pushing a little harder each time, pushing closer to the knuckles. I wanted her to go fast, to get it over with—to just push past the pain, like the first time I got fucked with a strap-on. But Janna went slower and slower. And she was so quiet I could hear Carla start to whisper.

"Come on, Susie. You can do it. Relax—you gotta relax

and let her into you. Open up wide and let her into your wet cunt, your sopping pussy. You want her to—you want her so bad...."

Janna was pouring more lube onto me now, cold at first, thick and wet, coating my thighs and cunt and the sheets and her hand fucking in and out of me.

"I saw it at the club; I watched you make up to my girl, and I knew you were dying for her, you wanted her so bad. So give it up, baby. Relax and let it go, let her have you, let her take you."

She was pushing harder, pushing hard enough that it hurt, just a little. Pushing down, and her fingers pressing against that spot that felt so good but made me feel like I was gonna pee. And I was twisting under her hand, or trying to—I couldn't help it—but she kept my hips pinned down with one hand and fucked me with the other. In and out.

"We want you to let us fuck you, baby, and it's the least you can do, little tease, little slut. You pretend you're a top but what you really want is for someone to take you and fuck you hard, push you up and over the edge—"

I was moaning now, pulling hard on the ropes and glad they were there, moaning so loud that I almost couldn't hear her anymore. I was so close, so fucking close.

"...and you want it bad enough you're willing to beg for it from someone you know you aren't supposed to touch. So come on, baby girl...come on..."

And that was it: Janna's hand slid into me with a quiet pop, a sucking noise, and it didn't hurt at all. It was in me. Then she started moving it. Moving inside me, her whole fucking hand. She opened it up and closed it, her fingers reaching up and into me, like she wasn't just fucking my cunt, like she was fucking *all* of me, and I was shivering and screaming before long, coming up and over and over again.

It went on for a long time.

When they were done with me, Carla untied me, still grinning. Janna and I showered, giggling off and on. I was pretty high on an endorphin rush; my thighs were trembling and my head was spinning. Dropping the soap was funny, and almost slipping on it was hilarious. I didn't know why Janna was giggling too, but I didn't care. I was just glad she'd enjoyed herself. Janna soaped my back and I did hers; we washed each other's pussies clean. That was all good.

By the time we started drying off, I was coming down from my high, the giggles disappearing and exhaustion taking over. I started wondering if this was it, if they were done with me. Maybe they picked up a different girl every week—it was possible. That should have been fine with me—all I'd wanted was to fuck Janna, right? And even if she'd fucked me instead, or they both had, I couldn't complain that I was unsatisfied. There was no reason for me to feel blue—but I did.

My mood got worse as I got dressed—Janna disappeared in search of Carla. When I joined them in their sunny yellow kitchen, they were sharing a glass of water. They looked so fucking cute; Janna leaning against Carla, the glass cradled in her hands. I shoved my hands in my pockets so they couldn't see them shake; I was ready to storm off, pissed for no reason I could explain.

Then Carla said, "Hey, that was great! Do you need to take off, or do you want to stick around and talk, maybe have dinner?"

Dinner. I wasn't sure what came with dinner—maybe something complicated—maybe more than I wanted in the end. It had been a pretty strange day. But for now...

"Dinner sounds good."

I took my hands out of my pockets as Janna handed me the glass, and drank deep.

Art History 101
Carol Rosenfeld

The biker stood by the motorcycle, wearing full leather—boots, pants, jacket. She removed her helmet, revealing dark hair cropped close to her head. I wanted her to take me right then and there, on the sidewalk outside the bar, in front of the smokers and the tourists walking by with their guidebooks in hand. But she didn't notice me.

Why would she? I was a Pillsbury Dough girl clothed in a cardinal-red silk blouse, black pants, sensible black pumps, and pearl earrings—hardly de rigueur garb for a biker chick wannabe.

I followed the biker into the bar, where two young women more likely to attract her attention immediately began preening themselves for her benefit. Tiny tops stretched across barely-there breasts, stopping short at the perfectly flat midriffs. These world-weary beauties were half my age but looked jaded enough to have lived twice as long. And their combined weight would probably be less than mine.

The biker didn't notice them either. She ordered a pint of Guinness, perched on a stool, and began watching the basketball game on the television.

I walked over to where she was sitting, leaned across the bar, and ordered a Rolling Rock. I thought I heard her mutter, "Poodle piss."

At the commercial break she turned to me and asked, "Is there anything to do in this town?"

I looked at her. She was in New York City. I said, "Why don't you go to a museum?"

The duo to my left snickered in scornful unison.

"Which one?"

"Well, I like the Metropolitan Museum of Art."

"Want to show me around? You look like a teacher type."

In fact, I was a law librarian and the unpaid editor of a small and largely unappreciated poetry journal, *The Obscure Boulder*.

"Okay," I said. "Meet me on the front steps at ten o'clock on Saturday morning. Fifth Avenue and 81st Street." I printed the place, date, time and location on the back of one of my cards, and handed it to her.

She looked at both sides, then slid the card into a pocket inside her jacket. "I'll be there, Noelle," she said.

People began setting up for a band.

"Who's playing tonight?" the biker asked.

"Fish Head Barbie," said Biker Bait One. "They're having a CD release party."

"What's the title of the CD?"

Biker Bait Two shrugged. "I think it's something like *Sin Dee Seagull*."

"I'd better go before the noise—I mean the music—starts," I said. "Uh…what did you say your name was?"

"I didn't say," the biker replied. "But you can call me Lou."

"Is Lou a short version of a longer name?"

"Yes." She stared at me, and I knew there was no point in asking what that longer name was.

"I'll see you on Saturday, Lou."

Friday night I soaked in my favorite bath salts—green tea, scented with Moroccan roses. I liked that the list of ingredients specified where the roses were from. After I dried myself off, I painted my toenails and fingernails with a creamy polish the color of a seashell.

Saturday morning I showered using soap scented the same as the bath salts from the night before. I stepped into a cotton skirt pattered with red rosebuds, topping it with a short-sleeved, V-necked crimson cotton sweater that buttoned down the front.

I faced the full-length mirror, foolishly hoping that I might see Jacqueline Bisset reflected in the glass. But it was still me. Well, I was clean and color-coordinated, right down to my underwear. That was the best I could do.

Riding across town on the M79 bus, I worried about whether or not Lou would actually go through with the plan we'd made. Over the past couple of years, I'd begun to suspect it was my karma to be stood up. So when I saw Lou walking up the steps, I was very relieved and a little surprised. She was wearing her leather jacket, a black sweatshirt, black jeans, and mirrored sunglasses. I couldn't tell whether she was looking up at the banners hanging over the entrance, or down at me. In the sun's spotlight, I saw she had a generous sprinkling of freckles on her cheeks. I smiled.

"What?" she asked me.

"Nothing." I wasn't going to tell her the freckles made her less formidable.

"This is a big place," Lou said as we entered the Great Hall.

"We're not going to be able to see everything," I said. "We could concentrate on one area, if there's something in particular that interests you, or we could just stroll and stop whenever one of us wants to take a closer look at something."

"Let's do that," Lou said. "Tell you what—let's make a

game of it. We'll take turns pointing out something we like, and explaining what we like about it."

"Sounds like a good plan."

"Okay then. You go first."

Lou's suggestion fitted in with my hidden agenda. I intended to test the power of suggestion by directing her attention to images of nude women—preferably voluptuous ones. Fortunately, there was no shortage of examples.

Lou's initial selection turned out to be a painting of two hounds quarreling over a dead hare. "Y'know what I like about this?" she said. "That rabbit really looks dead."

And so we made our way through the Nineteenth-Century European Paintings and Sculpture galleries, alternating between naked women and the lurid, gruesome or bizarre.

I became nervous as we approached the Modern Art galleries, partly because my art history instruction hadn't progressed past the Impressionists. The first thing I saw when we entered the room was an image of a skull that took up an entire wall.

"Cool," Lou said. "Let's rest our feet for a minute." She sat down on the leather-covered bench, facing Warhol's *Skull*. I sat beside her, hip to hip, facing the opposite direction and a different Warhol work—a series of images of Jacqueline Kennedy, wearing a pillbox hat. It was a close-up view, but I knew the original photograph had been taken just before President Kennedy was shot. I remembered that they sent us home from school early that day, and when I walked into the kitchen, my mother was crying.

Lou swung her legs up and over the bench, turning her body so that we were both facing the same direction. Her thigh was pressed against mine, and her arm was behind me.

"I wrote him a letter during the Cuban missile crisis," I said. Lou didn't ask whom I was talking about. "I was scared. I got a letter back too. It's somewhere in my parents' house. I look for it every time I go to visit, but now that I really want to find it, I can't."

We came out of the Modern Art galleries into European Sculpture and Decorative Arts. It was my turn to choose something, and I decided to take a closer look at a small terra-cotta sculpture of *Leda and the Swan*.

"They're looking at each other so tenderly," I said.

"Doing it with animals is a little too kinky for me. You have to draw the line somewhere."

"It's a myth," I said. "Zeus wanted to seduce Leda, who was the wife of the king of Sparta. And Zeus was married too—to Hera, who wasn't a goddess you wanted to piss off. So he disguised himself as a swan."

"So Zeus was playing a role in order to get something he wanted?"

"Yes," I said. I looked closely at Lou. She wasn't actually smiling, but I felt that something was amusing her.

We stopped for coffee in the small café adjacent to the Sculpture Court.

"What do you want to see next?" I asked. "Greek statues? Egyptian mummies?"

"How about etchings?"

"Etchings?"

"Yeah. You know—as in, don't you have some etchings you want to show me?"

Now was the time for me to give the "friends first" speech I'd rehearsed on Friday night. But who was I kidding? I had changed the sheets that morning. And I did have an Inuit print over my bed.

We headed back to the west side of Manhattan through Central Park. As we passed people walking dogs, pushing strollers, or both, often while talking on a cell phone, I silently prayed to the great feline goddess that no hairballs or similar offerings would greet our arrival at my apartment. As we walked under one of the arches, Lou put her arm around my shoulder, pulled me toward her, and kissed me. Was it the boldness of the move or the kiss itself that took my breath away? Her lips felt like heated velvet. Because she was almost a foot taller than I was, I had to stand on my toes while Lou bent her head. She pulled away and sighed, "We need to either sit down or lie down. I've had a lot of experience with this situation." She took my hand and led me out of the cool darkness back into the bright sunlight, pulling me up a hill and through some bushes. "Let's get warmed up," she said, spreading her jacket out on the grass and guiding me down. She lay next to me and kissed me again. Lou's lips and tongue had the same delicious warmth as the sun heating my hands as I caressed her hair and then her back through the cloth of her sweatshirt. Her hand cupped my breast, and her right leg lay between my open ones. She was moving it in a way that created delightful sensations.

We might be in New York City, and I might be halfway to paradise, but I was still of this earth enough to worry about being gay-bashed. "Wait—what if someone sees us?"

"Anyone who sees us is going to think I'm a guy," she murmured, squeezing, pressing, rubbing.

"Lou," I said. "Please."

"Okay," she said, pulling me up. "Lead on."

It took me a couple of minutes to get myself together. As I straightened out my skirt and sweater I saw that Lou was grinning.

"What?" I asked.

"The flush on your neck matches your sweater."

We didn't say much as we left the park. I was thinking about her hands on my skin, her lips on my breasts, and her tongue on my clit. Hopefully she was thinking along the same lines.

"Hold up," Lou said, as we passed one of the ubiquitous Korean salad bar/deli/grocery stores with buckets of flowers out front. She considered the tulips carefully, finally choosing a red cluster. She went inside to pay for them, and when she returned, she handed them to me.

"Thank you."

The outside petals seemed almost powdered, hinting at the deeper color waiting to unfold. As I looked at them, I realized the color reminded me of... "Oh God," I whispered.

"What's the matter?" Lou asked.

"I've been reduced to finding sexual imagery in flowers," I said. "How trite is that?"

"Actually," Lou said, "I picked those 'cause I thought they matched your outfit."

And they did.

When we reached my apartment, Lou inspected the Inuit print while I found a vase for the flowers. She flopped down on the bed, leaning back on her elbows, and looked up at me. She said, "It turns me on to watch someone get undressed."

"It turns me on to have someone undress me."

Stalemate.

"We could flip a coin," I said.

"We could wrestle for it," Lou replied.

I knew that wouldn't work. She was bigger and stronger and I wasn't inclined to try and hold her off me.

"Let's compromise. I'll take off my sweater and bra if you'll take off my panties."

Lou considered this. "Deal."

Reminding myself that a thing worth doing was worth doing well, I began unbuttoning from the bottom up. I made a point of fumbling with the little buttons, silently counting, "One Mississippi, two Mississippi, three Mississippi," between each one to slow myself down.

When I reached behind me to unhook my mesh demi bra, embroidered with red flowers, Lou said, "Wait. Don't unhook it yet."

She sat up and moved to the edge of the bed, legs apart. Positioning me so that I stood in between them, Lou began nuzzling the areas of my breasts that were not confined. She kept her thumbs on my nipples beneath the mesh, pressing them and circling.

Then she dropped her hands and lifted her head.

"Now," she said.

"What?"

"Take the bra off now."

Once my breasts were totally exposed, Lou placed her hands on the outside of each, gently pushing them together. Alternating between breasts, she licked the aureoles and nipples, then bit and sucked. I held on to her shoulders. It felt a little awkward, being nearly naked while Lou was still in her sweatshirt and jeans, but there was something exciting about it too. Soon I was leaning forward, cradling Lou's head.

"Please," I said. "I don't think I'm going to be able to stand up much longer."

"Did you say stand up or stand it?"

"Both. Aaahhhh! Either—oh!"

"Okay," Lou said. She pulled me down next to her, then pushed me all the way onto the bed. When I was flat on my back, Lou put one hand on each knee and opened my legs.

"Aren't you going to get undressed?" I asked.

"In a minute."

She placed her palm on top of my pubic bone, fingers cupping my vulva, pressed down and began massaging me through my panties.

After a couple of minutes she changed position, sliding two fingers under the silk and inside my pussy.

Lou eased herself off the bed and out of her pants. "Close your legs for a minute." She leaned forward, grabbed the sides of my panties and pulled them down and off. "Okay. You can open them again."

I did.

"Now," she said, settling back down on the bed, "I'm gonna make that pussy purr."

When her finger touched my clit, I opened my legs even further. Lou encouraged me, murmuring, "Yes baby, that's right. You know what you want. You're making me so hot." I didn't recognize myself. Who was this greedy, wanton woman?

Liquid squirted out of me; I could feel warm drops on my legs. It was my bed, but I still felt the need to apologize.

"I'm sor…"

Lou put her hand over my mouth. "Don't." She took my hand and put it between her legs. The cotton of her boy briefs was soaked through. "See what you did to me?"

"Lou," I whispered, sucking her ear lobe, "Please." I pushed the ribbed neckline of her sweatshirt down so I could kiss the hollow at the base of her throat, punctuating action with words. "Want you." When I reached her stomach I pushed the sweatshirt aside again, kissing here and there, and smelling. I took her boy briefs off oh so carefully and began licking her gently, until her legs opened wide enough for me to be able to slide my tongue a little ways into her, to take her labia between my lips. I felt her hands on my head, heard her sigh then whisper, "Can't," but when I fluttered the tip of my tongue against the tip of her clit, she did.

Afterwards I lay with my head on Lou's shoulders, admiring her long legs. "Lou?"

"Um?"

"What do you do?"

"I'm a teacher."

I tilted my head. "Really? What grade?"

"I'm a college professor."

I propped myself up with my right arm so that I could look directly at her face.

"And what subject do you teach?"

"Art history." Lou laughed. It was a wonderful laugh, loud enough to startle the cats out of their languor. I wanted to punch her. She looked at me and she knew it.

"Don't be mad at me, Noelle," she said. "In the bar...when you told me to go to a museum...I thought you were adorable. I wanted to have some fun—tease you a little."

"Well, I don't like to be teased," I said, more sternly than I meant. Two could play at this game of pretending in order to get something you wanted. "I'm very sensitive."

"I know," Lou said, breathing the words into my ear and brushing her thumb over my right nipple. "Can I make it up to you?"

"You can try," I said.

Cinderella's Shoes
Kate Dominic

I was certain Cinderella never had to wait in her room for her ugly stepmother to come upstairs with a spanking strap. Not that Deirdre was really ugly. Even when I was mad at her and feeling more than a little scared, I appreciated that the potential trophy wife my father had briefly dated was a beautiful dark-haired woman in her midforties with a slender, curvy figure and flashing brown eyes. She'd built her own multimillion-dollar security consulting company from the ground up. She gave me good advice about boys—and when she realized I wasn't interested, better advice about girls. She even taught me to drive her Porsche, much to my father's dismay. After her and Daddy's totally amicable breakup, I was ecstatic when she gave in to my begging and agreed to let me live with her while I attended classes at the university a half mile down the street from her house.

My only complaint about Deirdre was that she was convinced the only way to get the attention of an undisciplined young college girl was through her bottom. That meant every time I was in trouble, I found myself over Deirdre's lap with my panties around my ankles, her arm tight around my waist, and my butt high in the air. She whipped the bejeezus out of me with a nasty leather hand strap that packed a world of hurtin' into twelve short inches of supple, black cowhide.

Fortunately, my crimes were paid for as soon as my bottom was on fire and I was crying in the corner. If I needed to make restitution or had to apologize to someone else, her company's chief investigator, a rude, macho dyke named Amanda who was also Deirdre's ex-lover, used state-of-the-art surveillance systems to verify that I'd done what I'd said I was going to do. I got a double dose of Deirdre's strap if I didn't. I learned to follow up quickly, partly to stay off Amanda's radar, but mostly because I'd realized how much I liked kissing and making up with Deirdre.

It had taken me a while to realize I was in love with her. She was so different from the women to whom I usually was attracted. I liked young, mouthy butches who wore masculine clothes and comfortable shoes. Deirdre was older and sophisticated—a total clotheshorse femme, just like me. We went shoe shopping together at least once a month and stood in line at the crack of dawn for the semiannual clearance sales at our favorite department stores. We even got our nails done on Saturday mornings. She kept hers long and painted in subtle, classy colors. I couldn't figure out how she'd never once scratched me when we were panting on our Egyptian cotton sheets. I kept my nails typically dyke short, though lately I'd been getting a clear gloss finish rather than just buffing. We had so much fun together. When she held me close and told me she loved me, her kisses made me quiver

Her fucking strap also made my bottom hurt so bad. I was fairly certain how she was going to react to my having gone eight-hundred minutes over my cell phone limit this month, in addition to the horrendous long-distance and roaming charges I'd forgotten to mention. When she'd specifically asked me if

I'd incurred any during my outlet trips with my friends, I'd told her 'no.' I figured I could brush off a few. But then I'd gotten so busy, I'd forgotten to keep track of how many extras I was adding. If the additional charges had been an emergency or even if I'd made arrangements ahead of time, and most especially if I hadn't lied, Deirdre wouldn't have minded.

She was going to mind this, in a really big way. Right on time, I heard her car pull into the driveway. I tried not to bite my nails any more than I already had. I knew better than to not tell her now. But I'd taken the coward's way out and just left the open bill waiting on the table with the rest of the mail.

Five minutes later, Deirdre marched into my room. She was still in her pastel-pink power suit. She held the bill in one hand and her strap in the other. Staring directly into my eyes, she dropped the damning evidence on the bed next to me.

"Is there anything you'd like to say in your defense, or should we get right to spanking your bottom?"

I looked sullenly at the floor. It seemed like there should have been some other options for someone my age. Okay, so there were. Any time I wanted, I could take over paying for my entire phone bill, rather than just paying the additional charges the way I was going to be now. Well, at least, I could as soon as I earned enough money to pay that and my overdrawn credit card bill, which Deirdre had strapped me for last week. I sighed heavily and muttered, "No, ma'am."

"Very well." She took off her jacket and draped it over the back of my desk chair. She was wearing a cream-colored silk blouse and pale pink pearls and the buttery-soft Italian designer heels we'd picked up last weekend. I was still nervously admiring her outfit when she sat down on the edge of the bed and patted her thigh.

"Take off your shorts and panties and get over my lap, Melissa."

I looked up at her in surprise. "Take them off?"

"Yes, young lady," she said firmly. "Your behavior has been in a downward spiral for the past few weeks. It's time to nip this in the bud." She smacked the strap loudly against her hand. "Strip from the waist down and put your clothes in your hamper. You won't be needing them anymore tonight."

Deirdre's look told me there was no point in arguing. My face flamed as I unbuttoned my shorts and hooked my fingers in the waistband of my panties. I skimmed them down together and quickly stuffed them in the top of the hamper, hoping Deirdre hadn't noticed that I still hadn't done my laundry.

"I see you'll be doing your laundry as soon as you're done with your corner time," she said firmly.

"Yes, ma'am," I blushed. I took a deep breath and marched stoically over to the bed. With each step, the edge of my T-shirt brushed the top of my behind, making me even more aware of the nervous tingle in my skin. Deirdre took me firmly by the elbow and guided me over her lap.

I scooted forward, wrapping my arms firmly around my pillow. I got extra on the backs of my thighs if I reached back to cover my bottom. I usually didn't do it. But sometimes I did. Deirdre always got me really crying when she strapped me. With it being summer, I didn't want to have to wear long pants or skirts to cover the marks on my legs. To be honest, I have to say that Deirdre had never given me a spanking I didn't richly deserve, but I was still embarrassed enough over getting strapped that I really wanted to keep my punishments private between us. Deirdre resituated my bottom so it was right up over her leg. Then she lifted my shirt up over my waist and wrapped her arm tightly around me.

"You're going to get a good sound spanking, Melissa. Cry all you want to, but don't cover your bottom or try to move off my lap."

"Yes, ma'am," I squeaked, pressing my thighs together. I was determined to keep my mouth shut. I'd never succeeded, but once again, I promised myself that this time, I'd stay quiet.

The first crack tore the breath from my lungs. I lurched up against her arm, gasping as fire screamed across my right cheek. I gasped again as the next crack burned across my left. Two strokes later, I was yelping, hugging my pillow as hard as I could and squirming wildly over her lap.

"Ow. Ow. OW!" I arched forward, tightening my butt as much as I could, trying to squeeze the pain away. It didn't do any good. Each crack was hard and hot and it burned deep into my tender bottom flesh. Before long, I was yelling and twisting, frantically kicking my legs as Deirdre strapped me with the same thorough effectiveness she always used. I shivered hard when she reached down and pulled my outer leg to the side.

"Deirdre! Pleeeeease!!!!" I howled. Her grip was like a steel band, exposing my poor sore bottom even more.

"You know you deserve this, young lady," she snapped. Then that nasty fucking strap cracked into the tender flesh of my wide open sit spot and way up between my cheeks. I wailed, lurching and thrashing like a wild woman as she strapped me until my bottom hurt so much I knew it had to be on fire for sure.

When she finally stopped, I collapsed over her lap, sobbing and apologizing profusely for being so irresponsible. I promised I'd never do it again, not ever. I was so sore I almost meant it. In fact, I meant it so much I knew I was really going to try to behave for a good long while. The sound of the door opening in back of me barely registered.

"Your apology is accepted, Melissa. But at this point, I need to be certain your irresponsibility is going to cease. Thank you, Amanda."

I looked up, astonished to see the chief investigator standing next to me. "Deirdre?" I gasped. She had never spanked me in front of anyone before. I tried to reach back to cover my bottom, but she held my hands firmly away.

"Come now, Melissa. You didn't think your little escapades had escaped surveillance, did you?"

I gave Amanda my dirtiest look, but she just glanced at my butt and whistled sympathetically. "You're getting one heck of a strapping, young lady. Your bottom looks almost as sore as mine used to feel after a good session over Deirdre's knee."

I was stunned almost to silence. "You?" I gawked. I could not imagine the big, strong, suit-clad dyke standing in front of me hanging over anybody's knee, especially with her pants down, getting a spanking.

"Yes, indeedy," she said seriously. "You better believe that as long as I lived under her roof, I ended up with a blazing sore bottom whenever I misbehaved. She didn't use a strap on me, though." For the first time, I realized Amanda was holding a long, slender stick in her hand. "She used a willow switch, just like this."

I gasped as Deirdre swatted my blazing bottom. "Since the strap isn't getting through to you well enough, I've decided you should have a good sound switching as well today, so you know just how serious I am about your behavior changing."

As I stared at them, too shocked to speak, Amanda sat down at the head of my bed and took my hands in hers. "I know we haven't gotten along well before, honey, but you better hold on, now. A willow switching really burns, and Deirdre is going to light your butt on fire by the time she's done."

I stiffened as Deirdre held my leg out and open again. But before I could say anything, the air whistled and a lightning flash of pure, white-hot pain slashed across my bottom. I screamed and Amanda winced, but she held on tight to my hands, murmuring "There, there, dear," as I shrieked and bucked over Deirdre's lap. Deirdre lashed four more horrifically painful strokes from the top of my backside to the bottom, then she added two more to my already blazing sit spot. I was still wailing at the top of my lungs when she whipped the last one down diagonally, igniting my whole backside into a solid wall of flames all over again. When I collapsed over her lap this time, I was crying so hard I could hardly breathe.

I was certain my bottom would never stop hurting again, not ever in my whole life. Amanda patted my hands before she left. Then it was just Deirdre and me again. When I'd finally settled to hiccupping sniffles, she stood us both up and pulled me into her arms. I cried out when my shirt brushed over my scalded skin. Then I clung to her for dear life, soaking her silk blouse with my tears as she petted me and told me I was a good girl, and she knew I'd do better from now on. Oooh, my bottom burned. I told her I was sorry. I promised I'd be more responsible, I really would. Then I cried some more because my behind hurt so bad.

Eventually, I'd calmed enough for Deirdre to lead me to the corner. As I pressed my face to the juncture in the walls, she leaned over and gently kissed the side of my neck.

"Would you like to be alone now, dear? Or do you want some additional comforting?"

I clenched my bottom involuntarily, wincing at the pain of my well-whipped cheeks pressing against each other. Even though I was really sorry for what I'd done, my backside was sending waves of electric heat surging into my pussy. Each time I tightened, the feelings got more intense. Deirdre's kisses were making me shiver so hard the hair on the back of my neck was standing up.

"More comforting, please," I sniffled, swiping my hands over my tear-filled eyes.

"Very well," she said quietly. Her next kiss was so wet and soft and tender I moaned into my fingers. "Compose yourself a bit more, darling. I'll be back when I've changed and your corner time is up." She set the timer on the dresser for ten minutes and closed the door, leaving me alone with my thoughts.

The wait seemed like an eternity. As the timer ticked loudly into the quiet evening air, I thought about how sore my bottom was and how mad I was at Deirdre for spanking me, and about how mad I was at myself for being so naughty and how embarrassed I'd been to have Amanda see me getting switched. It was so unfair, even though I'd pretty much asked for it. When I reached back to gingerly touch my bottom, my skin felt so hot and tender even my own hand hurt it. I sniffled as more tears leaked out of my eyes. The switch had left a crosscross of horrifically sore thin, raised welts. And I was so horny that just thinking about Deirdre's kisses made my pussy throb. I pressed my thighs together hard, ignoring the pain in my bottom as I squeezed pressure on my clit.

I was wiping my eyes again when she walked back into the room. I heard her pull out my desk chair and move it over near the nightstand. She rummaged around in the drawers, then quietly said, "Come here, darling."

I turned around and my breath caught. Deirdre still wore her pearls and her fancy Italian shoes and the gold bracelets that usually adorned her wrists, but she'd peeled off her skirt and slip and blouse. Her luminescent silk stockings were held up by a lacy garter belt with butterflies embroidered around the edges. She wore a matching satin demi bra, and she wasn't wearing panties. In her hand, she held a black leather thigh harness with a large, purple latex dildo secured into the ring. My bottom tingled at the sight. Deirdre sat down on the chair and buckled the harness on her right thigh, just above the top of her stocking. The nightstand drawer was open, the one where we keep all our supplies. She reached in the drawer and took out an accordion-shaped lube applicator. As I stepped in front of her, she peeled off the cap, then patted the tip with one long, polished nail.

"Turn around and bend over, dear."

Tears stung my eyes before I even put my hands on my bottom. I slowly turned my back to her and spread my legs.

Then I leaned forward, hissing as I gripped my sore cheeks and pulled them open for her.

"A little more, sweetheart." She patted my bottom gently. I yelped. I was so sore, even her fingertips burned.

"It hurts," I whispered, tears falling down my cheeks as I dutifully pulled my burning cheeks as far apart as I could. I shivered as the cool evening air tickled over my anus.

"Little girls who need spankings end up with very sore bottoms," she said tenderly. "Your bottom's bright red and very hot."

I moaned as her finger traced lightly over an excruciatingly sore line. I knew it had to be a switch mark. Then the tip of the applicator touched my anus. I jumped as a cool smear of lube glided over me.

"Keep your bottom open and bear down for me, darling."

I hated that part. It was so embarrassing, yet it felt so good, even though my bottom hurt so bad. The slippery nozzle teased until my asslips fluttered against it. As I pushed back, straining to kiss my anus over that hard plastic tip, my sphincter opened just enough for the nozzle to slide through.

"Oooh!" I trembled as it slid up into me. Deirdre laughed softly.

"Good girl."

I shook as she squeezed the cool dose of lube up into my bottom. She pulled the applicator slowly out and I stood there, holding my bottom cheeks open as my anus squirmed and clenched and squished on the cool, viscous lube filling my rectum. Deirdre set the applicator on the nightstand.

"Stand up and turn around, dear. Take off your shirt and bra, and when you're naked, you may straddle me."

I peeled off my shirt and unhooked the back of my bra. Deirdre had picked it out for me, a simple cotton uplift style with a chaste white ribbon between the cups. It made me feel so innocent and sexy—and hers. As I undressed for her, she took the big lube bottle from the drawer and slathered her huge purple cock until it was dripping. I moved my legs over her thigh, spreading them wide and bracing my hands on her warm, feminine shoulders. Then I squatted slowly, until just the tip of the dildo brushed against my anus. Deirdre reached in back of me, her bracelets jingling softly as she cupped my bottom, pulling me open. I gasped hard. Her hands hurt so badly, and her latex cockhead felt so good. It pressed against me, just enough to gently kiss my anal lips.

"Ow," I moaned. Deirdre's hands stilled instantly.

"Does the dildo hurt you, Melissa?"

"Nooooo," I sobbed, leaning down more in spite of myself, reaching for the delicious, slippery stretching. "My bottom hurts. You spanked me so hard, Deirdre!"

"Yes, I did." She licked tenderly over my nipple. I shivered as it hardened. She licked again, and I lowered myself further onto the plug. The tip slid in.

"Ooooh! It feels so good!" I gasped.

Deirdre laughed softly, pulling my bottom cheeks further apart. I yelled at the pain, shuddering as the slippery cockhead slid further into my lube-stuffed bottom. Then the head popped in.

"Deirdre!" I wailed her name, shivering as she held me quietly, letting me adjust to the huge, relentless stretch in my hungry sphincter. Eventually, I slid lower, taking her cock gradually into me. Deirdre raised and lowered me, kneading my pain-filled bottom as she fucked me over her cock. I cried out at the pain, my asslips trembling at the exquisite sensation of sliding over her huge latex toy. Each time I descended, she slid further in. I was so close to coming. Her cock always got me so close. It got me craving the touch that would push me over the edge.

"I expect you'll be remembering for a good long time what happens to little girls who need their bottoms punished." She licked soothingly from one breast to the other. "And to little girls who take their punishments and are forgiven." As she started to suck, her fingers gripped right into my sit spot, right where the strap and switch had burned in so hard into the sensitive tender skin. She squeezed, very, very hard.

"I'll remember, ma'am." I sobbed. The fullest part of the dildo suddenly stretched me wide and slid in. My tender bottom landed hard against her thigh. As I cried out, Deirdre slid her hands up to my waist, holding me tightly onto her leg as she sucked hard on my nipples. Finally I lifted my legs, shifting my weight so my sore, spanked bottom rested almost entirely on her, letting the pain wash over me the way I knew she wanted me to. As tears streamed down my face, I clutched her shoulders, ignoring the pearls trapped in my fingers as my anus trembled over her dick in a frenzy that had me so horny I could hardly stand it. Deirdre rocked me back and forth on my bottom and the dildo until I was shaking.

"Deirdre!" I wailed. "I'm sorry! I want to come so bad!"

"I know you do, darling." She lifted her head and kissed me. "Milk your nipples now." The well-sucked tips were so sensitive that when I took them between my fingers and pulled out, my bottom clenched hard. I cried out, squirming hard over her thigh.

"You're so beautiful, darling."

I moaned in relief as Deirdre's fingers slid from my waist. She poured lube into her spanking hand until it glistened. With the other hand, she peeled my slippery labia open, baring my clit. Then her cool, lube-slicked fingers slid down and rubbed tenderly over my quivering nub. I cried out, grinding against her thigh as my anus clenched hard around her cock.

"Rock on my thigh, love, while I give you your orgasm."

Her beautiful fingernails moved in slow, deliberate circles over my throbbing clit. I ground against her, frantically tugging my nipples. The sensation vibrated deep down into my pussy and my wide-stretched asshole and my screaming sore behind. I let the pain and the heat and the glorious pleasure of her thigh cock press deep into me while Deirdre slowly and relentlessly drew the orgasm from me.

"I'm gonna come," I blurted out. Deirdre laughed softly. She didn't let up on her circling, not even once. The orgasm washed over me, and I threw back my head and howled. My legs quaked as I rocked against her, and her fingers, her fucking wonderful fingers made me come so hard I thought I'd quit breathing.

"Please stop," I whispered, my hands falling free as I leaned forward and rested my head on hers. I was shaking so hard I knew I'd fall if I weren't held firmly in place by the dildo embedded deep up my ass. Deirdre tenderly slid her hands back around my waist and held me until I'd stopped shaking.

I cried again when she pulled my bottom cheeks wide open so I could rise up off of the plug. I pulled free and squatted over her, my hands holding tightly on to her shoulders as the tears again streamed down my face.

"Stroke your anus, darling," she said softly. I groaned. She always made me do it, and it was always so embarrassing. But it felt so fucking good. I gingerly reached in back of myself, working my arm past hers as I slid my fingers down my crack. I shivered at my own touch. My anus was puffy and still slightly opened.

"Stroke your fingers in and out."

I did, whimpering as she squeezed my burning cheeks and I finger-fucked myself. Touching my slippery, open sphincter felt almost as good on my fingers as my own touch did on my anus.

"This is what happens to naughty girls who need their bottoms strapped and switched. Have you learned your lesson, dear?" She squeezed my bottom very, very hard.

"Yes, ma'am," I shivered, sliding my fingers in and out of

my open hole. A small wave of pleasure once more washed over me. "I've learned. I promise."

"Good girl," she smiled, letting my bottom cheeks close. I lifted my glistening fingers back to her shoulder. "You may now lick my pussy and give me an orgasm, darling. But you may only use your tongue. Your fingers have been in your bottom. While you're licking, remember that if you want to put your fingers in Deirdre's pussy, you have to be a good girl."

"Yes, ma'am." I dove between her legs. Oooh, her pussy tasted good. It was sweet and sticky. Her stockings and the strap from her harness and finally her Italian pumps rubbed against my arms and shoulders as she wrapped her legs around me and held my face to her pussy. She let me eat her to three orgasms. Then she gave me a deep, soft kiss and told me she loved me forever and ever.

We went downstairs, me naked and Deirdre in her underwear and heels. After I'd started my laundry, she let me serve us homemade European salads and she even let me take a sip of her chardonnay.

Three nights later, I looked in the mirror, gingerly touching the last of the deep red marks and the long thin switch bruises still crisscrossing my bottom. I was thinking if I wore nice soft panties, maybe I'd be able to sit still in the car long enough to go across town with Deirdre. As always, my spanking had been the end of the matter. We'd worked out a loan plan to pay my outstanding bills, and I was making damn sure that fucking Amanda wouldn't have anything bad to report about me. Well, maybe she wasn't all bad. But I still wasn't going to give her any ammunition for narcing to Deirdre. I pulled on a pair of loose silk tap pants, another gift from my sweetie, and went downstairs to go shoe shopping with her. There was a moonlight madness sale at the mall, and we wanted to be first in line.

Keeping Up Appearances
Kenya Devoreaux

She was pretty faced and beautifully endowed, my English Literature professor, and as she leaned over for more sugar for her lemonade her C-cups fell in her brassiere like ripe peaches from a tree. I could see her nipples—*oh, Jesus, her nipples*—protruding through her crisply starched linen blouse. It was as if they were whispering to me, *"Norma. Please...."* My own ached, they hadn't been sucked for so long. I wanted to kiss her breasts all over. But I couldn't, could I? She was my professor, after all, and I didn't wish to breach the parameters of the teacher-student relationship. Despite the rumors of Professor Carlyle's affair with Dean Mary Shannon two years prior floating around the university, she appeared to be extremely straightlaced. And appearances *are* everything....

"The clouds are making interesting shapes this afternoon." Ms. Carlyle looked skyward, blue eyes sparkling in the California sunshine. She was nice to let me into her home this way just to discuss my research paper. I wasn't sure whether or not she would rather have been spending Saturday afternoon frolicking in the surf, her body being tossed about by the huge, playful ocean, white froth lingering on those gorgeous breasts. But literature was her favorite subject, after all. She loved words, she loved ideas. And her enthusiasm for language as an art form was infectious. I enjoyed the two of us sitting on her veranda, the sea-salty odor of the ocean before us mixing with the scent of her cologne. It was intoxicating, the converged fragrances of two of nature's wonders: the Pacific Ocean and Professor Katherine Carlyle.

"So, Norma, as for your paper. Before anything, I want you to know that I am flattered by your seeking my counsel. And I enjoy knowing one of my brightest students holds me in such high regard."

"That is encouraging, Ms. Carlyle. Thank you." I found her perfect formation of the vowels and the sharp expulsion of breath on each consonant between her gleaming creamy-whites provocative. I hoped she didn't notice my pupils dilating.

"Now tell me, dear, which genre of literature will you be discussing?"

I was researching lesbian erotica, and although I was not ashamed of my interest, I did not want to cause Ms. Carlyle to blush. Well, she didn't.

"Lesbian erotica, eh?" She raised an eyebrow and chuckled softly before lifting her glass for another sip. "That is some of the best literature in existence. You have wonderful taste." She smiled and looked off into the distance behind me. Then she turned and looked me square in the eye.

"Does it taste good to you?" Ms. Carlyle kept her glass in front of her face, only partially hiding the impish grin frisking about the corners of her bow-shaped mouth.

"Yes, ma'am. It does." It may have been the sugar in my drink or the sugar in her tone, but something was exciting me and causing the type of exquisite discomfort one usually wishes to keep secret.

"What pretty thoughts come to mind as you feel the grit of the sugar slide between your teeth and over your tongue?"

"I feel it very distinctly. The grit is what conveys the sweetness to my taste buds. The lemonade wouldn't taste so sweet if I weren't force to actually partially chew it."

"Do you like that?"

"Uh...yes. Yes...I do."

"Try and develop a mouth fetish. It will make poetry much more fun to read." Ms. Carlyle continued, "And other notable experiences will be all the more intensified." She searched my eyes for a moment and, finding what she was looking for, said with a strange sort of gentleness, "So...let the games begin."

"Okay, professor. I am comparing and contrasting lesbian erotic literature from the Victorian Era with contemporary lesbo-erotic works. Now, I went to a poetry reading and I totally fell in love with the work of this one poet—I think her name was Delaney. The texture of the language was crunchy...you could almost taste it. But the words were huge, mutlisyllabic. Not like small granules of sugar, but like chips of ice in a cold and sobering drink."

Ms. Carlyle looked interested.

"So anyway, this magnificent lesbian poet said at the end of her set that she was influenced by a Victorian writer by the name of Emily Wittingham. I wanted to go up to her and ask her for more information about that writer, but I didn't want anyone to think *I* was a lesbian—"

"Oh. Yes. Of course," Ms. Carlyle interjected with a sweet smile.

"So I went to the library and I looked on the internet; I even called the Library of Congress. I can't get my hands on her!"

Ms. Carlyle pushed a real swig of lemonade up over her teeth and then gulped. "Yes, dear. I am very well acquainted with the work of Emily Wittingham. She had a way of using rhyme and meter to stimulate the subconscious of the reader. One could read a piece about a woman playing the piano—a popular pastime of middle-class women in those days—and end up turned-on without knowing why. There is one poem called "Crushing Cotton"—I could swear it is about two lesbians pushing their pussies together."

My mind slipped out of my body and I was visited by visions of naked blondes, brunettes, and redheads with throbbing, hot–red cunts slung, sprawled, and spread-eagled on clouds of cotton before me. The all wanted my hand inside them.

"Norma. I know you're hot, baby."

"I beg your pardon? How do you mean?"

She laughed good-naturedly. "You need something wet on your hands."

I was immediately embarrassed—and so damned aroused by the possibility that she knew about the dozens of lesbians I had humping in my head.

"When the extremities are cool the entire body cools." She wiped the perspiration from my top lip with her soft fingertip. Her glance down at my hefty cleavage, which was now heaving violently, elicited from her a very soft but audible, "I *ache* to fuck you." Suddenly she sat up straight, squinted her eyes playfully, and then leaned back languidly in her chair. As she spoke with me her hand busied itself with stroking away the droplets of water that had formed on the shaft of her glass. She resumed her commentary about Emily Wittingham.

"What Wittingham is able to do, and better than any lesbian writer since, is penetrate you so deeply...that you are actually forced to abandon everything you've learned about how poetry should be interpreted and *feel* what you're reading. Don't initiate a partnership with the poet in creating the meaning, just allow me—I mean, Emily—to caress your mouth, your eyes, your ears, and even your skin as you see,

speak, and feel the piece." Ms. Carlyle licked her lips in enthusiasm. "A real high-caliber writer knows how to take her own
ideas and disguise them within the perspective of the character, do you know what I mean? And she'll pump and pump
and keep pumping into you that part of herself that makes her
original."

I nodded—trying not to lick my own lips.

"Have you ever seen the movie, *God, Give Me Wings*? It
starred Daisy Andersen and Celia Davis. They are a couple
offscreen. Daisy does the writing, I believe. And Celia directs
most of the pictures. Well, a little after the second act, the
climax—which women artists are noted for fabricating better
than men—Daisy slips her hand into Celia's drawers and
steals the cherry—"

"Oh, yes. The only clue that she had been visited by the
virgin nymph."

"Okay, darling, well that came from a Wittingham poem.
Emily believed in immortality. But she lived in a period in
which scientific and technological knowledge was not as vast
as ours. She knew the only way she could become immortal
was through her poetry. The poem itself still resonates—to
those who can even find it. Technological advancement doesn't
necessarily inspire good taste." She sipped a little of her lemonade at that and sucked a juicy piece of pulp through her
teeth. "Fascinating isn't it, dear?"

"Quite."

"Have you ever had an artist suck you so deeply into her
fantasy that way? The good stuff can be difficult to get, but
the resolution of the tension is exhilarating just the same."

"I think I've just broken into another sweat."

"That's Emily. She knows how to touch you."

"Glory. When I was handling my load without you I was
so tense—"

"Come in the ocean.... Swim with me."

At that moment I realized that one needn't ever say yes to a proposition such as that; a slight drop of the jaw will suffice. Professor Carlyle, serious, fiercely intelligent, and—I'd just noticed it—incredibly soft skinned, had just asked me to go skinny-dipping with her...and I couldn't wait. She rose from her chair and stood before me, looking terrific in her white linen blouse and matching pants. She took me by the hand and led me barefoot down to the beach. She came close and did to me what I'd fantasized about since the first day she had entered the lecture hall and introduced herself to the class.

With her tongue pressed into my mouth she slipped her hands under my half-shirt and pulled my breasts so firmly that I fell into her. She slid her hands from under my shirt slowly, savoring every inch of my perky, tight girlishness. She cradled my temples and pressed her face into my hair. Her long, aristocratic nose was nestled in my ear as she fumbled with the belt buckle on my denim shorts. I had to help her undo the buckle. She never broke the connection of our faces, but seemed pleased as punch when she grasped my rear to remove my panties and found I wasn't wearing any. My shorts dropped once they were completely unfastened and I stepped out of them. I stood naked as I watched her undo her own blouse, and parted my legs slightly to enjoy the sea breeze as it caressed my very moist, downy mound and labia. I reached out to assist Professor Carlyle in removing her garments, but she nudged my hand away. As she let her blouse and lace brassiere fall from her body, I gasped. *Don't show me every-thing, I don't want to come yet.* I was pleased to see I was not the only one standing on the sand with breasts that stood up when unbound by a bra. She got out of her pants quickly, then exposed her whiter-than-white teeth at me expectantly. I looked down at her pussy. I could see the long strands of dirty-blonde down through the lace front of her Victoria's Secret underwear. She looked down at herself, and grabbing a good portion of the material, very smoothly and with much pomp, ripped her drawers down her pelvis and hips and off. She stepped toward me gracefully—like a lady, stroked my left cheek with the lace, and pressed it gently against my nose. She dropped her underwear beside us and we just stood there, each with her hands about the other's waist. Each woman's cunt pressed firmly against the other's cunt. She kissed me.

I sucked my middle finger and tickled her asshole a little.

She chuckled. "Shall we?"

"Let's."

The surf had risen a couple of inches on the waterfront, washing our feet and our clothes away at the same time. I would be naked with her forever. We'd removed all our garments and waded into the deep, wet sea. Stripped of our clothes—and all pretenses.

Along a Rocky Hillside
Catherine Miller

I had given up the idea of being a detached observer long ago. It was impossible anyway, I decided. What I cared to learn about when I traveled was purely subjective. Given time, I assumed that what really mattered would seep in the tastes, sounds, and sights of this remote village and its surroundings—as well as being captured by my camera lens in the images I took away with me.

I was the subject of more than a few untoward looks from the locals. I could not be sure whether I attracted attention most because I was a woman alone in this Middle Eastern country without a man to guide or control her, because I was from the West, or because I had developed an ease with the rocky terrain that surprised the people who lived there.

I had walked to this hillside several times since my arrival in Gilgamesh, hauling my collapsible tripod and camera with me in my rucksack with my water bottle—the bare necessities of my life. I could not understand what compelled me to keep returning to this scene. Large rocks dotted it and yellow summer grasses weaved their way across it, but it was not obviously different from other hills in the area.

It was on one of these jaunts that I first saw her, walking with some of her friends, sisters, or coworkers. I could not be sure what relationship she shared with these other young women, but there was an easy familiarity that told me they knew each other well. I heard them before I saw them. They were coming from the direction of the cotton fields at the close of the day.

In describing her, some might say her face was a little sunburned, but it seemed to me as though the sun had brought the very lifeblood inside her to the surface of her skin. She was the most curious of her friends at the sight of me, as though she wondered not only who I was and where I had come from, but also what it was I saw through the camera I peered through that I did not see without it. And perhaps, I thought long after we had said our final good-bye, she wondered what I saw of the world through it that perhaps she did not.

It was this curiosity that struck me first, the way it lit up her face, her mouth curled inquisitively into a lively smile, her eyes shining with questions, her hair blowing against her cheek that she brushed away so it would not impede her vision.

Our eyes met and I found myself smiling, in part to myself, in part at her. She had a fierce natural beauty, like a desert flower forcing its bloom upon a spartan landscape. It was so different from the easy beauty of the Western ideal, where skin and hair were coddled by years of luxurious care and a life unchallenged by a lack of resources.

Her friends tugged at her, first with words, then with their hands, to move on and she did, looking back once at me with a smile. I never expected to see her again, which left me with a sadness that seemed so completely out of proportion to the circumstances, I chided myself for being sentimental. It was a deep, dull ache that felt strangely familiar.

So I was surprised when, the day after next, as I was framing a landscape for another shot of the hillside, I saw her in the corner of the frame, standing under a tree, smiling. When I stood back from the camera and looked at her, she came towards me, saying gentle words that I could not understand. She pointed to the camera and then at herself, and I understood that she wanted to look through it. I showed her how to look and then how to shift the view and focus, and finally when she nodded, how to snap the photo.

The young woman looked at me with what might have been gratitude and then reached up and pushed a fallen lock of hair across my forehead. Her hand brushed my cheek and she smiled. It had been so long since I had been touched, I melted inside at this unexpected gesture from a stranger who, while clearly an adult, could have been my child by way of some teenage indiscretion. Despite her youth, and how romantic a notion it seemed, it felt to me for all the world as though she embodied all the love of the original Mother.

Emboldened and grateful, I took her hands in mine and saw that they were raw from picking cotton. It had been with these obviously pained hands that she had shown me such kindness. I kissed them and felt charged through with a desperate desire to soothe them. I pulled my first aid kit from my rucksack and lightly rubbed antiseptic-anesthetic cream onto her palms. She gazed up at me in a way that told me she was not used to this kind of attention.

But it was more than that. I saw a hunger for something different; a loneliness that led her, worn and tired, to seek out a foreign woman who walked the hills above her village, who waited for the sunset to cast its color and shadows on this hillside. That evening when we parted, I felt a certain clarity. I had not known why I was there, what drove me to the same hillside to try again and again to capture the beauty of the place. In this young woman's presence, I finally understood. There was something about her for which I had come thousands of miles.

The next afternoon, when she came to see me again, I saw an eagerness in her eyes, of which I was not sure she was aware, but that I could not misunderstand. I told myself that I was imagining things, but her nearness to me, her almost constant eye contact, and her easy affectionate touches were unmistakable. I had observed the physically affectionate manner in which members of the same sex interacted, but I was sophisticated enough to know that this kind of touch was not meant to be interpreted as erotic in nature.

So I was mindful of the risk I was taking in reading too much into her behavior when I reached for her face with my hands and placed my lips over hers, drawing her suddenly lighter form against me with my arms as I felt her sink into the kiss. She tasted of peppers and tomatoes, of cinnamon and dates, and of a woman who had never been kissed like this before, full and wet and urgently, my tongue exploring her lips and mouth in search of an answer to what I now knew were my dreams.

At last I broke away, dizzy, sure I would not be able to stop myself from pressing my now throbbing clitoris against her leg if I did not. She sighed, and we sank down to the ground under a tree. I examined her face more closely. She couldn't have been more than twenty, although her hands looked older, and her brow was furrowed with the heaviness of a life not of her own making, until she laughed at something and the lines vanished. An intoxicating mixture of innocence and wisdom imbued her.

While I explored her with my eyes, she took my hand and then shyly put her head in my lap. I held her like this while tears coursed down my cheeks, unbidden. I was undone by the gift of this young woman's trust and affection, which I could not see how I deserved—a transient foreigner who had made a mess of her life—from a country at odds with her own, and with a history shorter than the years this sweet girl's family could trace itself back in this village.

I stroked her raven hair and she looked up at me, saw my tears and began to kiss them from my cheeks, an act of such tenderness from a face of such beauty that I lost control of my senses, of the real possibility that we could be discovered, of the consequences for me and, worse, for her, and of any time that had ever existed before or would ever exist after this moment.

Through her blouse I felt for her breasts, and watched her mouth fall open and her eyes glaze over at my touch. I pulled off her peasant blouse and kissed and sucked on her hardening nipples, which dwelled in the center of breasts I knew had never seen the light of day. She moaned and said something I could not follow.

She offered no resistance, and when I returned to kiss her lips again and again, I felt her mouth water. When I pulled down her loose pantaloons, I was struck by the sight of her full hips and thighs, centered with a hearty triangle of dark hair that spilled onto her thighs, unwilling to be tamed. A breeze blew her scent into my nostrils.

The evening had cooled the hillside, but I was on fire. I tugged at my clothes like they were chains, then placed them under her body so she would not be scratched by the rough grasses underfoot. She looked up at me expectantly, her eyes widening at my nude form. I wondered what it was that she expected? Surely in her short and sheltered life, she could not have been led to expect anything between women like what had already transpired or was about to.

I stroked her legs lightly and she squirmed, shifting her hips and rubbing her thighs together slightly. It was as though desire crept inexorably out of her center. I knelt down over her with my hands on her inner thighs and gently placed my fingers on either side of her lips. I split her pussy open gently, and thought how like a pear she was there, fresh and with a clear, sweet juice dripping from between her lips that overwhelmed me. I buried my face in her sweetness and my lips and tongue joyfully sought out and teased her clitoris.

My darling moaned and cried and begged in her own language. Her whole body shook and her long hair was tossed from side to side, partly concealing her face. It was not long before she arched her back, pressed herself up at me and came, her sex released from a lifetime of constriction, her pussy throbbing in a seemingly unending series of contractions. My tongue continued its wanderings through her lips and soon she bucked up at me again, more boldly, with the movements of one who now knew what to expect.

A rosy flush suffused her breasts and face as I half lifted her into my arms and she clung to me. My clitoris was throbbing intolerably. I held her on top of me with her thighs intertwined with mine. My pussy reached for her, and I rocked her, rubbing myself in desperation against her, finally coming in a rush of relief, my lips on her neck, my face buried in her hair.

When she left me that evening, darkness conspired with us to conceal our whereabouts and I returned to my pensione, I believe without being seen. I lay awake, wanting her, grateful for the taste of her that remained on my lips. No one could convince me that what we had done was unnatural, two women vibrant and alive, discovering each other sensually in a world which separated men and women for all but the most perfunctory, male-focused acts and pleasures.

Surely, I thought, looking out the window of my room, there were many other women like us buried under these brown hills, embalmed in postures of intimacy and ecstasy in the architectural ruins of civilizations past.

A wedding was being celebrated nearby. By custom, there was music and dancing all night long, voices raised in laughter that belied the difficult living these hardworking people scratched out of these hills. Suddenly I wondered how long it would be before my darling with no name was to be wed herself. I tossed and turned for hours. I knew I was being ridiculous. It was not as though I were going to stay in this country indefinitely. I had an itinerary, and I was sorely behind as it was. The nature magazine I had pitched the photo shoot to would be expecting me to return soon. The passion I was feeling, however, did not respond to reason. I was jealous of my sweetheart's husband-to-be in advance.

She did not come the next day, or the next, and I feared that she had been discovered missing too late in the day to be respectable, and that her movements were now being watched more closely. On the third day, however, she returned. Her face reflected a joy and a sadness combined that opened my heart and made me rush to embrace her and take her lips in mine, thirstily, possessively. She broke away after an amount of time that could have been a minute or an hour—and pulled a swatch of cloth from inside her waistband.

My heart sank when I saw her holding it out to me, a sample of the characteristic color and type of fabric worn by brides. I almost laughed at the cruelty of my foresight.

I'll never know for sure why she stayed away for two days. Was it a matter of being too busy with wedding preparations or other work, or merely that the opportunity to slip away unseen did not present itself? By the gravity of her expression, I suspected that she had stayed away because she was struggling with whether to see me again, to deepen our connection, which would make the joy of our time together and the pain of our parting more acute.

When we came together as lovers this time, we moved more slowly, as though to stretch out the time—which was all too short—forever. She surprised me by reaching for me first, her slender fingers, unsure of what they were doing but exciting me beyond reason all the same, exploring my folds, brushing against my clitoris. I sat back against a tree, my breasts warming in the late afternoon sun, while her sweet hands urged me on to a climax. Her unpracticed touches moved me, impassioned me, until I lifted myself helplessly against her, grinding myself into her gentleness until the tingling that stretched from my hips to my toes exploded, and I came more joyously than I had any right to expect, given the bittersweetness of our circumstances.

When it was my turn to lay her down, I tongued her every curve until she squirmed with an impatience that was new for her. I dove into her sweetness and led her on a long, tortured journey in the name of pleasure. I kept her hovering just under an orgasm, unsure exactly why, except that I didn't want our lovemaking to ever end, and she looked so beautiful when she was almost there, so wild and alive. This slow teasing demanded more of her, more cries, more body movements, more commitment to her lust as she undulated and ground against my face in hopes of joining with me for the climax that was just outside her reach.

At last, she grabbed my head with her hands, grasping my hair so that my tongue pressed flat and hard against her clitoris, abandoning any semblance of tenderness in her grip on me as she came with three piercing cries that sent birds in the tree above us into flight. I had provoked her to this, to cry out her passion with a full throat to this hillside that had seen so much of women's suffering, to this breaking of the code that said she must subjugate herself to a man.

Afterwards, she pulled my hand towards her opening and tried to put my fingers inside her, as though some new ache had overcome her. I wanted to go inside her with my fingers and to give us both this pleasure, but I shook my head and withdrew my hand. As the older, freer one of us, I felt I had to behave responsibly. I knew that if I entered her, she would be risking disgrace—or worse—on her wedding night, if her husband chose to reveal that he was not the first to cross her threshold.

She looked at me as though she knew what I was thinking

and tears formed in her eyes. She took my hand again and nodded slightly, in a "Yes" that was unmistakable for all its silence. My pussy throbbed anew as I realized the magnitude of the desire she felt, the gift she was giving me, and the risk that she was taking.

She lay on her side facing me and bent her legs at the knees, lifting the top one slightly. I moved my fingers towards her lips and reached in gently first with one, concerned about hurting her. She grabbed all four of my fingers and shoved them at her lips, begging me with her eyes. Overcome by my response to her longing, I thrust them deeply into her pussy, and felt the tear of her hymen. She yelped with surprise and discomfort for a moment, but soon switched to a deep series of groans that called to me to continue each time I thrust into her. They were the sounds of a lone wolf calling to its mate, and I was there and hers, and that was all that mattered.

My thumb grazed her clitoris each time I slammed into her, faster and faster in concert with her cries, until she came again, deeply, through and through the very center of her body and—it seemed—her soul.

For a long time she refused to release me from our last embrace; before slipping away, she looked into my eyes with such sadness I knew this would be our last encounter. The next wedding music I heard in the valley would be hers. I packed my things the morning after the dreaded music woke me from a dreamless sleep.

Though I hid myself behind a tree alongside the road she and her unmarried friends used to walk on the way back from the cotton fields, she was not with them that last day. I knew she had her own home now, with responsibilities to someone else. I only hoped it was someone who cared for her, a man who had the scruples or compassion not to reveal that she was no longer a virgin on her wedding night.

For myself, on the bus back to the city I hoped that the

dark, closed place she had opened in me would not shut again, that I could bring back with me to the rest of my life the hope and joy I had felt with her for the first time in many years.

After completing a shoot in a neighboring area a year and a half later, I could not resist traveling the extra miles to her village. I hoped for a glimpse of her, but feared it as well, for what it might mean to both of us. I saw her in the marketplace with several other young women, some with small children in their arms. She was unmistakably pregnant and she was smiling. In response to some utterance by another woman's little boy, she stopped and reached up to caress his cheek. One of the women said something to her and she laughed. I turned away and brushed a tear from the cheek she had once caressed, just as she had the little boy's.

I was glad to see the color in her cheeks that I remembered surfacing as we made love, to catch a glimpse of the moments of joy she was able to find in this life that had been carved out for her before she was born, and grateful for the way the first flush of her desire had reawakened my own.

Of Ghosts and Shadows

R. Gay

I am watching my lover, Amélie, move through the market sifting through items neither of us can hope to afford. It is stinking hot, the kind of hot where it feels like even my eyeballs are sweating and I want nothing more than to jump into the salty water of the ocean for respite. I am watching my lover because it is too dangerous to do anything but watch. Her face is thin and drawn but when her fingers dance across a trinket she likes or a sweet confection, her eyes light up and the muscles in her shoulders relax. I imagine that she is imagining what it would be like to own these petty items she covets. There are a few tourists in the market, walking around confused, as if they read the wrong brochure. Most Americans come to Haiti expecting it to be like Aruba or St. Kitts. They lump all of these small islands into one paradise where libations flow freely and cabana boys are waiting to attend to their every need. Unfortunately, for them, the cabana boys have all fled the country and there is no ice to cool their drinks.

Amélie and I have known each other since we were children. Our mothers are best friends and together we watched our fathers taken away for supporting free elections, we watched our brothers disappear into the countryside or across the ocean—and we watched each other. We always watched each other. Once, as we sat on her front porch drinking mango juice, holding the cool glasses to our foreheads between sips, she turned to me and said, "Sometimes, Marie Françoise, you are the only thing in this world I care to see."

A gaggle of schoolchildren noisily push their way past me, and just looking at them makes me want to cry. They are so young, if not so innocent, and they too want things they cannot have. Amélie looks up and smiles at me. No one else could recognize it as a smile, but I know. Her eyelids are raised, lips slightly curled at the edges, her thumb grazing her chin. I cock my head to the side and pretend to be interested in a box of cornflakes selling for thirteen dollars. I smooth one eyebrow and draw my finger down my cheek. This is my way of smiling at her, telling her that I wish I could touch her face, hold her hand as we shop, whisper futile fantasies of what we wish for but cannot be.

Slowly, I move towards her ignoring the bony elbows, gaunt faces, tired old women sucking their lips. My heart pounds and with each step, the sharp twinge between my thighs melts into a gentle throb. I should stay away, but I am feeling rebellious today. I enjoy torturing myself with this dance of being so close yet so far. When I am finally next to her, I carefully inspect a handful of patterned beads with my left hand, my right loosely by my side, two fingers reaching towards the worn pink fabric of her dress, one of only three she owns. She leans into me and I can feel the light pressure of her thigh against my finger, her bare arm against mine.

She turns and I can feel her staring at me. I force myself to look forward but it feels like she is reaching inside my body with her eyes, reaching past skin, bone, and blood to my heart. I slide my fingers upwards, along the round edges of her hip to her waist. In another time, or another place, or if I were another person, I would stand behind her, graze the back of her neck with my lips. I would wrap my arms around her for a moment of comfort before taking her hand to continue strolling through the market. But since we are here and now, I step away as I notice a group of young, angry men walking towards us. I doubt that there is any particular reason for their anger. It is the anger that most men feel these days; they are angry about their impotence and their desires and their reality. It is an anger we all feel. But it is an anger they can freely express.

I start walking in the other direction and though I want to turn around and whisper *I love you*, I keep walking. On days like today, I think I could walk until the muscles in my legs burned in protest, until I drifted into the ocean, until I walked into that time and place where Amélie and I could be together, out in the open.

For now, we are women who don't exist. We are less than shadows, more than ghosts. We're the wayward relatives neighbors gossip about in hushed, horrified tones. We are the women people ignore because two women loving each other is an American thing—not the sort of behavior god-fearing island folk would engage in. There are a few people who live openly, men mostly, artists who are indulged in their bright-colored sashaying about town because their work is so brilliant. But even they meet with contempt now and then; an insult hurled here, a sharp rock thrown there. And when they get sick, they are greeted with smug smiles, a harsh reminder of all good things, as their bodies waste to nothing.

Amélie and I were caught once, when I was twenty-three and she was twenty-two. It was late at night and we met in the dark shadows between our houses. Our mothers were asleep; our neighbors were asleep. It was a moment when we were the only two women in the world and we felt a certain freedom to do as we pleased. Even beneath the cover of night it was so hot that we were sweating. There are nights in Haiti when it feels possible that the moon burns just as hot as the sun. She was wearing a T-shirt and worn sandals. I was wearing my housecoat, the top three buttons open. We clasped hands and sank into the darkest part of that dark space and we traced each other's faces with our fingers as if in the space of the few hours since last seeing each other, perhaps our features had changed.

I ran my tongue from the tip of her chin to the hollow just beneath her throat. I tasted the salt of sweat and could feel her breath humming just beneath the surface of her skin. We said nothing, but there was no need for words. Everything that could possibly be said had already been spoken between us over the course of so many years. She clasped the back of my neck and lifted my head, and bringing my lips to hers she kissed me so hard, I imagined she could swallow me whole. Our lips were so dry and cracked that I tasted blood. My tongue pushed past her lips, running over the sharp edges of her teeth, meeting with hers in a tangle of desire and emotion and hunger. And then she pushed me lower, pulling her T-shirt over her narrow shoulders. I took her breasts into my hands, and the soft mounds of flesh spilled through my fingers. I traveled along each ridge and curve of her sepia-toned nipples, moaned softly when she hissed and arched her chest into me. I suckled her nipples until my jaw ached and she was trembling in my arms and the heat between her thighs threatened to sear me. Amélie whispered only one word, "Please," so I lay her on the ground, licking from her breastbone, so flat, down between her breasts, over the slight swell of her belly, my hands greedily spreading her thighs—her thighs, so dark and warm, slick and strong.

The earth beneath our bodies was warm, inviting, generous. I crawled down between her legs and drew my tongue along the soft crevices where her thighs meet, then to her pussy lips, swollen and glistening with moisture. I slid two fingers inside her and paused as the thin membranes of her cunt pulsed around me. She moaned loudly, perhaps too loudly, but I said nothing. Instead, I pushed my fingers deeper inside of her and began feathering my tongue over her hard little nub in light, slow circles. And then we heard a gasp, and I knew if I moved, my heart would fall from my chest and into the ground. It was a moment when I knew that all my fears were about to come to pass. I have had many such moments. Amélie scrambled away from me, reaching for her T-shirt, wrapping her arms around her chest as if she could disappear if she sat ever so still. Slowly, I turned my head and saw my mother beneath a thin shaft of moonlight, and the look on her face was so horrified, so distant, that I hardly recognized her. She turned and walked away. We never spoke of it—neither me and my mother nor me and my lover—but Amélie and I never met in the dark between our houses ever again.

Now, five years later, when we want to make love we steal away to a friend's house when we can, or we get together once in a while with other people like us, women and men who are also less than shadows, more than ghosts. They are sad little affairs, our get-togethers, on Saturday nights in the backroom of someone's house in Port-Au-Prince. The rum is watered down. We have to pay ten dollars American to get in, and the entire time, we try and pretend that we are in New York or Miami or Montreal, at a club with friends. We try and show each other affection. We try to pretend that we aren't staring at the doorway, afraid that we'll be caught. And Amèlie and I will steal to the bathroom, dark and dank, with little room to move. We'll fumble with our clothing, and shove our hands between each other's thighs, kissing for so long that we start breathing for each other, trying to extract as much pleasure from our bodies as possible before we have to return home.

On a strangely cool December evening not too long ago, a group of thugs raided our private party. Amélie and I were sitting on a couch, our arms around each other, when five men came through the front door. We could smell drink on them—we could smell hate. Albert, a friend of ours, was by the door, and they grabbed him by his shirt, shoving him against the wall, saying the crudest, cruelest things they could. One of them, tall, fair-skinned with wide features, threw the stereo on the floor and began beating it with a baseball bat. But for some reason, the music played on. The air was filled with their taunts and the tinny sound of *konpa*. "Faggots," the man with the bat sneered. For a moment, we froze, eleven of us, hoping our passivity would bring the moment to an end. And then we were running through the house and out the back door, away from that place. We knew we were cowards but we didn't dare look back.

The next day, we heard that Albert was in the hospital with three broken ribs, a broken hand, and a chorus of bruises. I mourned for his pain. But I didn't want that to be me, and I didn't want that to be Amèlie. It was simply one more shame I chose to bear. The same could be said for all of us. But we continued to meet, continued to defy *the rules*, because we knew that such stolen moments are the one small thing we have in this big, big world. .

When I arrive home, my mother is in bed asleep. For the past several years, she has spent most of her time sleeping and her slumber is an understandable one. I stand in her doorway, listening to the sound of her breathing. It is shallow and timid. The wrinkles in her face are smooth. She looks so relaxed, so at peace that I can't bear to wake her and disturb her stolen moment. And to wake her would do just that. I see the pain in her face when she looks at me. It is the sorrow of living with a daughter she loves but doesn't want. There are times when I think of settling down with a man, any man. It would please my mother to no end. But then I think of the scent of Amélie's neck and the flutter of her fingers over mine. And I know that despite the unbearable distance between us, I would not have things any other way. Neither would she.

In the kitchen, I prepare myself a mug of *café au lait*, and though it is hot, even indoors, I hold my face over the steam, my pores puckering open. From the window I can see directly into Amélie's house. So I sit there, and wait to watch her return home from the market. Her mother waves from the porch and I offer her a shy smile, a careful wave, and then I look away before my face says too much. I sit for hours and I think of the last time Amélie and I made love, how fleeting it was, how hungry it has left me. I think of her sticky thighs rubbing against each other as she walks and I think of her in the market, and the warmth of her thigh pressing against the edge of my fingertips—stolen moments.

The first time we made love was a shy and awkward affair. I was nineteen, she had just turned eighteen, and as we walked home from school, the cracked pavement burning through the thin soles of our shoes, I grabbed her hand with mine, clenching it so tightly my knuckles turned white. She stopped and stared at me. I opened my mouth, but there were no words. But there were words, I simply didn't know how to wrap my lips around them. In the distance, a lone Citröen ambled towards us, but I closed my eyes, leaned into her, and brushed my lips across hers. I traced the arch of her eyebrow with one finger, and then I ran away, trying not to cry. She called after me, but when I turned around, she wasn't following, so I kept running, off the road and through a cane field, ignoring the brambles that scratched my skin, until I reached my house.

My mother clutched her chest when she saw me, but I shook my head and retired to my bedroom where I sat on the cool cement floor in a corner, my arms wrapped around my knees, rocking back and forth.

Moments later, there was a light knock on the door.

"Go away," I said hoarsely, but the wooden door slowly creaked open and there Amélie stood, pale, lips pursed. She stepped inside my room and closed the door behind her.

"Why did you do that?" she asked.

I lowered my head, staring at the floor. She moved closer, close enough for me to smell sweat and the lingering scent of her perfume. She knelt, her knees pressed against mine and she cupped my face between her hands and in that moment she was holding the whole of me.

"Why did you do that?" she asked again.

I looked up. "I feel things I am not supposed to feel. I want things I am not supposed to want."

"How do you know that?"

I laughed, bitterly. "If you knew, you would turn around. You would never look upon me again."

"Do you not know me at all?"

"It is not as simple as that."

She took my hand in hers, held it between her breasts. Her skin thrummed lightly through her shirt and my fingers trembled. It took all my self-control not to move my hand mere inches to the right or left. And then, her hand covering mine, she slid my hand under her shirt, up the smoothness of her stomach and cupped it around her breast. I sighed a heavy sigh, enjoying the weight of her in the palm of my hand. I had imagined that moment for so long, lying in bed alone on dark, humid nights, that I felt a sharp, intense pain between my eyes, and for a moment, the world went white.

"Perhaps it is that simple," she said.

A single cry escaped the dryness of my throat. I kissed her chin, her neck, pulled her shirt over her shoulders as my mouth fumbled lower to her nipples. She held me to her breast, her fingers drawing small circles against the back of my neck. I could hear my mother shuffling around in the kitchen and my heart pounded as I prayed she wouldn't disturb us. I slid my hand beneath the elastic waistband of her skirt, past the line of her panties, moaning as the wiry curls covering her mound tickled my skin. She remained silent and kneeling, but she parted her thighs and pressed herself against my fingers. Though I had no clear idea of what I was doing, I parted her pussy lips, reveled in the moisture I found there, eagerly searching for that place of pleasure that was already as familiar to me as my own. I could hear my mother like a distant echo calling me to dinner, asking Amèlie if she wanted to join us. I pressed my fingers harder against Amèlie's clit, faster. She was slick and swollen beneath me, slipping closer and closer into me as her hips rocked. The muscles of her thighs were taut, her spine rigid. I could not breathe. But when she came— and then scrambled away from me, fixing her skirt, just as my mother entered my room—the world opened up.

It is hours past dark when Amélie finally comes home. As she stands on the threshold of her house, she looks at me, sees me in the shadows, and changes her mind, making her way to my house. I greet her at the door and she looks so sad, so hollow, that I open my arms and she tumbles against my chest, perching her head against my shoulder.

"I cannot sleep alone tonight," she whispers. "I simply cannot."

I lift her chin with a finger, look into her eyes. "We could call on Patricia, see if she'd let us spend the night there."

Amélie shakes her head. "I want to sleep here in your...in our bed."

There are butterflies in my stomach. I did not realize until now that I have always wanted to hear her say those words. "My mother is here."

"I don't care, do you?"

I think of all the tiny pleasures we have denied ourselves over the years. I cannot deny her this one thing, the only thing she has ever asked of me. "Come," I say, leading her to the bedroom.

We tiptoe past my mother's bedroom. She is snoring now, but I do not bother to shut her door, nor do I shut mine. Amélie's courage tonight, however blind it may be, makes me want to be just as brave. Her courage makes me wonder if we really have anything to fear—if it is only ghosts and shadows forbidding our passion. She strips out of her clothes, as do I, and we crawl into my bed, which creaks beneath our weight. She lies on her back, I on my side. The mattress is so thin that I can feel the coils of the bed frame.

She traces my lips with her thumb. Her smile is genuine. The depths of her light brown eyes are fathomless. I see wisdom there, fear, a little happiness, desire.

The tension between us is palpable.

"Love me," she says.

I trace the sharp angle of her chin with my tongue, sliding one of my legs between hers, my right breast pressing against her left. Our nipples brush and I shiver. I kiss the silence beneath her eye and, dabbing a bead of sweat from her forehead, I bring my finger to my mouth, tasting her sweat. She shifts, turning her head towards me. One of her arms snakes around my body and she draws long lines along my spine with her fingernails. Our skin clings together. I wet my lips with my tongue and kiss her slowly, softly. Our lips barely move. It is such a moment of stillness and passion that I ache. Her mouth opens wide enough to surround my lips, swallow my entire body. Her knees, already quivering, squeeze my leg. We kiss harder, our tongues shyly meeting, the tip of hers pointed, the tip of mine rounded. I relish the juxtaposition. The taste of her satiates me. She slides her fingers up my back and through my damp hair, with gentle pressure. I inch lower, leave a thin trail of saliva from her lips to her neck. Gently, I tug at the tight skin there with my teeth. She curls her fingers, still in my hair, into a loose fist. I let my teeth sink deeper, then wash away the threat of pain with my tongue, suckling softly. I kiss the spot of her pulse before drawing my lips across her shoulder, tasting the soft patch of hair beneath her armpit, the concave of her elbow, another pulse of soft skin beneath her wrist. Carefully, I follow each of the deep lines in the palm of her hand, sucking each of her fingers into my mouth, grazing her knuckles with my teeth, savoring all the flavors I find there.

When I am done wetting her with my desire, her hand fumbles for my breast, and she rolls my nipple between her thumb and forefinger. Waves of pleasure wash over me, and I crawl atop of her. We kiss again—we kiss until we are both gasping for breath and our lips are numb. Her cunt is pressed against mine. We are breast to breast and thigh to thigh. When my hips rise, hers follow. But we move as slowly as we are kissing. Every motion is deliberate. We are defying time and circumstance. I straddle one of her thighs and groan loudly as my clit throbs against her bare skin.

"Do you feel how wet I am?" I ask her.

She nods, arches her back and lifts her leg. My eyes closed, I writhe against her. For a moment, I almost forget that she is there. I am alone with the idea of her—the shadow of her—and the burning that echoes inside my cunt. I clench my thighs around her, and bury my head between her breasts. Sweat falls from my body onto hers. The walls are thin enough that I can hear my mother turning in her bed. My right hand finds Amélie's and our fingers entwine. We hold each other so tightly my hand becomes numb. But I ride her thigh, my pussy lips spreading wider and wider, until I reach that point where the pleasure is so intense it overwhelms me and I fear I will suffocate.

My left hand sneaks between her thighs, and I slide two fingers inside her as deep as I can possibly reach and hold them there, filling her as I grind my hips faster, as fast as the flutter of a hummingbird's wings. My thumb finds her clit and I press hard enough to feel the bone just beneath the thin folds. A sharp keening sound rises from deep within me. I don't have the strength to stop it. I hear my mother's feet hitting the floor. Tension crawls from my toes, along the backs of my thighs, over the round of my ass to the base of my spine. My heart is beating so very fast. I wonder if Amélie's mother knows where Amélie is, what her daughter is doing. I exhale loudly. I did not realize I have been holding my breath.

"Shh," Amélie says, pressing one finger to my lips. She stares right into me, grips my shoulders, and raises her leg forcefully. The bone of her knee bruises me. I curl my fingers inside of her upwards, pressing against the doughy pad, and her entire body shudders. A gush of wetness oozes around and between my fingers. We are staining each other's bodies. I think about how dangerous this is for us—of the shame our mothers would feel if others knew. I think about stones striking flesh. I realize that my mother could be standing in the doorway but I do not turn my head. There is a stirring that hovers beneath my navel and slowly spreads throughout my body. I see the edge, and spill over it before I can stop myself, coming hard, so hard that my limbs feel like lead and I collapse against my lover.

I try and catch my breath but the air is thick with the smell of sex. I try and slide my body lower so I can pleasure her more, but she shakes her head, moving aside, pulling me into her damp embrace. I pull my fingers from inside her and paint her belly with her own juices. She covers her hand with mine.

I fall asleep before I can tell her I love her, listening to the sound of her beating heart and rushing blood. I cannot tell her that she should leave before dawn arrives. I am too tired and too satisfied to be afraid. In the morning, my mother will find us like this, limbs entangled, bodies as one, breathing each other's breath. She will think she is seeing ghosts or perhaps shadows. In many ways, she will be right.

At Long Last
Madeleine Oh

This was it.

As the train slowed, I snapped my novel shut and pulled my suitcase from between the seats. In a few minutes we'd be face to face after thirty years. Was it curiosity or obsession that had me haring up to Scotland to see the man who'd shattered my twenty-two-year-old heart when he married my cousin, Penelope?

Why was I here? To see how the years had treated Alec? Did I hope to find him sporting a massive beer gut or sagging jowls? Perhaps recovering from a triple by-pass and double hip replacements? Sitting in a wheelchair pushed around by his brand-new trophy wife?

If he looked the same as he had at twenty-five, I would rail against the injustice in the world. He didn't. But he wasn't the one who was recognized first.

"Jasmine Waters! May I call you, Jasmine?"

It was Emily, wife number two. One of my faithful readers.

"Of course you may. It's my name."

"But is seems so…You being so famous and…"

"You must call me Jasmine. Alec does." She all but blushed. How deliciously English and young she was, like a fat ripe plum, ready to drop off the branch into my hand.

"He calls you, Jazzikins."

He would. He had. Couldn't call me Jazz or Jasmine the way everyone else did. He had to make up a special name that still had the power to tweak my soul. Standing beside her was my old heartache himself. "Hi, Alec."

A man who had left his wife with an autistic teenager and a senile mother-in-law had no right to thrive on it. But heaven help us all, he was still gorgeous. His dark hair was halfway gray, but it looked good on him. And as for his laugh lines, where had they come from? From smiling to himself as he walked away from his responsibilities?

"Jazzikins!" His smile was so sincere, I wanted to spit. "Fantastic to see you!"

I held out my hand before he had a chance to even think about hugging me. "Alec. It's good to see you." That wasn't a lie. I was satisfying my curiosity and, to be truthful, he was as easy on the eyes as ever. He still had a smile to invoke impure thoughts in virgins' minds. It had in mine. He'd just never delivered.

"Jazzikins." I restrained a wince. "After all these years." He grabbed my hand and pulled me into a hug before I could evade, planting a great smacking kiss on my left cheek. While I took a deep, cleansing breath, he stepped back, looking me up and down as if contemplating a purchase. "I still can't believe it! You're here, and all because of Emmsy. Who'd have thought it?"

Thought what? That I could write? That his wife could read? That he was incapable of using anyone's full name? I made a point of not snarling. "How could I not come? Invited to Scotland by a loyal and ardent reader?" He'd better not think I'd spent all day in a train for him. But he did.

"Alec," Emily put a hand on his shoulder. Marking her territory, perhaps? "let's head for the car. I bet Jasmine wants to kick off her shoes and have a drink."

I decided I might like her, even if she had supplanted my cousin, and hoped her idea of a "drink" entailed something more than a cup of tea. I couldn't help wondering what Alec had told her about me. Was I his ex-wife's cousin, the sister of a school friend, an old, lost love? Most likely, none of the above. Maybe he never remembered breaking my heart.

His dark-green Jaguar was an improvement on the Deux Chevaux he owned the last time I'd ridden with him. His transport might have changed but his laugh hadn't; neither had his voice, or the way he drove too fast, and slid through lights as they changed. He made a very Alec crack and Emily laughed, throwing her head back a little, shaking her long, chestnut-colored hair and showing the vulnerable expanse of a long, pale neck. I'd always longed for a long neck. Still, I had bigger boobs—but she had Alec.

Did I honestly care now? Come to that, had I ever really been in the running? I'd fallen for him like a felled oak. And gotten over him, or so I always told myself. I wasn't the type to do unrequited love. But I'd hurt. Standing as bridesmaid at Penelope's wedding was an agony I hoped never to repeat. Now was payback time! Alec owed for breaking my virgin heart, leaving a gaping hole in my cousin's life, and for the handicapped son he'd abandoned. Penelope wouldn't seek revenge. She was far too kind and up to her eyes with providing care. Simon missed his father desperately, Alec's mother was too senile to realize he'd gone and poor Penelope was aging daily.

But I was here and willing, and as we settled in the living room, overlooking the garden, I prepared to settle the score. One way or another.

Trouble was, I liked Emily. I could hardly fault her for falling for Alec; I'd done the same when I hadn't been that much younger. And she was a fan. She had every one of my books in hardback and all but kissed my hands when I gave her an advance copy of the new one. Hard to hate a woman who admires your work and mixes a mean g-and-t.

By the time we were halfway through dinner, I was seriously thinking about smushing Alec's face into his tiramisu as he pontificated about local politics, the virtues of his new car, and the tremendous responsibilities of his job. How many more "Jazzikins" and "Emmsies" and "old things" was I prepared to endure? It was the last that got to me the worst. He had two years on me and I didn't have gray hair. Thanks to science.

Emily was far more tolerant than I. That's what love does to you. But I caught the occasional spark of irritation, and the glances of female complicity she shot my way.

I grinned back as her dark, gray eyes flashed amusement and when she hugged me for helping her load the dishwasher, I squeezed back. Her body was warm and soft and her breasts pressed nicely against mine. She was my height, her body firmer and her breasts higher, but we fit together, the old and new loves of Alec Carpenter.

"How's the coffee coming along, girls?" he called from the sitting room. Emily looked ready to give him hot coffee where it hurt.

It was an odd after-dinner conversation. Emily wanted to talk about my books. I was more than happy to oblige. Alec didn't exactly sneer at mysteries but he came darn close. Then he committed the cardinal sin. "How much do you make on a book?"

"Tell me what you earned last year, and I'll tell you what I made."

He declined the invitation with an irritating laugh. "Oh, Jazzikins! You've changed."

In more ways then he could guess.

I broke up the evening by pleading weariness. Emily kissed

me good night with a promise of tea in the morning. Her lips were warm and ripe and young. Hugging her was a joy. I looked forward to my early morning cuppa.

She brought it wearing a short pink robe with satin rosebuds scattered over the yoke. It suited her, bringing out highlights in her dark hair. She blushed deliciously when I told her so. Alec had seldom told me that I looked beautiful either. She sat on the edge of my bed and I watched her firm nipples ride underneath the thin cotton. I'd found my revenge. I just had to find the means.

Alec handed it to me at breakfast.

Emily was annoyed.

I was thrilled.

"Why this weekend? Didn't you tell them you had a visitor?" Emily gave him the closest thing to a pout I'd seen yet.

"Never mind." Time to smooth some amicable oil over the marital waters. "If Alec has a crisis at work, he needs to go."

Emily muttered disagreement.

"I knew Jazzikins would understand." I got Alec's best smile, and heartfelt regrets. He did both really well. "I feel terrible mucking up your weekend when you've come so far."

"You haven't mucked it up. Emily and I will frolic together in the fleshpots of Aberdeen." Emily's face brightened. Alec glowered. No other word for it. I gave him my sweet smile. "She'll look after me, I'm certain." He looked worried. He should. "You go take care of your crisis. Don't bother about us." I sure wasn't going to bother about him. And if I had my way, neither would Emily.

He streaked off in his Jaguar. Emily and I set out in her little Fiesta. Size was of no importance.

"Take me on the tourist tour," I asked. "Show me the sights, and all the bookshops. We can stop somewhere for lunch and somewhere for tea and somewhere for a drink, and if we really feel like it, another somewhere for dinner."

She giggled like a schoolgirl let out of boarding school. We visited the bookstores, and had coffee in a dark-paneled cafe where we sat close in a corner and she confided in me that Alec worked terribly long hours. His new wife felt neglected. She took me to the rose garden and the maze. We got nicely lost, and held hands muddling our way out.

She drove us to the beach. "It's almost deserted," I said looking at the great crescent of golden sand. "No one's swimming."

"Too damn cold. This is the North Sea."

It wouldn't stop me. "I've got to put a toe in after coming this far."

I left my shoes in the car and ran across the beach. Emily hesitated a few seconds, before following me. The tide was out. I zigzagged over the hard sand, glancing over my shoulder. Emily followed, cutting corners to catch up. I let her, just as we neared the water.

"Chicken?" I teased as I jumped in. Emily hadn't been kidding! An icy wash hit my ankles. She stared. I took a step deeper and held up my skirt.

"Never!" She followed me, and gasped. "This is ridiculous!"

I wouldn't argue. We ran along the water's edge, keeping to the firm sand. My toes were tingling with cold as I was outran Emily again. The girl was no marathoner, that was for sure, so I slowed to take her hand, as I made a beeline for the car.

By time we got there, my feet were numb and turning red, and my calves stung from salt water and North Sea wind. Emily was shivering. "Alec will never believe we did that!" Her right eye watered from the cold, but she grinned.

"Why need he know? Do you tell him everything?"

She shook her head. Slowly. "Not everything."

Smart girl.

We wiped our feet on Alec's cricketing sweater. The

closely-knitted wool warmed our skin as it absorbed the damp and the sand. The sweater was unwearable by the time we were finished. Emily shook her head at it. "He'll throw a wobbly when he sees that."

"Let's save him the worry, then." I took the sand- and salt-encrusted heap and tossed it toward the beach, where the wind caught it momentarily, whipping it higher before it fell, wet and heavy, on the sand.

Emily watched it arc up and fall. I wasn't too sure of the look on her face. Regret? Shock? Worry? Until she smiled. "I doubt he'll miss it until next summer." She shrugged. A wry smile twisted her mouth. She took my hand and squeezed.

I pulled her to me. Slowly. Giving her time to draw back, I wrapped my arms around her and dropped a soft kiss on her forehead. "I'll never tell," I said. She kissed back, a soft whisper of skin on my chilled lips. The warmth of her breath was lost in the wind but the heat of her body wasn't. We stood, arms entwined, warming each other against the wind. It wasn't enough. Emily shivered. "We need to get out of the cold," I said, "Where's the nearest place for a drink?"

The all-but-deserted bar of a vast Victorian hotel.

Dark Lincrusta covered the walls and the rings of generations of damp glasses marred the oak tables. Emily ran her fingers up and down her glass. I raised my drink and savored the best single malt whisky the bald-headed bartender had to offer. Watching Emily over the rim of my glass, I drank. The old codger's best was pretty good. I took another taste, holding the whiskey in my mouth and working it over my tongue before swallowing.

Emily's manicured nails tapped the side of her glass. She hadn't tasted it beyond a first sip when I'd proposed our mutual health. "Drink up."

"You want to go home?" Her eyes were dark with unspoken wants.

"I think we both need a nice, hot bath."

Her full lips parted. Slowly lifting her glass, she tilted it and drank half the whiskey down with one swallow. I expected her to choke and splutter but she just smiled. "That's good." Her glass made a dull thud on the table as I nodded.

"I never settle for less than the best you can have...or give," I said. Her hand rested on the table, palm down. I covered it with mine. Her skin was still cold. Emily moved her hand so our fingers meshed. There was no mistaking the look in her eyes. She would appreciate what Alec had refused.

She bit her lower lip with one very white tooth. "I'm glad Alec is at work."

"So am I." I swigged the last of my whisky almost as fast as Emily did hers, ignoring the burning as I swallowed.

We were back in the house in minutes and upstairs in seconds. On the landing, with its ornate railings and decorative cornice, I paused. Her room or mine?

She settled that. Sweet, quiet Emily dragged me into the bathroom. Squeezing my hand, she leaned over the claw-foot tub. Steam rose, misting the gilt-framed mirror as Emily stood upright, and hesitated.

I didn't. I reached out and released her hair from the pale-blue scrunchee. As she shook her head and ran her fingers through her hair, I unbuttoned her blouse.

Did she and Alec share this tub? How hard did he get, seeing her firm, creamy skin swelling above her pink lace bra? Did he lust after her young body? Who was I kidding? They were married! They did this every night. Except when he hared off to save the day and left her alone. But today Emily wasn't alone and she hankered for me. Her nipples weren't hard from the cold this time.

I unsnapped her bra and cupped her breasts. They were round and sweet, just like her. I pushed aside the lace and slipped the straps and her shirt off her shoulders and unsnapped her jeans. She wore a pretty lace thong that matched her bra. They ended up together on the floor. Her legs were long, her thighs smooth and her tummy flat. Her breasts hung high and firm with nipples the color of the inside of a Venus shell. I'd looked like that once, back when Alec had rejected me. Now I had crepe thighs and a belly stretched by three pregnancies, but along with the cellulite, I'd gained experience and I knew what pleased women.

I eased my hands down her belly and watched her face. My mouth curled with anticipation. Emily smiled back. I didn't wait any longer. Cupping the back of her head with my hand, I pulled her face to mine. I started soft and slow, just a brush of lips on lips, but she opened her mouth and swallowed the kiss and my breath. Her lips were warm, moist, and as eager as a virgin's. Hell, she most likely *was* one, with a woman. I kissed back, trailing my other hand down between her shoulder blades and holding her steady in my arms.

As I broke off the kiss, I whispered. "Get in the tub." Like a good child, she obeyed. As she stepped in, I couldn't resist skimming my hand over the curve of her lovely, smooth haunch.

"Aren't you coming in?" When I nodded, she reached for a bottle and poured fragrant oil into the bath. The room was now filled with lavender-scented steam. I dropped my clothes on the tiled floor and joined her.

Perfumed water rose to our breasts as I sat down. Brits may not have figured out about ice in cold drinks, but they have hot baths right. As I soaped Emily's breasts with scented foam, she closed her eyes, sighing as my fingers trailed lower. I soaped her all over like a child, having her kneel up as I washed between her legs and down her thighs.

After I rinsed her with a damp washcloth, she washed me with a touch that left me impatient and ready. Damp and heated, we patted each other dry with warm towels that wrapped us from shoulders to knees.

Emily raised her fingers to my face. "Jasmine," she said, her voice tight and her eyes bright with curiosity and need.

"Come on!" I grabbed her hand and led her down the hallway to the room I'd slept in last night.

She tugged me in the opposite direction.

It took a couple of seconds for me to register where we were headed. She pulled open the door and pulled me inside. After all these years, I was, at long last, ending up in Alec Carpenter's bed.

I grinned as I yanked back the covers, climbed in, and pulled Emily beside me. She tumbled onto her belly and the smooth expanse of her back and lovely, curvy butt inspired me. "Don't move! I'll be back in a minute."

I was down the hall to the bathroom and back with a jar of lavender lotion in less time than it takes to tell.

"What are you doing?' Emily asked, looking over her shoulder as I walked through the doorway.

She hadn't moved.

"Pleasuring you." I squeezed out a dobbit of lotion and rubbed my hands together to warm it before easing my palms across her shoulders and down her back to the curve of her waist. She sighed with pleasure, so I reached for the lotion again. I anointed her. Kissing her neck and shoulders as I stroked lotion into her back and arms. Fluttering my tongue on the soft pale skin behind her knees as I massaged her thighs and butt. She went limp and relaxed under my touch. Lovely. But I didn't want her too loose. I needed her sweating with want as her body arched under me and her eyes blazed her need.

I rested a hand on the curve of her hip and nudged. "Roll over."

Emily didn't need asking twice. She flipped onto her back, giving me an uninterrupted view of her delicious, firm breasts. I ran my tongue up from her rib cage to her nipple and felt her excitement as I worked it between my lips. She gasped as I

Madeleine Oh

pulled it into my mouth, and let out a slow moan of contentment as I worked my lips to her other nipple.

"Don't stop," she whispered as I pulled away.

"I won't," I promised.

I could smell her arousal over the scent of lavender but I took my time, running my fingertips over her curves and tasting her skin. As I rested my hand on her bush, she was whimpering with need. I spread her legs with my shoulders and opened her with my fingertips, reveling in the scent of her sex. Gently I breathed on her moist flesh and ran the tip of my tongue from fore to aft. Her head came off the pillow with a jolt, and the eyes that met mine were wide as her cunt.

"Jasmine!" It came out on the tail of a gasp. "There? No one ever…"

Can't say I was surprised. Alec always was a selfish bastard but… "Shhh." I didn't say anything else. My tongue was busy.

She was sweet and fresh as morning and as ready as sunrise. I'd hoped to take longer but in minutes she climaxed with a series of little cries and frenzied jerks of her hips as frantic hands grasped my hair.

She was still gasping, her breasts rising and falling with each pant as I eased up the bed and took her face in both hands. I kissed her very gently, letting my lips linger before opening her mouth so she could taste the joy I'd given her. She was halfway to fainting when I let her go. I settled for gathering her close, delighting in her warmth and scent and, I have to be truthful here, thrilled that I'd upstaged Alec.

Nasty of me. Bitchy of me. But in the circumstances…

"Jasmine?"

"Yes." I smiled at her as I ran my hand over her hair.

"You haven't come?'

I shook my head. "Not yet." It could wait. I was enjoying a different satisfaction.

Emily disagreed. Propping herself on one elbow, she bent her head to my breast and carefully worked her way down. When she reached my cunt, she delved in with the enthusiasm and ardor of a convert. I came three times before she finally paused and I insisted we take a nap. She might not need a rest at her age, but I did.

We slept the day and night around, waking as the early sun streamed in through the open curtains.

After a slow morning loving, Emily lent me Alec's toweling robe to eat breakfast in. We sat in the bay window, sipping coffee and spreading creamy butter and tart Seville marmalade on butteries. These were heavy, fatty pastries I'd have disliked in anyone else's company but now they tasted of Emily.

We were debating the wisdom of more coffee, or back to bed when Alec walked in, clothes rumpled, hair on end and eyes red from lack of sleep. I was scared he'd smell the sex on us but all he seemed to notice was food. Muttering a couple of sentences about idiot crews who don't maintain equipment properly, he wolfed down the remaining four butteries and the better part of the second pot of coffee his nice wife Emily fixed. Apparently Alec had not enjoyed the past twenty-four hours as much as his wife and I had, and unfortunately, he wobbled off to bed to restore himself so that put paid to an encore for us. But there would be other times. I was a patient woman.

"So glad you two get on so well together," Alec said that evening as we walked down the platform to my sleeper. "Some people have been unbelievably snooty. Peter hardly talks to me now."

Can't say I blamed Peter. He was bound to take his sister's part. Heaven help me! Had I really loved this man? He was so self-centered, patronizing and just plain thick! I had, once, when I was young and equally thick but now I was well and truly cured. "Nice of you to ask Emmsy to your book signing in Edinburgh," Alec went on, as I hugged her goodbye

"It'll be nice to see someone I know." I gave a wave and hopped on the train. "I'll let you know the date." Something good had come out of the hurt of Alec Carpenter. I was going to have to call my publisher and insist they add Edinburgh to my next book tour. They wouldn't need to provide any escort. I could arrange that. I settled back in my seat, thinking. I was a trifle torn between genuine fondness for Emily and our promising affair and the certainty that Penelope would get a kick out of knowing I'd made Alec a cuckold.

Egg
Tamai Kobayashi

They are lovers working in the same office, but few in the company even suspect. Professional, courteous and distant. Their coworkers think they hate each other. But one morning, during Shel's conference call, Junko comes into her office, pulls down Shel's lace panties and eats her out, tongue stabbing and then a full finger-fuck. Shel is enraged. Plots her revenge.

The next morning Jun knocks on Shel's office door. She looks contrite, and for a moment Shel pities her.

"Can I come in?"

Shel nods. But this time it is Jun who is slammed against the desk, Jun's pants yanked down. Jun, already wet, had expected this one-upmanship. But Shel only slips something inside her, an egg-sized something, and simply lets her go.

"That's it? That's all?"

"You've got a lot to answer for: the conference call, and fucking me on the photocopier." Shel hands Jun the Xerox sheet, a grainy image of Jun's hand in Shel's cunt.

In the bathroom, Jun sits on the toilet. What was it, this big surprise? But she can't get it out, this egg, it's too round, too slippery, she is too wet for her own good. But it is time for her report and she steps out of the cubicle.

Shel is waiting outside, with Sash, a new girl from down on fifth.

"Looking for something?" Shel smirks.

Jun brushes past her without a word. But she catches Sash's rebuke.

"Jesus, Shel, she's presenting today, give her a break."

At nine-thirty, Jun waits to give her report in front of the Board, with all the senior management in attendance. Shel is there, sitting beside Sash. Jun fidgets with her papers, as Clark drones on. She's worked on this for weeks so it better go well. Then she feels it, low, a vibration within her cunt. The egg.

Jun shifts uncomfortably. Glances up at Shel, who's smiling.

Jun smirks. Is that all there is?

Clark babbling on and on and a steady buzz between Jun's legs.

Jun shuffles her papers, her transparency falls to the floor.

The egg is doing its work. She shifts and the egg twirls inside her; shifts again, uneasy. The buzzing is faster, now, and higher, an urgent hum.

Clark steps down. Jun's turn.

But she drops her papers at the podium, and the transparency is lost. There is a burning inside of her, a whirl that spins her off, her mind can't focus and wet, so wet. Her hand shakes, cannot hold the plastic cup, the water splashes over her spiral-bound notes. Jun hands out copies of her report, her only hope, and staggers out the door.

Shel follows behind her. "Nice try." A parting shot.

But it's Jun's turn to be enraged. She tails Shel down to her office, pushes her to the wall.

But Shel hands her an envelope, says curtly, "Fuck her and I'll pull it out. In the focus room." She slaps a briefcase to

Jun. "Fuck her with this. Instructions in the envelope." And Shel exits.

Jun stands, envelope and briefcase in hand.

Jun opens the envelope, dreading. Sash. The instructions are clear.

A knock on Shel's door and Jun opens it. Sash, the new girl on fifth.

Sash asks, "Shel said you wanted to see me?"

The egg hums inside of Jun, she cannot pull away.

"In—in the focus room."

On the way down Sash is chattering. "…Wouldn't worry… great report…speaking in public…"

Jun opens the door to the focus room. A wall-sized mirror to her left. Two-way. Jun knows why Shel has chosen this room.

Fuck her toward the mirror, spread her and let me see it.

Jun places the briefcase down on the table. Seduction is not her forte. And Sash seems like a sweet young thing. Sure, Jun had caught Sash glancing at her in the washroom, staring in the boardroom when Sash thought Jun wasn't looking. But this, this was different.

Jun hangs back, sees Sash's lovely neck, her breasts in that loose silky blouse, the skirt clinging to her ass.

Jun stammers, "You…you have a run in your nylons… at…at the back. They're caught…here, turn around."

Sash's eyebrows arch. "That's it? That's all."

Jun thinks, she's expecting more.

Sash turns, but as Jun's hand begins its journey up, Sash turns again, embarrassed, explaining, "I don't wear underwear, not with nylons."

Jun blushes, and Sash is amused.

So Sash turns again and Jun's hands run up her legs, to her hips.

"Lean forward," Jun whispers hoarsely. Sash places her palms on the table in front of her.

Jun squats, peels down the nylon, but only so far. Sash's skirt is lifted and she can see her pussy; her smell is light, not yet thick with desire. The mirror can see them, Jun knows. Jun knows Shel is watching.

With one swift motion Jun grabs Sash's hips, rams her tongue inside her cunt, sucking blindly. Sash yelps with surprise, her legs bucking but the nylon's got her. Jun eats and eats, mashing her face into Sash's furrow, no subtleties now, her mouth devouring Sash, chin rubbing clit, her nose in those folds, her skin, teeth biting ass. A cry from Sash, lower, something akin to a moan, as tongue flashes in and out, Jun's mouth gobbling clit and juice, tongue circles, then bull's-eye, the centre, and Sash jerks, almost there but Jun remembers the envelope, the briefcase, and steps back, gulping the air.

Sash blinks, coming to her senses.

Jun glances at the mirror. *Will she do it?*

"Up on the table," Jun commands, and strides forward. She begins tearing off Sash's lovely silk shirt, the nylons, the skirt. She pulls Sash to her knees, turns her ass to the mirror.

"Do you touch yourself, Sash?" Jun asks.

Sash nods.

"Then fuck yourself for me, like this, for the mirror."

Sash hesitates, "Touch me," she whispers.

Jun slaps her hard, between the legs. Sash jolts against the sting.

But Sash begins. Her position is difficult, and Jun feels for her. Sash's fingers are nimble, the juices coming quick. Jun sees the sweat beading on Sash's back, the arching line of bone and muscle, straining thighs, round asscheeks, taunt belly and breasts in limbo. Sash is so perfect like this; the mirror catches her, her cunt a revelation.

With a start, Jun sees the video camera in the corner and knows Shel's preserving this.

Sash's staccato gasps—she's so close to coming, but Jun takes her hand away.

"Please Jun." Sash looks so desperate now.

Jun eases her off the table. "Catch your breath."

Jun goes to the briefcase, snaps it open. Inside, a harness and dildo. A bow and ribbon, reading *For Sash*.

Jun strips off her clothes, straps on the harness and dildo. Sash watches. Her chest is flushed, glossy.

"Jun," she says, "I've never...not with that."

Jun takes her to the table, lifts her up. "Not if you don't want to," Jun murmurs. And at last begins tasting those nipples. Grasping breasts, she presses them together, takes both of those small buds into her mouth. Sash moans, feels the sucking down to her cunt. Jun revels in the fullness in her hands, the play of pebbles in her mouth. She feels Sash wanting her, and it makes her want to fuck her more.

Jun pushes Sash back on the table, pushes open Sash's thighs—matted curls, a dark flush within, the liquid seeping out of her cunt hole, viscous.

"Eat me," Sash begs.

Jun only smiles. She nestles the tip of her dildo at the edge of Sash's lips, the barest hint of motion.

"Sash," Jun whispers. The dildo brushes. "Sash." The dildo's caress.

"Jun, I've never..."

Jun looks down at her, rocks a smidgen in. Sash feels it, and Jun rocks out.

"One word," Jun murmurs, "and I'm out of here." A promise or a threat? Rocks deeper, but only slightly. Rocks and rocks, no deeper, but Sash can feel it, and instinctively tries to pull the dildo in as it pulls away.

Rocks. Rocks. No more, no less.

Sash has to ask, has to beg.

Rocks.

"Deeper, please."

Jun complies, but barely. Sash's hips are up, but Jun forces her down.

"Deeper, Jun, please."

Again.

Sash, in tears, cannot hold back, "Oh fuck me."

Jun does just that, plowing into her, and fuck slam fuck of rutting joy, reaming bliss, a humping, bucking animalistic greed, not for the camera, not for Shel, but her her her, a piercing, cleansing need. The egg spins inside of her, like she's fucking herself, and Shel behind the mirror, she can see all of this.

Jun pulls out. Sash is on the table, barely able to move, yet she's still not come. Jun's mouth suckles Sash's slit, her fingers thrust into her cunt, she pumps and swallows, pumps and swallows, Sash's leg over Jun's shoulder, hips jerking at each penetration, Jun's mouth latching onto Sash's clit, sucking, fingers fucking as Sash is swept into her coming.

The room goes dark but then the door opens. At first Jun does not believe it—a cake with candles, Shel, and Olivia from fifth floor singing Happy Birthday to Sash. Sash, still on the table, legs open, feels the whipping cream on her clit, just as Olivia licks it off.

"Happy Birthday, girl," Olivia laughs.

Jun blinks in surprise.

Shel links arms with Olivia, partners in crime.

Olivia pushes back Sash's disheveled hair but her hand slinks down into Sash's vagina. "Oh, I'm going to have a fun time tonight," Olivia whispers, "watching Jun fuck you, and with my birthday gift too. What a birthday wish! Are you surprised it came true?"

Jun looks at Shel, the egg still planted inside her, asking.

Shel looks at her watch, shakes her head. "Eleven o'clock and we've only started."

Strap-Ons and Straight Chicks
Lynne Jamneck

Kay didn't know why she had the delicious inkling to do so, but that Saturday she decided to wear something extra to the club.

She had only recently become comfortable with wearing the strap-on at home, and had never really thought of wearing it anywhere outside her front door. The overpowering screams of feminist voices clanged in her ears, though she kept telling herself the seventies were long past and she lived in a brand-new era in which 'politically correct' were very bad words indeed.

It was one of those special evenings. Everything was in its place: hair, charming smile that (she had been told) made the girls weak in the knees...and a couple of other places too.

At a quarter past ten Kay watched herself in the mirror, as she strapped the harness into place, carefully tucking the pink-tinted rubber dick into one leg of her faded Diesel jeans.

Thank god for legroom. She might be ready to go out strapped in, but Kay wasn't too keen on the idea of everyone staring at her crotch the whole evening. Call her old-fashioned, but she preferred keeping the unknown just that—until the time came to sneakily place an unsuspecting hand on the button fly of her jeans and enjoy the impressed expression elicited from whoever was lucky enough to be sitting opposite her at the table.

My, but she was feeling exceptionally cocky tonight.

If Mia could see her now, she'd promptly expel Kay from dykedom. Mia was one of those girls who believed that a penis, real or latex, could never accomplish what five fingers and a hand could—ridiculous to even contemplate! Kay tried to explain to Mia that she, Kay, was absolutely right for once, but Mia was too busy mumbling traitorous remarks in Kay's direction to hear.

If PPCM (Perpetually Politically Correct Mia) had just shut her mouth for three seconds, Kay would have told her that you can do much more leaning on two hands than on one. Plus, there's the advantage of being able to watch your lover's eyes roll to the back of her head as she comes, screaming your name deliriously and possibly pulling the hair at the back of your neck. Not necessarily in that order.

Mia read too much feminism rhetoric—blondes are easily brainwashed.

For now, though, Kay assessed herself in the mirror.

Minor adjustment.

I am a goddamn killer boy.

The club was one of the few exclusive dyke spots in the city. In between the vicious bouts of underground house and tribal music you could very comfortably sip your drink to the tune of Macy Gray, Massive Attack and Madonna. Kay was glad to see that the place was already packed by the time she arrived. She tried to forget that she was actually packing for the first time in public, but she couldn't help noticing how it made her strut, as if she was goddamn Jimmy Stewart waltzing through a saloon door at high noon.

I don't need this shit! the lyrics suddenly screamed from the speakers just as the bartender handed Kay a shot of whiskey. The giant watch against the wall read 23:07. Kay caught the eye of a girl at the end of the bar, and their eyes locked briefly before the assault of electronic lights from above made any form of eye contact impossible. Moments later though, Kay noticed the exact same girl kissing what must go down in the heterosexual community as a "hunk." So much for her.

First they don't like us, then they want to attend our parties.

Kay ordered another scotch and took a seat at the bar. The weight of the dildo between her legs made her feel in control. She wasn't at all self-conscious or embarrassed.

This is part of what she could never explain to Mia. A penis (even a fake one) connected to a woman is something completely different from a man being led around by his dick.

But Mia only has to hear the word *penis* once, and she's up in arms—ready to fight the next lesbian civil war.

Kay looked up from her scotch, and saw the most beautiful, dark-haired boy looking at her from across the room, her eyes moving down the length of Kay's body slowly, then back to her eyes for a possible invitation.

Kay smiled appreciatively before looking away. She wasn't there to pick up boys, no matter how delectable they might be. In fact, she didn't even know if she had really come here tonight to pick anyone up. She came here to prove to herself that she had the balls (so to speak) to flaunt the energy she normally reserved for the privacy of her own home.

"Hi there."

Kay turned around to see the girl who'd been kissing her boyfriend a couple of minutes earlier standing next to her, her body language like she was coming on to Brad Pitt. Dark, shoulder-length hair framed her face, and she had a mouth that looked to Kay as if it had probably gone down a couple of times. Interesting, if nothing else, she thought. But just as she wasn't there to pick up boys, neither was Kay in the frame of mind to seduce straight women. She supposed a conversation wasn't too much to ask, since she wasn't doing much at the moment anyway.

"Hi, I'm Kay. Having a good time?"

"Lindsey, hi." She held out her hand for Kay to shake. Kay wondered briefly where Lindsey's hunk had disappeared to, and if she wasn't wasting time talking to a straight chick while there were plenty of extremely viable candidates all around her. Right across from her, a sexy girl who could have been Sinead O' Connor's twin sister was suggestively proposing to Kay that she come and join her and Me'shell Ndegeocello on the dance floor, which by now was packed with a feast of devastatingly gorgeous lesbians.

Kay was starting to grow more and more aware of the dil in her jeans, and she felt a sudden sense of power in her crotch when she noticed Lindsey fleetingly glancing at the bulge in her Diesels.

"Your boyfriend get bored?" Kay asked, figuring she had nothing to lose.

Lindsey smiled slowly. "I saw you watching us at the end of the bar."

Kay sipped her scotch silently. "Is that why the guy tried to perform a virtual tonsillectomy on you, to prove a point?"

Lindsey laughed. "Scott's just an insecure jock who can't get it up after one too many frat party beers. If I were to tell him that half of the women in here are packing he'd probably flip out completely."

Kay looked at Lindsey surprised, not sure if she had actually heard the word 'packing' come from this straight chick's mouth, or if it had been a clever hallucination brought on by the whisky and the sight of two women touching one another in a dark corner opposite them.

"I might not be a dyke, Kay, but I'm not stupid."

Kay felt her heart hammer a couple of beats off rhythm as Lindsey pulled a barstool up next to her and sat down, their thighs touching as Lindsey leaned forward to get the bartender's attention.

She ordered a gin and tonic, and another scotch, which the bartender placed in front of Kay.

"I've always been intrigued by the concept of a woman having a dick," Lindsey continued.

Kay was starting to get the picture. The reason Scott was nowhere in sight was probably because he had made some stupid comment about dykes, and Miss Lindsey got offended (not because she was particularly politically correct, but because she was toying with the idea of having a woman fuck her), and sent Scottie on his merry way.

"You sent him home didn't you?" Kay asked, trying to focus on Lindsey's dark eyes instead of the buzzing between her thighs. The dil was starting to take on a life of its own as if it had magically become a biological part of her, with nerve endings and a cocky attitude that was surfacing more and more by the minute.

"Like I said," Lindsey looked into her eyes, and then Kay felt the unmistakable pressure of a hand on her thigh, " Scott's an asshole."

Kay tried to concentrate on what to say next as Lindsey's hand moved slowly up her thigh, coming to rest just above her crotch. Lindsey's fingers were only inches from where the dil struggled against the confines of her jeans, but Kay didn't dare look down. She didn't know why, but she had the feeling that if she did, Lindsey would come to her senses and stop what she was doing, and Kay didn't want to risk that. As it was, she had to cling to every bit of self-control to keep herself from taking Lindsey's hand and putting it right on her dick. Straight or not, this girl was obviously working towards something, though Kay wasn't exactly sure what that was.

"So you brought an asshole chauvinist to a lesbian club? What the hell was that in aid of?" Kay couldn't help the slight edge to her voice. The sensible part of her brain had suddenly decided to make itself heard. She tried to avoid picking up straight girls, because a) they wanted to make their boyfriends jealous, b) they had been dumped by their asshole boyfriends and thought they *might* be queer, or c) they got a perverse sense of satisfaction out of setting up dykes and then saying, "Good night—it's been swell!"

Kay ignored the fact that Lindsey was looking at her intensely, but couldn't quite ignore Lindsey's hand as it pressed the strap-on cock lightly (*but very definitely*) against her clit. Still, she didn't dare look down, but instead caught the eye of the woman behind the bar, feeling sure that the bartender knew what Lindsey was busy doing to Kay's libido underneath the counter. Strobe lights started flashing. She couldn't keep herself from looking any longer. Kay leaned back slightly on the barstool, and as she looked down, Lindsey's hand unbuttoned two of the buttons at the crotch of her jeans, and slipped a slender hand inside.

"You have the hands of someone who doesn't do a lot of hard work," Kay mentioned matter-of-factly, trying to control her breathing as Lindsey's hand curled around and squeezed her dick softly.

"You like that, don't you?" Lindsey smiled as she signaled the bartender for another g-and-t.

Kay held her eyes. "Be careful Lindsey—you have no idea what I do and do not like."

Lindsey squeezed harder, and Kay arched her back and dragged hard on the cigarette she had just lit. All she needed now was for asshole Scottie to show up and realize his girlfriend was well on her way to jacking off a boy dyke.

"While that might be true," Lindsey said, pressing the base of Kay's dick solidly against her swollen clit, "I'm not too dumb or too straight to realize that I could make you come right here on this barstool, and nobody would look twice."

Okay. Kay finished what was left of her scotch in one gulp, put the glass down on the counter, turned to look Lindsey in the eye, and put her hand where Lindsey's moved inside her jeans.

"Whatever you're trying to do in your own mind Lindsey, don't think you can use me as an exciting little distraction from your socially inept boyfriend. Some dykes think they're privileged if a straight girl decides to fondle her dick—I'm not one of them. What I'm saying is: take your hand out of my pants, or be prepared for the consequences. I might not be a man who needs to fuck everything that walks past him, but I'm not putting up with that sort of shit either."

Kay waited, aware of the intensifying strobe lights, her heartbeat jumping along to a Paul Oakenfold remix of a Madonna song: *Do you know what it feels like for a girl...*

Lindsey's hand stayed put. They looked at each other for a moment longer, Kay trying to figure out what this girl was up to, then finally deciding she didn't care anymore.

Kay slid off the barstool, gave Lindsey her best come-hither look and started walking towards the back entrance of the club.

Past the bathrooms, a door led to a short entryway that Kay assumed was used for deliveries. She waited for Lindsey to catch up with her, then closed the door behind them, hoping there weren't going to be any more deliveries tonight.

She wasn't expecting it when Lindsey roughly pressed her back into the wall, one hand firmly on her hips, the other sliding down the small of her back and coming to rest on the swell of her butt. Kay was covered in gooseflesh; she felt the steady beat of the music pounding through the walls and into her body. With one hand she grabbed the loose curls at Lindsey's neck and pulled her close, kissing her delicious mouth, her tongue teasing Lindsey's into submission.

Kay felt the unfamiliar body of this woman pressing into her, felt the knobby ridges in the concrete wall jutting into her back, and her hips thrusting forward, seemingly of their own accord. Lindsey pushed with the weight of her whole body into Kay.

There were plenty of things for Kay to concentrate on in that moment, but the most urgent was the way Lindsey's hips were bearing down hard against the dil now, causing the base to rub Kay's clit achingly, which felt ready to explode. Kay moved both her hands down Lindsey's back, cupped her ass and started moving the hard ridge beneath her jeans into Lindsey's crotch, satisfied at the pleading moan that escaped from this—till now?—straight girl's mouth.

Kay wondered if she should say something before Lindsey lost her nerve, which sometimes happened when you found yourself in a compromising position with a complete stranger. But there was nothing she could think of to say; nothing she wanted to say.

Lindsey broke their kiss, moved down to Kay's throat—and kissed it. Dropping down further she brushed against Kay's nipples, instantly making them stand to ready and willing attention. Only then did Kay realize that Lindsey's fingers had completely unbuttoned her jeans. Before she fully realized what Lindsey planned to do, Kay saw her moving down and taking the dil in her mouth, at first just the head, then slowly moving her lips up its entire length.

Kay didn't dare breathe for fear that she might stop—that would be like promising rain to the Sahara, sending in the clouds, and then letting the storm blow over. She didn't know whether she was imagining it, but Kay could actually feel herself filling this girl's mouth. She placed one hand on Lindsey's face and pulled her mouth back to the base of the dil, amazed and elated at the same time that Lindsey was able to take all seven inches. Her previous girlfriend had loved getting fucked with the strap-on, but she had never really been into giving blow jobs.

Lindsey slowly released Kay from her mouth and glanced up.

"What?" Kay finally breathed.

"I don't think I've ever come across someone before who could give me what I wanted from blowing a dick."

"I did?"

"Mmm—you give before you take."

Kay took Lindsey's hand and pulled her up. She had a pair of stretch Levis on, and the zipper came down like it had just been oiled. Kay slipped her fingers down the front of Lindsey's white cotton panties, smiling with satisfaction when she felt how wet the girl was.

Never mind how hard.

She took Lindsey's jeans and pulled them down and off with several swift yanks, panties coming with as a mouth-watering afterthought. They switched places, Lindsey briefly shuddering at the cold cement against her ass while Kay took the dil firmly in her hand. As Lindsey's hand crawled up Kay's T-shirt, fingertips brushing across her nipples, Kay slowly inched herself into Lindsey.

The music outside in the club droned, reverberated...*there's a crack in the concrete floor that starts at the sink....* Halfway inside Lindsey, and she was ready to come.

Relax...breathe, remember to breathe...slowly...

Lindsey's eyes were closed, a frown on her face as if she were either concentrating heavily, or trying to figure out some great mystery. She was biting down on her lower lip, short gasps escaping from the small opening between her lips. Kay felt Lindsey's hips trying to thrust forward beneath her own hands but held her back forcefully before thrusting the length of her cock (as she had now started thinking of it) shamelessly into Lindsey, making her issue a low, guttural moan that made the hair on the back of Kay's arms stand on end. She forgot the trepidation she had felt at wearing the strap-on to the club; forgot that she wasn't here to pick up straight women and forgot that she was actually a decent girl who didn't normally lure other girls into deserted entryways.

All she wanted to do right now was fuck Lindsey.

Kay steadied herself against the wall with one arm, with the other she got a good firm grip on Lindsey's sexily protruding hipbone.

"You're...fucking...*unreal*—" she heard Lindsey shuddering. Kay thought she heard herself laugh.

She pulled her cock out almost entirely, then slammed back in. Lindsey cried out and grabbed at the back of her jeans, trying to pull Kaye even deeper into her.

The base of the dil was only allowed intermittent contact with her clit, but it was enough to make Kay feel she might become rooted to the spot if she didn't move soon. She took two steps forward, her body pressing tightly against Lindsey's and started fucking her slow and hard.

Lindsey lifted one leg, resting her knee against Kay's hip and surrendering completely to the best fuck of her newly-acquired adult life—with a woman. From the look on her flushed face Kay could see that Lindsey was going to come any second. She started moving her hips quicker, pulling her cock out almost completely before entering Lindsey again with smooth, quick thrusts.

She felt Lindsey's ass start to tremble underneath her hand, and brought her hand up to cover the girl's mouth just in case the music momentarily quieted at the wrong point and someone walked past the door. Kaye winced as she felt teeth bite into the soft flesh of her palm, and gave one—two—three final thrusts before grabbing Lindsey's shoulder as her own knees buckled. They collapsed against the wall, breathing hard and fast, Kay feeling the sting of scratches on her shoulders but not knowing when they had been inflicted.

Fuck, she thought, tasting the salty perspiration on Lindsey's lips.

This better not become a habit.

The Pitcher
Sharon Wachsler

I was the catcher, she was the pitcher, the way God intended.

"Oh, God," I gasped later, when she plunged three fingers into me. "Oh, God."

"Oh, God!" I jumped when she threw a windmill pitch so hard it knocked me onto my ass. "What in God's name do you think you're doing?" I stomped to the pitcher's rubber.

God was to have a big role in our relationship.

"Oh, Gaaawd," she drawled, mimicking me in a too-girly tone. Her Southern accent stopped me short, panting. "Don't be such a pussy," she said, looking at mine.

"Listen, the only reason I'm on this Goddamn team is because slow pitch is full. And *you* keep losing players." I pointed at her pussy, just for good measure.

"I'm just supposed to be a warm body," I added. "So don't call me a Goddamn pussy." I kicked dirt on her shoe, then turned toward home.

"Well, your body better get a little warmer behind that plate," she sneered, "pussy."

Pussy was to have a big role in our relationship, the way God intended.

I tried to yank off my face mask to throw at her, but the strap got caught on my ear.

I was a New York Jew, soft and round and loud. She was an Alabama Baptist, sharp and pointy like a stick. Usually I don't like skinny. Skinny can feel brittle, insubstantial. But she had a way of making skinny overwhelming, scary. I liked that.

I didn't know how to play softball. The team stuck me as catcher because I couldn't field or throw or bat. Also, the equipment fit me. I guess their last catcher was also short.

The equipment was heavy and dusty and smelled like boy sweat: astringent and raw. All the joints creaked, stiff with salt and mud. There was a spot of blood on the mask.

With the thick padding on my chest, my knees, my ankles, I felt invincible. The metal on the mask was cool and hard. I felt like a man. A man with a cunt. I didn't want to play softball so much as I wanted to squat behind the plate, my hand in my shorts, masturbating for her, the pitcher, while a succession of women stood in front of me, swinging a big piece of wood while a white leather sphere was thrown at them.

I couldn't believe this game was legal.

"Get a room!" the shortstop yelled when I told the pitcher to "fucking fuck off and just throw the fucking ball like a normal fucking person. We aren't all Dot fucking Richardson."

We played the game. I don't remember most of it. I remember the perspiration crawling all over my scalp, pooling beneath my breasts, under the elastic on the backs of my calves and thighs. My thighs ached and spasmed from the extended crouch. I could have asked someone to switch positions with me, but I'm not really a switch.

I looked at her through the metal grid on my face. She threw the ball into my glove. It stung where it landed. My hand was red, tingling. The mitt smelled like leather and soap and dirt. Not the dust on the field, but soil: dark, rich, almost like oil. That's how she smelled, too, I found out later—like rotting earth and tough hide.

After the game the pitcher grabbed my braid. "So, what does your warm body look like under that chest protector?"

"You'll never know," I turned to walk away. My cunt jumped at her hand sliding down to the back of my neck. She didn't need to know *that*, though. She already knew that. I needed her to know that.

She swung in front of me. Her shirt was stained. A smear of dirt spread across her upper arm and her neck. Her breasts looked small and hard, the nipples scraping against her tank top. I wanted to bite them, to feel them give, to taste blood. She put her hand at the base of my throat. Under the chest protector I was fire. My hidden body was molten, burning the armor onto me.

"Even with that mattress on you, I have a pretty good idea," she smirked. I grabbed her wrist to fling it off. She snatched my hand out of the air, brought it silently to my side.

"This equipment belongs to the league, you know," she spoke softly into my neck. "I'm responsible for making sure it's all returned."

"I know where it goes," I heard the tremor in my voice, cleared my throat. "I know where the storage closet is."

That's when I saw her smile. That's when I knew. God knows, I knew.

We walked to the brick school building and into the gym. She pulled out a key and let us into the locked cage that held basketballs, soccer nets, hockey sticks, and big blue mats with yellow foam sticking out. They were piled in haphazard lumps.

"Be a responsible citizen," she intoned, "turn in your equipment."

I tried to pretend she wasn't there. I played it like I was unself-conscious. I bent to unhook the elastic bands across the backs of my thighs and knees. It was only after the third clasp that I realized I was sucking air with each release. The pitcher was gasping in time with me. She was catching what I pitched.

My skin felt strange and new in the cold air, goose bumps rose and I shivered. The heat of my body came off in the fabric of the shin guards as I peeled them back from my legs. The guards stuck out horizontally, still attached at the ankle. I knelt to unhook the ties around my ankles, staring at her legs in front of me, light hair on clay-colored skin, veins riding over muscle.

I didn't want to take the chest protector off. I felt so hot underneath, molded into its shape, as if I'd been wearing it since I was born. The pitcher reached both her arms around me, releasing the ties on the back of the chest protector. I saw the grime on her neck and a red splotch where she'd been scratching. When she pulled the quilted pad away from me I actually expected to look down and see my naked body, my breasts hanging like white plums. She threw the chest guard onto the pile of blue mats. Numbly I reached up to take off the mask.

"No," she grabbed my hand, "leave it on."

She laid her palm against my chest, then pushed. I fell onto the mats. She turned, closed the metal gate, its white paint peeling around the lock, twisted the key. "Now we're locked in."

I knew that we weren't. I knew that the key was on the chain that hung from her belt loop. I knew someone could walk in and find us. I knew I should probably leave. While I was deciding to leave she slid her hand up my thigh, her gritty fingers on my new skin.

The pitcher's other hand was still on my catcher's mask, her fingers entwined in the bars across my face. She lay down on me, her arm pinned across my throat and chest.

The pitcher slid her hand up my thigh and under my cutoffs, slipping a finger under the elastic of my panties. I inhaled sharply, waiting for her to touch me. But she didn't. She just ran that finger under the elastic, from side to side. I was wriggling, trying to force her finger closer, higher. But, pinned under her sharp body, her arm like a bat across my throat, I couldn't move. The mats were swallowing me; I felt engulfed in the deep blue indentation. The pitcher kept her finger moving but wouldn't touch my pussy. She wouldn't send me home.

"You're not a very good catcher," she commented off-handedly.

"I...I never..." I stammered.

"I hope you're a better fuck," she added.

"Fuck you," I struggled to get up but she grabbed the crotch of my shorts and yanked me back down, knocking the wind out of me. My ass thumped against the top mat. She had ripped the right leg of my shorts almost to the zipper. I glared at her through the mask.

When I'd caught my breath I realized she'd moved her hand so that it lay on my mound. She was that kind of pitcher—smooth and sly. She let her skinny hand whisper across the ends of my pubic hair, not touching skin—but the vibrations tingled down to my skin.

I moaned, lifting my hips, trying to make her touch me, but she just kept sliding her hand away. She was not the kind to let a runner steal a base.

"Hold still," she hissed then, yanking my mask so that my cheek was pressed against the mats. She brought her face right up to the metal grid, looking me in the eyes. "Hold still and be quiet. You don't want some janitor wandering in here to find out who's moaning, do you?" she asked.

"No," I whispered, embarrassed.

"No," she repeated, turning my head from side to side, gripping tight to the mask. "No, no, no," she incanted.

"No, no, no," I agreed, softly, dizziness descending as she rocked my head on the mats.

In a hypnotic rhythm I continued shaking my head,

mumbling "no, no, no, no," and felt her middle finger and forefinger slide to either side of my engorged clit. Deliberately she rubbed up and down, capturing my clit between her fingers. I rocked my head faster, gasping, slurring, "no, no, no, no." I couldn't see her face. I saw the ceiling and the mats and the cage and this wiry hand over my face, all blurred in the constant motion of my skull and the thrill of her fingers riding my slippery clit.

"Shut up!" she hissed suddenly. "I hear something. Someone's coming." She didn't mean me. The pitcher held absolutely still. So did I. It hurt to breathe.

I could feel the pulse in my throat pounding against her arm, in my swollen clit against her fingers. The stillness made me ache that much more to have her inside me. I must have groaned because she jerked my head and spit, "Shut up."

In the rank locker-room air, her fingers huge and crimson in front of my eyes, her other hand still inside my shorts, I wanted to beg her to fuck me. Yet I was afraid of someone coming in, seeing me like that. I didn't know what to do.

The pitcher pushed three fingers inside me, hard. I gasped. It hurt. I wanted to tell her, *no, too many*. I wanted to tell her *more*, to take her whole fist. She started skimming in and out, slowly at first, then faster. "Be quiet, don't move," she kept muttering through gritted teeth.

I gripped the blue mats hard. Later I found bits of foam under my fingernails. She pumped in and out, bumping against my clit with the heel of her palm, pressing into me. My legs went numb from her bony weight across them.

Every time I gyrated against her hand, into those skilled pitcher's hands, into that hypnotic stroking and probing, she'd pull out and yank my pubic hair, growling "quiet." While I gasped in surprise she'd plunge back in. I was so grateful and scared.

I could feel my orgasm building. It all felt rich and full—the striated meat of her hand, her slick fingers, my numb legs, my head tilting crazily. She saw I was coming, yanked the mask up onto my forehead and pressed her hand over my exposed mouth. I broke open like a glass of water, spilling in every direction. I was calling to God, but she couldn't hear because her hand was muffling me. My cunt contracted around her fingers, waves of heat washing over me, her hand pressed hard against my face. I think I must have bitten her, sunk my teeth right into her palm, but neither of us said a word. (When I saw her at practice the following week she had a bandage on her hand. Said she'd cut herself slicing a bagel. No one believed that.)

When I was done the pitcher pulled her hand out from under my shorts. "Shut your eyes," she said, "and suck." I sucked her fingers—my own bitter juices, her sweat, the oily leather of her glove, and a tangy metallic edge that made me want to taste her mouth.

She stood up, then pulled me onto wobbly legs. "Here, don't forget to leave this." Gently the pitcher peeled the mask from my damp forehead. She laid the mask on top of the other gear and opened the cage door, which squeaked as it swung wide. She locked it and we went out into the bright sun. I couldn't believe it was still daylight.

"See y'all next week," she called as she headed toward a silver mountain bike, chained behind the batters' bench. I just stood there with the sun on my hair, watching her turn her key in the Kryptonite lock.

I walked toward the subway, smelling my rank, sexed-up smell. I was already hungry to see the pitcher again, to watch her throw, to taste the bite her hands left on me. My pussy ached as I walked, reminding me of her, the way God intended.

Free-Falling
Elspeth Potter

Two days after I was of legal age and could register my come-out, I turned up at the spaceport in Cleveland with a complimentary pass to Grrltown in the back pocket of my purple latex shorts. My white push-em-up had a little closure in front, decorated with a hologrammatic pull tag that read, *open here* in flashes of green and red and gold. I didn't bring any extra clothes. What would I need clothes for, in Grrltown? I was going to get *laid*.

The Grrltown satellite is all minty-fresh gel, ribbed for her pleasure, but the real flavors of the day are two great tastes that taste great together: women and sex. You're soaking in it!

I wasn't brave enough to check the fancy hostels out yet; I wasn't sure I knew how to pick up women, even here, and I'd feel like a real dumbnik staying there alone. I decided I'd start slow. I had three whole days before I had to pay anything, and I wanted a good sampling.

I wandered the corridors and saw ads for live shows using the hippest classic commercials, enhanced with nude housewives fucking each other on the kitchen appliances. Live people, or sometimes holograms, begged me to come try their immersible scenarios (except I didn't have a hookup for those yet), or practice sessions. Practice sessions?

"In case of disaster," the doorchick said, and winked at me. I was curious enough to go along.

They swiped my health card first, and I had to check my boots. They stamped my arm so I could get them back later. Then the doorchick gave my ass a little pat and I ducked into a tunnel with some kind of cushiony flooring, the walls and ceiling strobing in pink and red, the air rich with the musk of aroused female. Freshmaker! I didn't walk through the door so much as I was sucked in.

Then the floor was the ceiling and the ceiling was the floor, or maybe that was the wall that was the floor now. I spun head over ass in a half-lit zero-gravity chamber as tall as a two-story house and at least fifty meters across, dark pink and thrumming with subsonics, like a womb, only the womb of some kind of gigantor android. That's why they took my boots, I figured, so I wouldn't damage anything in there.

Or so I wouldn't damage anyone else. Somebody's warm hand grabbed my ankle right then and my spinning slowed down. She grabbed my hand, too, and started towing me over to a wall. Then I figured out there were two women. They were both naked except for black belts around their waists. They hooked those belts into the wall and let me float a little distance in front of them, one holding my right ankle and the other, down lower, with her fingers laced in mine. They both smiled.

Ankle woman had dark skin, patterned all over with bioluminescent butterflies, and little curls that clung to her skull and her pubes. Small tits, lush hips, and an ass I could probably ride like a motorbike. She said, in a BBC Interplanetary announcer kind of accent, "I'm Trixie. She's

Dixie. You just float back and think of England."

"Cleveland," I said.

"It rocks," Dixie said. She had a higher voice, kind of sweet, and much paler skin, with purple fuzz on her scalp. Her shape was pretty much the opposite of her partner's. I couldn't take my eyes off the way her enormous tits just floated out with nothing underneath them. Sure, people look funny in zero gee, because there's no gravity to pull their flesh down, but I'd never thought of it like this!

Trixie let go of my ankle then and Dixie, keeping hold of my hand, pushed off from the wall and neatly reversed her body in the center of the chamber, so we were drifting there. Dixie laid her free hand on the *open here* tag on my push-em-up. My heart was pounding from anticipation. Dixie slowly, slowly tugged the tag down, and my tits, little but round, floated out. Being wrestled out of that tight top was like having hands rub over me. I watched Dixie pull her arm away from us and then give her wrist a practiced flick. My white top traveled end over end to Trixie, who caught it and stowed it behind some little door that wasn't easily visible to me.

Dixie let go of me then, and I tried not to squeal. I pretended I was in a swimming pool back home in Cleveland, and if I relaxed the water would hold me up. I wouldn't sink here, not really, but flailing around wouldn't get me far. Dixie said, "Trust us, we're experts," and ran her hands down my rib cage, letting her fingers trace my skin just under my waistband. I shuddered. It was so much better than I'd imagined, so much better than virtual.

The shorts were tight and didn't have any fastener; Dixie had to roll them down my hips like she was peeling a banana. The stretch latex seemed to peel the top layer of my skin off with it, not in a way that hurt, oh no. I could feel every millimeter as it came off, and Dixie seemed to know it. When the shorts got down far enough, my clit burst out from its confinement like my tits had done, and I moaned, very quietly.

Dixie sent the shorts over to Trixie, who stowed them before she pushed off the wall and flipped herself neatly to a stop near my head. Her hips were hovering in front of my mouth, and when I glanced towards my feet for a second, Dixie's head was right at my waist. Trixie said, "You ready? The game is to stay here, in the center."

I nodded, really fast. They had to catch me so the motion didn't send me careening off. Then Trixie gripped my shoulder and turned me, so my mouth was aimed at her pussy, marked off by one of those butterflies, dead center. I could take a hint. Time to see if I'd learned anything from virtuals. This was a practice session, wasn't it?

Using my hands turned out to be a bad idea. Every time I pushed on Trixie's hips, even a little, we started drifting away from Dixie, and I didn't want to move away from her mouth. Dixie was holding my thighs open, but *she* knew how to reposition her legs now and then to keep us steady. I gave up hanging on and let my arms float free, easy and relaxed, while I made my tongue into a firm probe and darted it in and out of Trixie's plump pussy lips. Her fragrance filled my nose and her juices floated out in droplets, colliding with my face. Whenever I shifted, the droplets shuddered into pieces and drifted away, surrounding us in a mist of sex.

Meanwhile, Dixie pressed her tongue to my clit, wide and warm and supple. She slid her tongue up and down, hardly moving, but pressing sufficiently to make me throb from my tip to my inner sponge. I wondered if I could spurt fluid without her even reaching inside me. It was that good; nothing touched me anywhere except Trixie's pussy and Dixie's tongue, amplifying every sensation a million times; something about hanging in free fall made all my blood rush to my pussy.

I finally had to stop licking Trixie because I was gasping and sobbing so loudly. She didn't seem to mind. She held my head in her hands and kissed me. I felt like Trixie's hands on my head were the only thing keeping me from spiraling off into the emptiness of space, or like I would curl into my clit that Dixie was torturing so deliciously, and implode.

Suddenly, Trixie let go and somersaulted out of sight. Dixie slid a finger into me. My pussy sucked at it like it was starving, and then I screamed, because Trixie had pulled my asscheeks apart and was flicking my hole with a tongue like lightning.

We careened into a wall eventually, but I was coming all the way, yelling like a bungee jumper, while Dixie and Trixie kept me going with their fingers.

And that was only my *first* day.

On the second day, I found out I could get a free hookup for immersibles with my pass. I was legal now! I could do it! It was kind of a shock to realize I could do *whatever I wanted*, short of harming anyone, and no one would stop me.

I met some other freebies at one of those little robot tables that wheel around dispensing noshes. They were all talking about immersibles. The cute tall one in the red shimmersheath explained to me that some of the scenarios are continuing stories; the characters remember what you did last time and do something different the next, usually something more intense than you'd done before.

I'd been standing kind of close to her, and was about to ask her name when this bossy chick pushed between us. "I like the ones with weird sensory effects," she said, pressing back against cute one's belly. "There's some where you can't see but your skin sensitivity is magnified, or where sounds affect you like touch." It all sounded très cool, or it would have, if she would have shut up and not gone on and on about different models of hookup and how much they cost and where you could get cheap ones. Cute one tried to interrupt but didn't have any luck. I hadn't even had a chance to ask her name before another group of newbies came and swept her away.

I realized I could do immersibles at home, and it would be just as good, and the bossy chick wouldn't be there. I decided to get the free port on my last day, and wandered off alone. Cute one glanced after me, but didn't follow. Well, there were plenty of other women. Some of them must be as cute.

There was a bar that didn't have any holograms flashing outside, so I poked my head in the door. The music almost knocked me on my ass, it was so loud. The little room was crammed with women all jostling close together, like they were performing a big dance routine, except for the naked part. I stepped in and saw they were all fastened together by a thin wire, looped through one woman's nipple hoop or another's ears or, more often, passed through some sort of port-adapter I'd never seen before. Groans erupted from the crowd at intervals, and I realized there was some kind of feedback stimulation going on. It was too much for me. I was beginning to wonder if I really liked Grrltown. I crossed the corridor and found a more conventional bar with a live show.

The live show didn't have any music, but the performers' sounds were amplified. I could hear heavy breathing, and a finger sliding in and out of a juicy cunt. That sound slithered into my ears from above, behind, under my table, next to me—really hot—and it was making me horny, but also lonely. *I should probably hook up with a group of newbies myself,* I told myself.

Then I felt warmth at my side, and a chick pulled up a chair. It was the cute one in the red shimmersheath. Without her jealous-eyed friend. She said, "I'm Jude. Can I let my fingers do the walking?"

I smiled at her. "If you'll melt in my mouth and not in my hand."

Okay, I liked Grrltown. I *loved* Grrltown.

The Inhabitant Candidate Learns Something New
María Helena Dolan

Oof. This is the part I loathe the most—that moment of *impact*, when you're really *in* the alien body, and you're trying to grope your way through, making all the connections so you can maneuver in their world.

It's *disgusting.* The upright posture with that pain-prone musculature and flimsy skeleton, the viscera that requires considerable autonomic control, the inability to proceed without the proper levels of nutrient ingestion and elimination of waste....

But the thing I hate worst of all is the inside of their mouths. The scummy coatings, the sour tastes, the bad humors welling up from incomplete digestion, the repellent array of teeth you have to learn to coordinate so you don't bite painfully into the being's own flesh—and that thick and repulsive tongue! Not only must it perform all manner of human functions; *we* have to rely upon it for two-way sharing of additional sensory and communicative data with our Collective.

If only there were some other way to complete my Studies!! I *despise* the new Field Research Protocols.

It was strange enough when our Superiors had us assume human shapes, and walk amongst them, "passing." *Now*, if we Candidates in the Bipedal Oxygen-Iron-Carbon Transport Species Studies are *ever* to attain our Status, we must actually *become* human, inhabiting their bodies and experiencing their lives for an entire solidig. Some penal incarcerations are shorter than that!

And do *other* Program Candidates struggle with such *difficult* species? No! Give me a good old methane breather any day! They just glide along on pseudopods, never bothering with "uprightness." Or even *this* planet's oceanic species, who at least are at one with their environment, and do not act in ways inimical to their individual and species survival. Unfortunately, their culture is all aural, visual and tactile, so their constructs leave nothing in the way of artifacts.

And since the Ruling Council has decreed that we can't import any more species into Homeworld—well those of us already engaged in Xeno-Studies had to filaster mightily in order to rearrange these Masters Programs in Artifacting.

Gah! I'm even beginning to *sound* like them! It's this damn English language. Couldn't they have sent me across this paltry globe to a place where nuance, context and harmonics convey *meaning*? It's enough to drive a Master Xenotropist into unrated gryvmometer repair.

And this human identity I was saddled with at the Allotment. None of the *other* Level IV Candidates were required to become "Butch Lesbian Studs," an apparent rare subtype who seem to have some bearing on recreational behavior.

Well, I just hope suitable subroutines are hypno-embedded deeply enough that my response to external stimuli is a reasonable facsimile of appropriate conduct. I simply haven't had time to review the annotated materials accompanying the

Allotment, so I'm pretty much going to be winging it for the next nocturnal rotation.

Ah, here's the entryway to the place described in the local guidebook as "a Dyke Dungeon." You know, I plugged that phrase into the Uni-translator, but the match didn't make sense: first, "a place of confinement within a wall containing water"; then, "colloquially, an underground place where certain women go." Can *any* woman be a Dyke, then? And *must* they be under the ground? Can they not be on top of the ground? I don't understand.

Oh. A programming subroutine prompts me now to extend my palm to my hair, and press back towards the nape of the neck with a smooth stroke resembling a caress, which shows the upper arm muscles to good effect. I selected this sleeveless shirt for a purpose, I see. Ah, also the gesture has caught the scanning eye of several women, although *their* subroutines apparently prompt them to disguise their level of interest. Hmm. These women seem to fit an identifiable sub-type referred to as "Fem," who are somehow connected to the Butch identity. Curious.

According to my implants, the Fem exercises considerable powers of attraction over the Butch. There is a certain amount of ritual preening and dancing attached to this...ah! The Butch Lesbian Stud doesn't simply concern herself with recreational activities—she's an integral part of woman-to-woman mating rituals. Of course! No wonder this body has reacted so strongly to the atmosphere in here: it's crawling with pheromones, an important part of human mating signaling and preparation. Hey, this might be fun!

Now there is the specific type of walk with which I take a turn around the room: a swagger that swings from the arms down through the hips, and suggests a feline-like stalking to the onlooker. And I am to *appear* largely unconscious of the attention that this walk engenders within the Fems nearby, registering it only in the form of a slow, secret smile as I place an order for an alcohol-containing beverage at the "bar." (I wonder at the etymological derivation of that word, signifying as it does a piece of polished wood separating the patrons from the alcohol. It hardly resembles the only *other* bar I have ever seen, which is a forged metal instrument for prying things apart. Oh well....)

I note a certain Fem seated three stations to my left. She has been nonchalantly looking in my direction, a series of glances engendering a certain quickening alertness in this body. Regarding her fully for a moment, I turn and instruct the bar-tender to supply her and myself with the alcoholic beverage of her choice. The tar-bender, uh, bar-tender winks conspiratorially and moves down to the Fem station.

The beverage purveyor mixes two Kahlua and creams. Something about the swirled milkiness threaded with subtle brown lines lends visual appeal. Upon receiving the glass, the Fem smiles, takes up the drink and lifts it slightly in my general direction. As she takes a sip from her glass, I swallow from mine, and discover that the faint sweetness of the drink's smell is amplified by the full-bodied sweetness upon my tongue. While I ponder this sensation, the Fem beckons, first by deliberately flicking the long silvery hair off of her shoulder, and then with the forefinger of her hand, employing a curiously exciting curling motion and providing an unmistakable visual cue.

I loose myself from the bar, and stride toward her station. I face her, and closely enter her sphere of consciousness. Prompted by hidden signals, I lightly rest my palm on the back of her hand, sending shivers of connection between our skins. I say something along the lines of "I know we haven't met before, because I would have remembered a woman as striking as you." And the odd thing is, while this may be a programmed subroutine, I find that it is true. Her frame, her face, her hair, her dress…it *all* pleases me somehow.

After names and length of residence are established, I query, "Voulez-vous dancer, mademoiselle?" Without a pause she smiles and answers, "Mais oui." I escort her onto the dance floor. The music is slow and sinuous. In fact, despite my extensive repertoire of programs of rhythmical step formations, I find myself feeling…I don't know, *clumsy* before her gracefulness.

And a certain level of self-consciousness is now compounded by her pressing into me as we sway, her breasts creating friction against mine, causing the tips to stiffen in a somewhat uncomfortable but decidedly stimulating fashion. And when she glides her hip into the place where my legs meet, I find a curious wetness beginning to seep there, accompanied by an aggravating sensation somewhere between itching and burning.

In fact, there's a distinctly burning sensation in various body parts. As I lean down and kiss her according to a rather pressing prompt, I find that the sliding of our lips across each other's and the introduction of my tongue into her oral cavity is extremely pleasurable, and not at *all* disgusting.

During this act of osculation, which goes on for some indeterminate amount of time, I experience a strange falling-away sensation in the pit of my stomach, accompanied with more flashes of localized burning. Apparently she also experiences this feeling, for I see that her eyes are closed, her cheeks flushed, and her hips moving even more rhythmically than before.

In fact, we do not stop kissing and rubbing against each other until a voice cleaves the music, ordering us to "Get a room!" We look at each other and laugh, and continue to dance, this time, not kissing, but holding each other more tightly. At the song's end, we proceed back to the bar station.

I reason that this must be some sort of outpost base, and I realize that I must get her to her home base in order to complete the ritual.

"You know, you've quite taken my breath away," I say. She smiles, and in a distinctly purring voice, responds, "I was thinking the same thing." Earnestly prompted, I declare, "I'm just enjoying your company and the night so much that I don't want it to end here." She purses her lips: "So it's the old 'your place or mine,' huh?"

"Well, *old* in the sense that human women have formed this kind of connection for thousands of years. *New* in the sense that it's the two of *us*, combining our energies and desires and seeing where they might lead us."

"You talk awfully pretty."

"I'm *very* good with my tongue. Allow me to show you."

"Oh, you will. But we have to go to my place, so I can let the dog out. Where's your car?"

"I don't have it with me. I beamed in."

"Great. She's a handsome nut job. But a hell of a kisser... why is it always the *maniacs* who're the best kissers and the best in bed?" She sighs, decides, and concludes, "Come on." I help her with her outer gear, and we go out to her car.

Once inside the small two-seater, I reach my hand out and touch her face. She closes her eyes and moves back into the seat. As I trace my finger from her cheekbone to her jaw, she sighs a little, shivers a tiny bit and exudes more pheromones. A split second before the prompts kick in, I lean over and kiss her. Softly at first, little rose-petal kisses on lips alive and wet and wonderful. Then, with more hunger, more insistence, more pressure.

Centered in my pelvic region now is a blazing firestorm, a heat so kindled that it threatens to burn down entire sectors. And she feels it too. But an inner voice informs me that we should not complete the ritual here under a sodium vapor light. So I force myself to stop kissing, ordering her instead to "drive." Which she does, with hands shaking on the steering control.

I don't touch her as she drives, even though my hand longs to start at her knee and work slowly up her dress and her thigh, each millimeter of skin wakening and shaking as I inch up higher and higher to the place where her heat and her wetness originate.

Instead, I tell her how I will "do" her. I tell her I know how it'll be, and how she will respond. The words are incantory, making the night charged and liminal.

"I know what you need.

"I'm not being arrogant, and certainly not obtuse. You require a lot of kissing, a lot of arms entwined, a lot of lips and fingertips brushing across trembling skin.

"You need a woman to reach your core where your real desires dwell. You need a woman to open you up from the center outward, a woman to summon all the earthly rhythms in your deepest recesses, a woman who convinces you to allow your own heats to devour you. You need me, just now."

The Fem groans and grits her teeth and hisses "Are you *trying* to get me to run off the road?" But her elevated pulse and quickened breaths indicate that she wishes for me to continue with the narrative.

"We can't even make it into your bedroom before I tear the clothes off of you, releasing your hair and skin and hungers. Pulling off my own garments, I encircle you with my arms, and press my thigh against your crotch, and you immediately open wider, and begin to rub your distending lips across my thigh. I feel your breasts against mine, feeling so alive with this skin-to-skin touch, and so painfully aware that my mouth isn't upon them yet.

"Your hot desire decides the matter, and you push me away to arm's length, so that you can grab my hands and haul me bodily into the bedroom. And then I'm on you, showering you with kisses and touching you all over as you stretch upon the bed. These activities cause me to shiver as though cold, but in fact, I am so hot I feel steam rise from my flesh.

"Unable to delay any longer, I press my face to your pussy, and breathe deeply for your scent. Your sweat and your hormones and your juices all combine into the most intoxicating brew. I inhale deeply and fill my nostrils with your essence, so now I can smell nothing *but* your pussy, and it strikes me like a gryvmometer going into hyper-drive.

"But now, now your thighs are spread and I slip my arms under them, placing my hands on your hips and my face into your spread lips. A lingering kiss, lips to lips, and then my tongue begins to move, stirring with a life of its own. Licking firmly and dexterously, I cause you to moan and open your legs wider. Now that small but swelling and oh so sensitive clitoris engorges, flaring up from her base, demanding the constant motion of my tongue in tight circles so the innermost ridge gets as much attention as her surrounding folds.

"You squirm and rock and push against my mouth as searing bolts of quickfire detonate at the spot where tongue and pussy meet, spreading throughout your entire body, which thrashes and bucks and kicks with the force of it.

"Slowly, I begin to realize that my mission, my goal, my only desire, is to pleasure you. That is the thing that matters, the thing I can't do without.

"Your pleasure. As you tear at my back with your nails. Your pleasure. As you grip my upper arms so hard that the bruised imprints will be there for days. Your pleasure. As you tremble beneath my touching. Your pleasure. Of a sudden, I know: your pleasure *is* my pleasure.

"So I turn you over, and am ready to take you. I start at the depression at the knees, licking and nipping and worshipping my way from there upward, that sensitive thigh skin crying out from the ministrations. At last, I come face to face with your ass.

"I hardly know how to proceed, so awe inspiring is the vista. Feeling slightly faint, I lightly cup my hands around both splendid mounds, and gently pull them slightly ajar. Your pink puckered little peach pit smells incredibly sweet, and I run the tip of my tongue against your reticulated folds.

"But this is not what you want, *really*. What you want is for me to open you up, to fill you, to take you. And I will. Accordingly, I insert my tongue deep into your cunt.

"While I tickle your butthole with my nose, I push and push, my tongue extending farther and deeper, around and around. You scream and shudder and writhe, forbidding me to stop, pleading for more—which I must give you. I keep at you and at you and in you and in you, and now, finally, you're *so* wide open, I can lick your cervix and send you over the edge.

"Your cries and sobs and shudders strike me deeply in the viscera, and a series of spasms overtake me. I feel as though this body of mine is compressed and expanded at the same time, that I float above it while also inhabiting it fiercely. Hardly knowing why, I turn you back to face me, and get on top of you, thrusting my heated breasts and pussy against yours, bearing down where our cunts meet. Lip to lip and clit to clit, I rub hard and furiously, and we both see lightning and fire and earth, until I fall away from you, slowly. You gather me in your arms, and kiss the mouth that tastes of you.

"Yes. This is how it will be. Keep driving, Woman. I'm ready for you."

"How can I drive after *that*?" she shrieks, and brings the car to halt at the edge of the parking lot.

"You must," I insist.

"Can you really do all of that?" she asks in a shaky, husky voice.

"I assure you that I am indeed capable of those things, and apparently much more," I add, dredging up both a wealth of prompts and a welter of rather compelling images on my inner view screen. Picking up her hand, I insert her forefinger into my oral cavity, and suck on it. The sucking and the moisture of my mouth exerts a powerful effect upon her. The smell of estrogenic hormones now permeates the air, and she begins to roll her vulvar area against the seat. Moisture films the windows, creating a certain obscurant privacy.

"Ah god, I'm so hot! For Christ sake, just do it. Do it now!" she implores.

While extremely exciting, I judge her reaction to be overly hormone-induced, and pronounce, "Let us at least move away from the lights."

"No! NOW!!!" she howls. "Now. Prove you're not all talk, and do me now." Lifting her skirt and pulling off her panties, she commands, "Eat me and fuck me. Do it until I scream for you to stop." With that, she takes my head in her hands and pulls it down to her center.

What a wondrous vista! I had no idea that there was so much color and vibrancy in this location. Pink and purple saturating the folds, black and silver rimming the opening, and a mouth-watering reddening which seems to deepen as the clitoris begins to swell. And that smell! Positively intoxicating.

"For god's sake, don't look, just do it!" she screeches, and the prompts kick in furiously. I kiss the swollen area, rubbing my mouth and chin against it while smelling a sea.

Then my tongue, of its own accord, leaps out to lash against the stiffening clitoris. The Fem exhales deeply, and begins a series of groans and moans.

This spurs me on, and I reach my hand towards the source of the increasing wetness. I insert two fingers, and she shudders and begins to push against them, thrusting her hips and groaning more deeply.

"Ah god yes! Just like that! Don't stop, oh god, don't stop."

I have no intention of stopping, in fact, I feel compelled to redouble my efforts. There is something so...*forceful* in this sex business that I don't think I *can* stop.

So I continue with the licking and moving my head up and down and applying increasing pressure to the engorged source of her pleasure. Additionally, I penetrate her harder, faster and deeper, using four fingers now. In response, the shape and texture of her vagina begins to change, while she simultaneously grasps my hand more firmly.

Oh, this *is* exhilarating. And she must also perceive it thusly, because she keeps up a stream of sounds: "Ah Jesus yes, you're hittin' my spot, you're hittin' my spot, ah ah ah!" and she releases an ejaculation of sounds, as well as an ejaculation of fluid.

With a final shudder and grip, she lies quietly against the seat, and softly intones "Oh. My. God."

But now I find that the pressure which has built up in my pelvic region throughout this encounter requires immediate and unequivocal relief. Struck with inspiration, I rub my clitoral area against the upright mast of the gearshift.

In very short order this causes an explosive force to be released, which originates in that clitoral region and extends outward through my entire body and the surrounding atmosphere. The pleasure is so sharply intense that I gasp, and then collapse against her.

After some moments, I raise my eyes to hers. With a strange look upon her previously relaxed face, she asks, "Did you just get off on the *gearshift*?!"

"I suppose I did," I reply, marveling at the ingenuity of the act.

"You fucking pervert. Get out of the car!" she barks.

"I don't understand," I intone. This is not a script I have access to.

"You heard me," she says harshly. "*That* is *too* perverted. I would have done you. But you'd rather hump a goddamn gearshift," she grumbles, pulling her panties back on.

Not wishing to endanger the results of my research, I sit upright, blink, and then open the door.

"Uh, it was nice meeting you. Perhaps we can do this again?" I proffer.

"There is no fucking way. You eat pussy like a pro, but hell no." And she hurriedly slams the door and sets the vehicle in motion, leaving me in a vapor trail as I turn to walk back to the bar.

This was such a successful field test overall, I think that I will perform it again, with another Fem, before the night is out.

Gravity Sucks
Skian McGuire

"Oh, shit! Fuck! Goddamn!" I sucked my bleeding knuckle in spite of the grease and shut my smarting eyes against the shower of rust and undercarriage gunk that sprinkled down on my face like fairy dust from hell. Between that and the sixty-watt droplight frying my ear, I never noticed the garage door closing.

There was no point wiping my eyes. Nothing on me was clean enough. I blinked against the tears and groped for my lost wrench, cursing again. How far could it have gone? I scooted the creeper a little ways out and froze. The radio had come on. Holding my breath, I listened while somebody tuned it to a country station.

For one foolish moment, I imagined I would be invisible if I stayed completely still, like a rabbit. As if half of me wasn't hanging out from under the rattletrap '67 Mustang I called Baby. I forced my voice to work.

"Who's there?" I tried to sound gruff. Big and butch. Yeah, they could see my big threatening butch legs. Right.

No answer. With a shaking hand I switched off the light

and squinted into the dark, willing my eyes to adjust. If I could see, I could recognize the intruder's ankles, maybe. If they happened to be in the quarter of the garage available to my sideways, immobile vision.

No such luck. "Fuck," I whispered, barely audible over my jackhammer heart. I dug in my heels and pulled the creeper as hard as I could, right into something solid and warm against my upraised knee.

Someone giggled.

"Natalia?" I breathed, relief flooding in.

The leg that had stopped my creeper pressed against the inside of my thigh, shifted, and then there were two, pressing my legs apart.

"Jeez, Nat," I said in a rush, "you nearly gimme a heart attack. I thought maybe an ax murderer..." I trailed off. What would an ax murderer do, hack off my feet? Still, the thought gave me a shiver. "Natalia?"

The feet stepped back. Awkwardly, I pulled the creeper out and came smack up against the legs again.

Again, the giggle.

Now I was getting pissed. "Come on, Nat. I gotta get this frigging thing off so I can put a new parking brake cable on." I was whining, and I knew it. I tried to sound calmer and more reasonable. "If I don't put a new cable on, the parking brake won't work. If the brake doesn't work, it won't pass inspec—" Cool fingers pushed aside my waffle-knit shirt and grappled with the button of my jeans.

"Whoa!" Startled, I sat up. "Yah!" My head hit the frame. I dropped back, eyes streaming. "Fuck," I whispered and spit a mouthful of rust and gunk bits, hands useless at my sides.

More giggles. The hand worked my zipper down. I lay there, forehead throbbing. I heard a rustle and a little grunt as she knelt between my feet.

Fingers pushed past my underwear and dove unerringly

for my snatch, zinging my clit with what seemed like an electric charge.

"Eeep!" I squeaked. Reflexively, I tried to close my legs. She shifted her weight and shoved them apart even harder. Her forefinger set up a hypnotic rhythm, insistent but not drubbing, teasing but effective. My clit hummed to its tune. My legs fell open, suddenly nerveless.

"Eeeeeeeeeee," I breathed. She laughed out loud. My head didn't hurt at all.

Fingers spread my lips and dipped into the flood of juice I was producing. Wet fingers slithered and danced between clit and hole. My hips bucked. "Ohhhh, jeeez!" I moaned.

The hand yanked out of my pants. "Awww!" I protested, my heels shifting for purchase. I don't know where I thought I was going.

Her hands seized the waistband of my jeans. "Upsy-daisy," a familiar voice said. Familiar, but Natalia? While my fuck-fogged brain tried to puzzle this out, my hips obliged her, all by themselves. Hands tugged my jeans and underwear down past my butt, past my thighs, past my knees, coming to rest at my ankles. I sighed, quivering with anticipation. A cool draft wafted over my thighs as I waited. And waited.

"Natalia?"

Stillness. Silence. "Uh, Nat?" I tried again nervously.

"Whoa!" Hauled by the jeans around my ankles, my legs shot into the air. The creeper trundled backward. Under the car, my arms flailed for something to hang on to. "Whoa, whoa, whoa!" Hands scrabbling on the concrete, I tried to pull my legs down. My bare knees thumped against cold metal.

"Relax," that familiar voice said, "you're bungeed to the door handle."

"Oh," I said, as if that explained it. I craned my neck for a view. All I could see was a denim bell-bottom and the hem of a long crushed-velvet coat. I ransacked my mental inventory of Nat's wardrobe and came up blank.

The air in the garage was more than cool on my naked ass, but I was sweating in my long-john and filthy Carlux hoodie. Before I knew it warm breath had enveloped my pussy, and her mouth touched down like Soyuz docking Mir. "Na'zdorovye!" I shouted, inspired.

Her tongue flicked back and forth and sluiced up and down my labia, darting into my hole like a fish. Her lips closed over my throbbing nub and sucked. Her teeth teased my clit hood and tugged at my short hairs. My legs bounced on their tether as I strained to meet her mouth, the creeper rocking and rolling ever so gently as I moved. I was weightless, trapped in a tin can, floating in space.

My arms stretched out, Christlike, for ballast as I swayed. *There* was my wrench: the thought drifted through my brain. I panted and licked rust-gunk off my dry lips. Orgasm was inevitable; my lower half was on autopilot. Now that less of me was under the car, maybe I could see my benefactress? No. My own pale goose-pimply thighs blocked the side view. Straight down the middle, tucking my chin hard into my chest and scraping my forehead—"Ouch!"—against the car, only the top of a dark brown head was visible. Carefully, I drew my arms in.

Her tongue moved faster. She stuffed it into my dripping hole, and I clenched and opened, rising to it, trying to draw the slithery coyness of it deeper.

"Oh, yeah," I moaned. In slow motion, my hands met on the silky bobbing top of her head. I twined my fingers in her hair. Her rather longish hair. Had it gotten that long since I'd seen her last? How long had it been? I'd seen Nat two weeks before. No, wait, it was only...

Under her relentless tongue, the heat and pressure in my groin achieved supernova. Her thumbs dug into the soft flesh of my thighs as I came, bucking, a tiny lightship tossed in the solar wind.

"Cosmic," I breathed.

Her giggles were warm, moist puffs against my engorged clit. I shivered.

"Oh, Natalia," I breathed, the last spasms twitching through my rapidly cooling flesh. "Natalia?" I unwrapped my fingers from her hair—gee, how long was it, anyway?—and groped toward her face like Helen Keller with a load on.

"Ah, ah, ah!" she said, pulling away. Without thinking, I grabbed for her.

"Aaaack!" The creeper teetered sideways. My head hit the car. My shoulders slid toward the floor. My arms, trapped between my pinioned legs, came back too slow to keep my sweaty ass from stuttering off the canted creeper onto icy concrete. My splayed thighs slapped against the car door and bounced maddeningly on the bungee.

"Shit," I muttered. A giggle tinkled out from across the dark garage, somewhere behind me. I didn't dare open my eyes. I spit oily crud and called out, "Natalia? Wait a minute, honey. Help me get out of…"

The garage door opened. And closed.

I snaked a ten-inch breaker bar out from under my left ass cheek and scooted sideways. Far and wee, a twangy male voice tunefully exhorted God to bless Texas. I thought of Houston, and Ground Control, and empathized with all those nameless astronauts who came down hard on dry land in dark little capsules and waited, waited, waited, to be set free.

In the end, I toed off my sneakers and tugged numb feet and ankles out of their denim prison, my numb legs flopping uselessly back to earth. I thought about the glory days of Mercury and Apollo while the circulation gradually returned and my cold bare behind absorbed spilled transmission fluid and waste oil from the grimy garage floor. I thought of

Natalia—it was Natalia, wasn't it?—and unearthly bliss and my own shocking touchdown on the unforgiving planet.

But what can I do? I am a fool in love, or even in lust, as I suspected it might boil down to. I called Natalia after work the next day. She'd be happy to meet me at Taco Villa for "tapas, or maybe something more?" She breathed into the phone, "I just love eating South-of-the-Border, don't you?"

It took three-quarters of an hour to get the crud out from under my nails. She was waiting at the bar when I finally got there, nursing the last inch of a Corona and bobbing her head to Hank, Jr. on the jukebox.

I stopped dead in my tracks.

"Natalia," I finally managed as she bounced up to give me a hug, "you got a haircut."

"Yes, this afternoon," she whirled and patted her hardly-longer-than-a-crewcut locks, "Do you like it?"

"Ah, sure," I began faintly, until the look on her face told me I was about to make a horrible mistake, "yes, I love it. It's terrific. Absolutely gorgeous."

She took my arm as the waitress led us to a booth in the back. In the dark. My unruly imagination slipped the surly bonds of Earth, and I wondered what I would do if she slid down the padded vinyl bench and disappeared beneath the table.

She ordered a Corona for both of us. "Upsy-daisy," I murmured, remembering.

"I beg your pardon?" She cocked her head, smiling the kind of smile no virgin had a right to.

Our drinks arrived at something approaching the speed of light.

"Na'zdorovye!" She tipped her bottle toward me. I sprayed beer across the table.

She graciously helped me mop up the mess and even signaled the waitress for more napkins. Already as mortified as I could be, I forged ahead, boldly going where I fervently hoped no man had gone before.

"Natalia," I began, "did you by any chance stop by my house yesterday? While I was, uh…" I paused, feeling my ears turning hot, "…working on the car?"

"Did I ever tell you, darling," she reached for my hand and gazed deeply, earnestly, into my eyes, only the faintest hint of amusement playing on her lips, "that my father was a member of the KGB?"

"No," I answered weakly, "I didn't know."

"He was assigned to Martina Navratilova. When she defected, so did he. What else could he do?"

"Really." Her fingers were stroking my palm.

"So, you see," she smiled, "secrets run in my family." Her toe nudged my ankle. My heart threatened to achieve escape velocity.

Appearing out of nowhere, the waitress hovered over our table, her pad at the ready.

"We'll have the number five combo, and the number three," Natalia told her, "and the number six as well, hmm?" She looked at me for confirmation. I licked my lips. She took that as a yes. "Unless you'd rather…" She squeezed my hand and cut a look at the exit.

"Could we get that order," I asked the waitress, "to go?"

"Pre-par-ing for takeout…" she enunciated as she wrote.

Time is relative; you don't need a Grand Unified Theory to know that. Several billion years later, we loaded our steaming cartons of enchiladas and chimichangas into the Baby's backseat, where they were swiftly forgotten in our warp speed race across the galaxy to my bedroom. We left a trail of clothing through the house behind us, planetary detritus forming an asteroid field in our wake. I never found out for sure if it was Natalia's mouth I rendezvoused with in the lightless depths of my garage, and I don't know if pistoning fingers and slick thighs actually convert matter into energy. Minutes and seconds can't measure the rate of propulsion of a body rocketing toward orgasm. But this one thing is immutable physical law: when the Big Bang happens, time stops.

Einstein didn't know the half of it.

Wide White Sky
Cheyenne Blue

Her horse was ground tied. He stood with his head low, eyes closed, flap-lipped whiskery muzzle twitching in equine dreams. A pack was thrown carelessly onto the sagebrush, a Navajo blanket spilling out, a water bottle, and the military-surplus rucksack she used for collecting.

Calamity sat with her back resting against a pinion pine. The ground around her was covered with cones, nuts and husks, gnawed by squirrels and small things that creep. I sat and watched her for a moment from the back of my horse, an elderly and arthritic animal, the only one that the ranch would consider lending to an untried, middle-aged city woman to roam the high desert alone. I dismounted stiffly, my inner thighs aching in protest, and let the reins fall. The stock horse understood and drooped his head to dream with his companion.

She was watching me, her dark unfathomable eyes intent on my face, cataloging my awkward gait. "I knew you would come," she said.

In truth, I had wondered at my foolishness. A woman my

age was supposed to be established in her career, successful in her marriage, with grown children maybe. She was not supposed to leave them all behind to pursue some nebulous dream of the West. Utah was a long way from New Jersey. A fractured mirror universe of possibilities and paths to be trodden.

The small Utah town had one motel and one bar. Calamity worked the bar: stalking the sagging timber floor with intent, flirting with the few customers, seducing them into leaving larger tips. She was a child of mixed race, whose heritage had given her not the smooth olive skin and curling hair that is so beautiful, but a patchwork of skin tones, a tapestry of birthmarks and varied pigmentation. Calamity. A name her mother had given her in anger and despair. The hurtful name she had made her own.

I was lonely of course, with the sad aura of a woman alone, whose dreams of escape were crumbling before reality. I did not know what I was doing here, I would not find myself in Utah, whose white respectability was safer and more straightlaced than my three-thousand-square subdivision in suburbia. So I sat at the bar, nursing my gin and tonic and watched her. And then she touched me and flirted with me as indiscriminately as any of the jowl-faced ranchers mumbling into their 3.2 beer. And the evening promised heady excitement, far from home.

"I harvest pinion nuts," she said. "I beat the sage for the Bureau of Land Management. Cut firewood. Come with me tomorrow."

Her eyes spoke of more than gathering seeds. I agreed. So here I was, sitting awkwardly on the ground, my hair streaked with dust, leather and horse sweat ingrained in my jeans. Calamity licked her lips, a fey gesture of momentary doubt, then leaned forward to kiss me on the lips with the bravado of an orphan.

It was why I was here, of course, to take some comfort

from this strange child, she of the sad little name and piebald skin. At first it was experimental. I had never kissed a woman before; the confines of marriage and respectability had kept me from indulging. I cataloged the sensation. Yielding lips, sweet with honey and bitter with coffee. Small lips coaxing mine apart, rimming mine, softer, less assured than a man. Icy from the air temperature, cold little nubbins of flesh. Satisfied with my response, Calamity rose to spread the blanket, a splash of color on the hard ground.

I watched her, the slight frame blending into the harsh landscape, her body golden in the weak wintry sun. Puffs of dust from her feet, as she moved around, shedding her clothes almost as an afterthought. Angles of elbow and shoulder, dried yellow sagebrush tangled in her coarse black hair. The air was sharp, but she seemed impervious to the temperature. I saw the jut of her ribs as she pulled the flannel shirt over her head, nipples pebbled with the cold.

I mimicked her movements, pulling off my fleece and layers of cotton, fumbling with the clasp of my bra—underwires and ribbing designed for support, not seduction. Her eyes were on my breasts. I knew what she was seeing: blue veins on white, breasts for nurturing, no longer exciting. She crouched and her small fingers touched me, tracing the weave of veins and fine lines, circling a nipple. She cupped one, testing its turgid weight with the flick of a callused finger.

I suppressed a small gasp as she bent and put her mouth to my breast. Warm wetness, cool lips, swirling tongue. Gently she pushed me back on the blanket. I felt sharp stones digging into my back under the scratch of the blanket, saw the criss-cross of branches against the washed sky, smelt pungent sage and something else. Arousal, the sharp scent of excitement, mine and hers, strong in this place.

She used her mouth as others might use their fingers. Crawling over skin; learning textures, imperfections and taste;

her lips mumbled over freckles and moles. She suckled me, moving to the waistband of my jeans, tickling her way over the creases of my belly, scars and lines of childbirth. I closed my eyes and let her work, seeing the kaleidoscope of sunlight behind my closed eyelids. She tugged at my jeans and I raised my hips and let her remove them, leaving me naked and ridiculous on the geometrically-patterned blanket.

I sucked in my belly, trying to flatten the folds, so that the fast-food curves were minimized. She traced her lips over my C-section scar, still keloid and livid after more than twenty years.

"You don't have to do that," she said, and poked me so that my exhalation was rapid and my belly expanded. "You have an honorable body."

The appreciation in her eyes gave the truth to her words. *Is this what it is always like with a woman?* I wondered. This unconditional acceptance?

She shifted to lie next to me, and my hands moved to her body, tentatively fingering the small ribs, tracing the mottled skin tones, the patches of pigment, shades of chestnut like the horse who dreamed nearby. I stroked one nipple. It was dark, a hard little coffee bean, fine hairs around the nipple. It hardened, sharp little cone-breast, rigid peak of nipple. The other nipple was pink, dusky ashes of roses. She closed her eyes and moaned, a breathy little sigh. I continued to tease, drawing gentle circles with my fingertips, watching the shadows of the branches make further patterns on her skin. Sunshadow shapes.

My fingers moved down to the waistband of her baggy pants. They were loose enough that I could slip my hand underneath them, over the concave planes of stomach, down to the elastic of her underwear stretched tight over the narrow span of her hips.

Tentatively I undid the drawstring on her pants, and dipped

my fingers down between her legs, over the cotton underwear. The undulations of her hips encouraged me, and I moved a finger under the gusset of her panties. My finger touched curls of hair as coarse as the hair on her head, springy and resilient like the sagebrush she harvested. I explored, feeling my way around familiar anatomy. It was not like touching myself. Oh, she was younger, firmer, skinnier, but it was the subtle little differences in folds and creases that I noticed. I pictured what she looked like through my fingers, feeling creamy wetness, a landscape of textures.

My wrist was straining at the angle. She gently removed my hand and shed her remaining clothes. Pinto girl.

I started to shake slightly, desire warring with uncertainty. "Show me what women like," I said.

"You already know," she replied, and straddled me, shifting around to lower herself to my mouth. She dipped her head. Her hands cradled my buttocks, raising me to her mouth.

I grasped her and used my thumbs to spread her open, to see her, then explored with my fingers, tentative movements, trying to please. She had no such reservations, and buried her face between my legs, so deeply I wondered how she could breathe. And the pleasure was abrupt and intense. I could see her in my mind's eye as if in a mirror. Folds of my sex mashed against her checks, her mouth pressed up against me, her tongue lapping around the small folds and secret valleys, the small pointed tongue flickering around the hood of my clit, not too hard, not too direct, just that slight off-center stimulation that I like. Quick laps, teasing points and then, unbelievably, the gentle scrape of teeth. Ah, the shock, the instinctive withdrawal. She drew me closer and the scrape became a suckling, gentle suction on my clit and I came, a gasp, a shudder, a tightening of thighs around her head.

When sensibility returned, I found I had been grasping her skin so tightly that I had left individual prints. Cloudy, crushed-purple marks on the hues of her skin. Two of my fingers were inside her. I felt immediate guilt for my selfishness and moved them gently, a pistoning action so beloved of male lovers. She wiggled upright on top of me, moved around, settling herself firmly on my face. A lap, an exploratory movement of tongue. Salty sage taste, different from my own. I circled my tongue, flickered, tasted. It was hard to breathe, the musty smell of her pussy surrounded me, stale sex. I wondered if she had taken one of the self-righteous ranchers into her bed last night. The thought was both repugnant and exciting. How could she, I wondered, be so careless with her body? How could she, I wondered, be so free and unfettered? My tongue savored her, trying to pick out the familiar thick taste of semen, but I couldn't. My senses were filled with everything that is intrinsically female. There wasn't room for anything else.

Calamity moaned a little, and I lapped harder, striving to give her a fraction of what she had given me. It was difficult; my tongue ached and she was wriggling around so much that I couldn't keep a steady rhythm. I kept trying—soft flickerings, more forceful rubbings. I used my fingers, my tongue, even teeth, trying to emulate the feelings she had roused so carelessly in me. And still, she ground herself on my face, grunted, gave sharp little animal squeals, tightened her thighs around my head. But she didn't come.

My concentration started to waver. I opened my eyes and studied the patterns of the tree boughs above my head. There was a sharp point of a rock digging into my back under the blanket and I jerked convulsively when some small insect skittered over my thigh. But still I persisted. I wanted to give her something purely for herself, and this was all that was within my power.

And just when I was about to stop, when my discomfort was so great that I couldn't last any longer, I felt the first clench of muscles around my fingers, felt the ripples of her orgasm and heard her long wail. I opened my eyes. She was arched up into the light, the curve of her body silhouetted against the wide, white sky, her head thrown back, her mouth open as she panted. The tangle of hair fell in static disarray over her shoulders, covering the deep chestnut nipple, the pale shell one still visible. And she was beautiful.

Much later, we dressed, and she shook out the blanket, releasing a shower of horse hairs, throwing the scent of our lovemaking into the breeze. Her horse had wandered off. We rode back together on my borrowed elderly pony. She curled trustingly into my body, riding behind me, her head resting on my shoulder. Her hair tickled my nose.

I was content. A relaxed permeating comfort that went far beyond the euphoria of climax. I held the reins confidently and pretended to guide my horse home. Calamity murmured into my shoulder, reaching around to cup my breast.

I knew that tonight she would don her false cloak of self-assurance and play the sassy flirt for the ranchers once again. Maybe she would come to my room afterwards and we would make love in the sagging bed with the faded sheets. Or maybe she thought that to show her need was a weakness she couldn't allow and so she would stay away. But for now, at this moment in time, she was mine.

I curled my hand back around her thigh and moved my body to the horse's rhythm, letting the friction of the saddle reprise the memories of Calamity that I was already storing away.

Bull Rider

Sacchi Green

Amsterdam.

Am-ster-god-fucking-*damn*!

Sin city of the '70s, still sizzling in the '80s. Cheap pot you could smoke in the coffeehouses, but that's not what lit my fire. Sex shows and leather-toy shops? That's coming a whole lot closer, but what really ignited a slow burn low in my Levis were stories of the working girls displaying their wares behind lace-curtained windows. Something about the dissonance between elegance and raunch struck a chord. "Fine old buildings," ice maiden Anneke had told some of the Australian riders, with her slight, Mona Lisa smile and a sidelong glance at me. "Many visitors tour the Red Light district just to view the…architecture."

I should have tried harder to figure Anneke out. A damned fine rider, in total control of herself and her mount, she was all blonde and pink and white with cool, butter-wouldn't-melt-in-her-mouth self-possession. But a certain Preppy Princess with a long chestnut ponytail and a cute round ass—and delusions of being a world-class equestrienne—had been using up too much of my energy at the time.

That was all over now. With a vengeance, a fair share of it mine. Now I needed to drown my sorrows in whatever flesh-pots I could find. I was not going to leave Europe without at least a taste of decadence.

You don't get to taste much, though, without a few guilders clinking in the pockets of your jeans. Which I didn't have. Damn near didn't even have the jeans. First French-tourist jerk-off to point at my ass and say, " 'Ow much?" came close to losing his business hand. "Chienne! Pour les Levis!" he hissed, rubbing his numbed wrist.

"More than you've got!" I tried to step away, but he scurried in front of me with a fistful of bills. "No way," I said, lengthening my stride until he dropped back. Before I made it across the Centraal Station plaza I'd had two more offers, in Spanish and Japanese, and damn sure would have taken one if I'd had any alternate covering for my BVDs. But after that fiasco at the Equestrian Tournament, I'd left behind everything except my hat, buckskin pants, and fringed jacket. And I'd pawned the leathers to raise plane fare home. Too damn cheaply, if even torn jeans reeking of horses and stable muck were this much in demand.

Maybe the stable muck was the selling point. Authenticity. I could've made a fortune if I'd known enough to dirty more jeans! The question now was: Could I parlay all that authenticity into getting laid? I had twenty-four hours before my flight in which to find out. And a conniving little preppy to purge from my system.

Oh hell, there it went again, like a movie in my head. My jaw and fists clenched—and my clit, too—as I sat on a bench at the edge of the square and spread a map across my knees. I lowered my head as though the names of streets, canals, and landmarks were all I saw.

She'd planned it from the start. All those weeks I'd spent coaching her to signal the horse with her knees—(to wrap her thighs, naked and moist, around my neck)—to lift her tight little butt in rhythm with the horse's gait—(to tilt her hips to the thrust of my demanding hand)—and all along she'd known that moment would come.

She'd been about to come herself, which only made her moment better. I saw it in her eyes as they went from deep and velvety to glittering and triumphant. She focused on something over my shoulder. My fingers slowed, and she switched all her attention back to me. "Eat me, Toby! Eat me!" she commanded, pulling my head toward her pussy. The musk of sex and the rich aromas of hay and horses blended into a powerful aphrodisiac. I delayed a bit, inclined to make her beg; then she flicked her little pink tongue over her lips like a kitten licking drops of cream, and I forgot everything but getting my own mouth into her cream, and my own tongue deeply into where it would do the most good.

She had never wriggled with more abandon, never let her gasps and moans and ultimate shrieks rip so free. No faking it, either. Her internal spasms surged right through her pussy into my mouth and hands and rocked me to my toes, but it was no tribute to my skill. When I came up for air I saw her eyes fixed again on someone behind me, and a look on her face like the proverbial cat who's deep-throated the canary.

Some instinct made me roll away just before his fist could connect. It's a wrench to shift from surging lust to fight-or-flight, but I made it fast enough to have ten feet and the business end of a pitchfork between us before he could swing again. I recognized him from the picture she'd shown me. Charles, the fiancé. I almost felt sorry for him.

"You goddamn fucking dyke!" he sputtered at me, as much pain as rage in his voice.

"Oh, Chub, do you always have to state the obvious?" Miss Ponytail languorously brushed hay out of her hair. "Afraid you can't do as well as a stable hand?"

Stable hand. I swung the pitchfork toward her, then back toward Chub's more physical threat.

I'd worked my way through the same elite Eastern women's college she was lounging through. Stable hand, stable manager, eventually assistant riding coach; what she called me didn't matter as much as the contempt in her tone.

"So, 'Chub,' " I said. "Let me know if you need any more pointers." I hurled the fork just barely over his head into the bales of hay behind him, and got out of there fast before he could pick himself up off the floor where he'd taken cover.

Any sympathy evaporated late that night when he caught me alone in the barn and came at me with rage in his eyes and a serious bulge in his pants. Poor dumb bastard. I left him hurting so bad he wasn't going to have the means to please Miss Preppy any time soon.

If I'd left it at that, I might still have been able to fly back to the States on the chartered plane with the rest of the equestrian team. If I hadn't charged into the Bitch Princess's room, shoved her face into the pillow, immobilized her with my knee between her shoulder blades, and taken my knife to that long chestnut hair until no fancy hairdresser was going to be able to conceal all the ragged gaps without cropping it even shorter than mine, the police and the International Equestrian Organization officials wouldn't have been called into it. But I did, and they were, and I barely got away ahead of arrest with my passport and leather duds and the clothes I'd been wearing to load the horses into the vans for the transport plane.

So here I was in Amsterdam. I'd fed the chestnut hair strand by strand to the wind from the back of some Hungarian biker dude's motorcycle when he'd picked me up hitching on the outskirts of The Hague. The breeze here in the city was pretty light, smelling of canals and the ocean, but I folded my map and stood and ran my fingers through my hair and tried to imagine the hot scent of her expensive perfume and greedy pussy being blown away over the North Sea.

Then I headed for the Walletjes Red Light District in search of replacement memories.

Okay, decadence is a subjective concept. Packaged, Health-Department-Inspected sex doesn't do that much for me, and the cruising scene seemed to be—no surprise—mainly the boy-meets-boy variety. There had to at least be a women's bookstore somewhere; I can handle that scene, as long as I can steer the conversation to the better bits of Colette, just as I can coach show riding and could compete myself if I could afford a show-class horse, even though at heart I'm Western all the way. But literary foreplay, especially with language barriers, wasn't what I had in mind.

The ladies of the night weren't disappointing, exactly; the tall, elegant windows glowed with discreetly red-tinted light, and the flesh casually displayed was enticing enough. One blond dressed only in a long white men's shirt saw my interest and treated me to a knowing smile over her shoulder as she straddled a chair and did a slow grind on its plump upholstered seat. But a paying customer caught the vibes and knocked on her door. After a close look, he invited me to come in, too; I declined. The window shade came down. I moved on.

The neighborhood provided plenty of rosy-fleshed occasions for fantasy, but none of the others quite did it for me. I began to have a sneaking suspicion that one particular pink-and-white-and-blond vision had been making my subconscious simmer. I sure as hell wasn't going to find her here, but I might know where I could. For all the good it would do me.

Anneke had always been civil, but reserved. Once, when I'd helped her with an emergency repair in the tack room, she'd said, "Toby, you should be riding that fine horse, not her," with a nod of her head toward Miss Preppy.

"Could never afford it." I wrestled with multiple interpretations. Riding the horse instead of riding the girl?

"No, nor could I." Her trace of accent was tantalizing. "The brewing firm that employs me keeps a show stable for…what is it in English? Public relations?"

"That's it," I said. "You work for them? I thought you must be family."

"No, I work summers in their Amsterdam clubs, as bookkeeper and assistant manager. The newest is a country-western bar on Warmoesstraat, all the rage, like that movie *Urban Cowboy*. They would go crazy for you there, Toby!"

Then she was gone, and like an idiot, I didn't follow up. Now it hit me hard just who I wanted to go crazy for me; just what smooth, white skin I wanted to raise a flush on; what cool, half-smiling lips I wanted to suck and bite until they were red and swollen and begging for more. And whose butter I wanted to melt in my mouth.

How hard could it be to find a country-western bar in Amsterdam? I even remembered the name of the street. Had she meant me to? Anneke had always been so collected, so focused on her riding. Maybe I'd been afraid to try anything, afraid it might matter too much.

The neon outline of a rodeo bull rider told me I'd found the right place. I hesitated in the doorway, well aware that I didn't have the means to buy a lady a beer, and even if I did, this might be the kind of place where a move like that could get me thrown out. Then again, the way the people inside were rigged out in wannabe-western gear, where could I get more mileage out of my battered hat and authentically work-worn (and pungent) denim vest and jeans?

It was early, but crowds were building. Behind the bar a large woman with a generous display of pillowy breasts scanned the room as she wiped the countertop. When her gaze crossed mine it moved on, stopped for a beat, then swung back.

Without looking away, she pulled a phone from under the counter and spoke briefly into it. *Oh shit*, I thought, *are the police here looking for me?* My "victims" couldn't have wanted that much publicity. Then a grin lit her round-cheeked face as she replaced the phone and beckoned to me. I might've resisted the good-humored gleam in her eyes, but the foaming stein of beer she offered was something else again. I hadn't had anything to eat in almost twenty-four hours, and nothing to drink but water from public fountains.

"On the house, honey." Her nametag said *Margaretha,* but her accent said New York. "You look like you might liven this place up. Ever ride one of those?"

I followed the jerk of her head. Through a wide archway I saw, rising above the sawdust on the floor like some futuristic mushroom, a mechanical bull just like the one Travolta and Winger rode in *Urban Cowboy.*

I wiped beer foam from my mouth. "You mean, does my ass live up to the advertising of my Levis? Lady, you have no idea."

"Don't bet on it, darlin'." Her assessing look assured me that one way or another, a good time could definitely be had. Much as I appreciate older women, though—hell, one saved me from fratricide—my hopes for something else grew. If it wasn't the police she'd called, who on this continent but Anneke would have described me to her?

"Yeah," I said, "I've ridden those, and the snorting, stomping, shitting versions too. For another beer and some of those hefty pretzels, I'd be glad to demonstrate."

"Wait a while." She refilled my stein and slid me a bowl of pretzels and cheese-flavored breadsticks, and I did my best not to stuff myself. Some things are better on a less-than-full stomach. Bull riding is only one of them.

"So, where are you from, Toby?" she asked, chatting me up while keeping a close eye on the door.

"Montana," I said. I definitely hadn't told her my name.

"They let women ride bulls in rodeos there?" she asked.

"Not yet. Not officially. Except at small local shindigs where anything goes." I paid close attention to my beer and pretzels, not wanting to talk much about it. But there was no way I could keep from remembering the surge of wild triumph when I outrode them all, even my brother Ted. The pounding of my blood—the pressure building until I had to explode or die—and the revelation that, to achieve explosion, I needed to wrap myself around Cindy's full, smooth curves.

Back when we were twelve, Cindy hadn't minded a little mutual exploration. She'd been away for a few years, though, and this time, as I tried to pull her close, she twisted away and ran around the grandstand to throw herself on Ted. Another revelation, that life was a bitch, seared me. No matter how much I could work like a man, even beat the men at their own games, their rewards were officially off-limits to me.

I was young and naive, and the shock filled me with rage. I leapt for my brother, and only the intervention of Miss Violet Montez, sultry lead singer for the intermission entertainment act, kept me from killing him.

"Hey, Tigrina, come with me." She pressed herself against me as Ted struggled to get up. "I have what you need. And what you don't even know you need." And she surely did, or close enough.

When I rode back to the ranch at daybreak, too drained to sort out the remnants of pleasure and pain and smoldering resentment, Daddy was waiting in the barn. He couldn't quite meet my eyes. "Looks like maybe you'd better go East to school the way your Mama always wanted."

"Looks like," I agreed. And that was that. Someday I'll find the words to tell him that it wasn't his fault. I'd never have survived being raised any other way. And how could he, after letting me know all my life I could do anything a man could do, tell me that the one thing I couldn't have was a woman of my own?

Besides, he'd have been wrong. Going to a women's college didn't make a lady of me, but I sure learned a lot about women.

Not that there isn't always more to learn.

Anneke came through the door and stood for a minute, cool as ever, with just a hint of defiance. "I'll be damned!" Margaretha muttered from behind the bar. "I knew you'd made an impression, but jeez!" From the dropped jaws and arrested strides of several waiters I got the feeling that they weren't used to seeing Anneke in tight, scant denim cutoffs and a gingham blouse molded to all the delectable curves below those peeking out over her plunging neckline.

Body by Daisy Mae; face by Princess Grace. A divine dissonance, but what the hell was I supposed to do with it in a public place and a culture I didn't wholly understand?

I sure had to do something, though, with the surge of energy pounding through my body. "Maybe it's time for a ride," I growled, and jerked my head toward the room with the bull.

"Good idea." Margaretha shoved some coins at me across the bar. "Go for it!" As I turned away, she grabbed my shoulder and swung me back. "Take it a little easy. She may not admit it, but she's new to this." She didn't mean the bull.

I set the controls on "extreme" and vaulted aboard the broad wooden back, my hat held high in the traditional free-arm gesture. It was a damn good thing the bull was mechanical; my body could handle all the twists and lurches without involving my brain. Matching wits with a live, wily, determined bull would've taken concentration I couldn't spare, with Anneke on my mind.

I was vaguely aware that a crowd had gathered. The music was "The Devil Came Down to Georgia," and Anneke was leaning against a nearby post watching with her Mona Lisa smile. Less vaguely, as the bull reared and jerked I realized I was going to be sore tomorrow—though nowhere near as sore as I'd like to be unless some vital moves were made. When my wooden mount slowed to a stop and the room held still, I tossed my hat toward Anneke, who caught it deftly and allowed her smile to widen. Then I shifted my ass backward to make room and held out a hand to her. With no hesitation she let me pull her up to straddle the bull.

Someone, maybe Margaretha, put more money in the machine and set it on "easy"; the music changed to "Looking for Love in All the Wrong Places"; and I was in the kind of trouble worth dreaming about.

Riding without stirrups can be an erotic experience all by itself. Riding with Anneke's ass pressed into me, kneading my crotch with every heave of the bull, was sublime torture. Her slim back against my breasts made them demand a whole lot more of my attention than they usually get, while her own luscious breasts… I nuzzled my face against her neck and gazed over her shoulder at the rounded flesh gently bouncing and threatening to surge out of the low neckline. From my vantage point, glimpses of tender pink nipple came and went. Much as I wanted more, I didn't necessarily want to share.

"Your décolletage is slipping," I whispered into her ear. Instead of adjusting it, she turned her head so her smooth cheek curved against my lips.

"Help me, Toby," she murmured. "Hold me." And I was lost.

I cupped her breasts, gently at first, as the motion of the bull made them rise and fall and thrust against their thin gingham covering. Then I felt her back arch slightly, and her flesh press more demandingly into my hands. There was no way I could help moving my fingers across her firming nipples. I felt her soft gasp all the way down to my toes.

Her ass began to move against me independent of the bull's motion. My clit felt like it was trying to scorch a passage through my Levis. My grip on her breasts tightened, and her nipples hardened and pulsed against my fingers as she leaned her head against my shoulder. "Toby," she breathed, "You are making me so sore!"

"Want me to stop?" I teased her tender earlobe with my teeth.

"No...don't stop...make me sorer still, please, Toby...."

How could I refuse? I unbuttoned her blouse at the waist and slid my hands across her silky belly before filling them with the even silkier flesh of her breasts. Then I drove her to as much sweet, sore engorgement as hands alone could provide. My hungry mouth made do with the soft hollows and curves of her neck and shoulders, feeling the nearly soundless moans she couldn't suppress vibrate directly from her body into mine. Her pale hair was coming loose from its intricate chignon, so I pulled out the fastenings with my teeth and let the golden curtain fall across the marks my mouth left on her skin. Her hair gave off a faint, clean scent of herbs and roses.

I hadn't forgotten our audience, but I was beyond caring. During my first wild ride there'd been whoops and cheering, but when Anneke joined me the sounds had dwindled to a low hum, an almost communal moan. Somebody put more coins in the machine, and "Looking for Love in All the Wrong Places" played on.

My problem was the accelerating need to get right down to it in ways even permissive Amsterdam couldn't handle. Or, if it could, I couldn't.

"We have to get out of here," I growled against Anneke's cheek. She gave a slight nod.

"Soon," she said, with a shuddering sigh. "Help me turn." I admired her flair for showmanship as she swung one leg over the pommel, poised briefly in sidesaddle position, twisted so that her hands could brace against my shoulders, and pushed herself up and over until she was facing me astride.

Okay. A little more for the paying customers. Just a little. My hat, now upside down on the floor, had become a target for a fair number of coins and bills.

I urged Anneke's legs up over my thighs and got a firm grip on her waist. She leaned her head back as I savagely pressed my mouth into the hollow of her throat and let anger flicker through desire. New to this, was she? New to what? Performing with a woman? What had she done here with men?

My mouth moved down and Anneke leaned farther back, both of us as balanced as if our moves had been choreographed and rehearsed a hundred times. I tore at her shirt with my teeth until the buttons let go and I could get at her arched belly. A collective sigh rose from the audience as the fabric slid aside to leave her round breasts and jutting, rose-pink nipples naked. I knew what they wanted, but there was only just so much I could share.

She lay so far back now that her legs were around my hips and only my grip kept her upper body from sliding off the gently heaving bull. I probed my tongue into the ivory rose-bud whorl of her navel as her thighs tightened and jerked.

My clit jerked too. I ran my mouth down to the waistband of her shorts and then over the zipper, biting down gently just where the seam pressed against her clit. The fabric was wet and getting wetter. Our musk rose like a tangible cloud, mixed with the scent of roses and the earthy reek of the stables.

I bit down harder, tugged at the thick seam, pressed it into her, and knew by the spasmodic thrusts of her hips I could make her come right now, right here. And knew I wasn't going to.

I may have a streak of exhibitionism wide as the Montana sky, but some desires are too deep, too intense, too close to the limits of self-control for any but private performance. I pulled Anneke upright and kissed her long and hard, letting her feel the sharpness of my teeth. "There's an old show-biz saying," I said against her mouth, my voice harsher than intended. "Always leave 'em wanting more."

I swung us both to the floor and stood, still holding her in my arms, until the ground stopped heaving under my feet. Her legs tightened around my waist, and so did her arms around my neck, reminding me, for all the enticing tenderness of her flesh, that she was a world-class athlete. The dazed look in her blue eyes retreated slightly. "But Toby, what if *I* want more?"

"You'd damned well better want more. You're going to get it. But not here." I started toward the door, not knowing where I was going. Hands reached out as we passed, some just stroking us, some stuffing money into my jeans.

Margaretha called out; Anneke turned, laughed, and caught the big old-fashioned key spinning toward her through the air. She shouted something in Dutch, and thrust the cold iron down inside the waistband of my BVDs. It slid, of course, much lower, producing new and interesting sensations as we ran hand-in-hand through the Amsterdam night.

The little houseboat rose and fell gently on the moon-lit canal. Anneke went down the steps to the deck, turned, caught me by the hips, and burrowed her face into the crotch of my jeans. My legs nearly failed me.

"Mmm," she said, inhaling deeply. "I never thought to breathe anything as sweet as the smell of a horse. But mixed with the scent of a woman..." All her cool reserve had melted. She looked up at me with eyes darkened by night and arousal, and just a trace of laughter on lips still swollen from my kiss. "I never thought to touch a woman, either, until I had such dreams of you I thought I must go mad!"

I came down the last few steps and pressed her against the low door to the living quarters, trying desperately to feel in control of a dangerously reeling world. When I kissed her as gently as I could, her tongue came tentatively to meet mine and my clit lurched as though it, too, had been touched.

"But Toby," she whispered, turning her mouth away just enough to speak, "I must get the key! I must...is it all right?" She touched my crotch lightly, then drew her hand up along my zipper to my belt.

"Yes..." I managed to gasp. It wouldn't have been all right for anyone else. Even now, I couldn't let her slide her hand down into my pants before I had mine deeply in hers. It was too late for control—I knew I was going to lose it any second, going to come at the touch of her fingers on my throbbing, aching clit—but I'd be damned if I was going to come alone.

Experience counts for something. And Anneke wasn't wearing a belt. I had my whole hand curved around her pussy before she'd gotten farther than the waistband of my briefs. She gasped, and paused, as I worked my fingers between her folds, not penetrating yet—the night was still young—just gently massaging the increasing wetness and circling her clit with my thumbtip. She arched her hips forward, but her hand slid down over my mound, and in desperation to distract her—and myself—I lowered my mouth to one breast and licked at her pink nipple until it was hard and straining. Then I sucked her, hard and harder, biting a little, and she pressed herself deeper into my mouth. Her gasping breaths turned into deep moans, but her hand still moved down and her fingers curved in imitation of mine.

I pressed my fingers deeper, moved my thumb faster, harder, demandingly against her clit, and her fingers moved too, tentatively, but more than enough to push me to the edge. The iron key, shoved back now between my asscheeks, only intensified the sensations.

I had to cheat. I gripped her wrist with my free hand and raised my head. "Wait," I said against her lips. "Just feel, feel it all." Then I covered her mouth with mine and sucked and bit and probed and worked my whole hand back and forth in her slippery depths, spreading her juices up over her straining clit, stroking faster and faster until she spasmed against me and sobbed into my hungry mouth. Finally I let her pull away enough to breathe.

"Toby," she gasped, "please, let me, I have to…Let me touch you!" She struggled to move her hand against my grip.

I had to let her. And had to bury my face in her soft neck in a vain attempt to muffle the raw cries tearing through me on waves of explosive release.

She withdrew her hand, and the dripping key, slowly and sensuously. "Oh, yes," she sighed, "much, much better than the dreams. And there is more?"

"More," I assured her, still breathing hard. "All you can handle. This was just a taste."

She smiled wickedly and touched her tongue to the key. "A fine taste!" Then she turned, and the door swung open.

In the snug interior, lit by a hanging lantern, I opened her to pleasures she hadn't yet dreamed of. I took it a little easy, since she was, after all, new to this; then, as her demand grew, she drove me to extremes. And invented new ones. Being with someone whose strength matched mine, who, like me, had as great a hunger to touch as to be touched, was a new and disconcerting experience.

By morning, when Margaretha dropped off some coffee and hot rolls and my hat filled with cash, we were both sore and exhausted. And as high if we'd just won the gold.

"Take all this." I dumped the money on the bed between Anneke's splayed legs. "If my half is enough, could you get my leathers out of hock and send them to me? I'll find the pawn ticket…in a minute…if I ever manage to move…"

"Maybe I shall find a way to deliver them in person." Anneke rolled over to straddle my thigh. "You won't mind, Toby, if I wear those snug trousers a bit, maybe ride in them? And think of you, and get them very, very wet?"

"We could send them back and forth," I said, "until they're seasoned enough to travel on their own. But in person would be a damn sight better." I found the energy to flip her over; maybe the coffee was kicking in. I nuzzled my face into the pale-gold fur adorning her finely seasoned pussy. "Just how wet did you have in mind?" Exhaustion forgotten, I was ready to ride again.

The Edge of Night and Day
Peggy Munson

The heat makes me gag, the air is rough, and the day dunks its panacea behind a cloud. But Daddy shows up on time, at eight, with his motor sputtering. He and the bike together look like a dark cat, and as the road unrolls in front of us the shrubs around the edge look like the salt on margaritas.

"There is a line," says Daddy, "somewhere along the Pacific Coast Highway, between night and day. At a certain time of early morning, when the sun peeks over the ridge, the moon is still going down over the ocean." Daddy has ridden on this line, the tightrope between conscience and depravity, one time before. He has ridden on it and known its curves. "There is a moment when you can witness time," says Daddy. "When time bends on either side of you like two parents. There is an edge between night and day."

I am afraid of falling, so I am afraid of edges. I am afraid of the stretches of road that teeter next to sharp drops to the water. There are people who believe that gravity will not win, but I am strictly Newtonian about it. When I read about catastrophes, I think about gravity. When you're buried in an avalanche, you're supposed to spit, because the spit will tell you which way is down and which is up, and then you can dig up. It would appear then that gravity is helpful, but not really, since nobody escapes an avalanche. And skydivers, when their chutes don't open, must grab another diver, still at terminal velocity, and hope the bones they break are few. A few collective bones.

So I climb onto the motorcycle. Daddy puts a helmet on my head. It's too big, like a Martian helmet in '50s space movies. Daddy sits in front of me. I put my palms on his thighs. I like the tops of thighs when they're not being laps but still remind me about laps. I like that borderland where something's use is changed by what's not there. Laps make me think of sex and comfort both. The way that denim is such durable material. They make me think of being on my knees, in front of him, and bracing both hands on his thighs while sucking his cock. And prying myself off of it is hard for me. I want to swallow all of Daddy, take him in.

Daddy moves my hands to a better place, so I can hold him. Speed whisks the air around us. Motorcycles make you think of sex because they never let you forget your body; you have to bend to make the cycle turn. And have to spread your legs to ride behind the driver. And have to feel the world spinning by, and your smallness, and your speed. I like the way my legs are spread for Daddy from the start and then I have to think about it, how I'm riding him already. Riding him to find the line between the things that are kept separate.

Daddy likes to say I'm irresistible. Often Daddies won't show need, but Daddy needs. He needs to take me to these places and to fuck the twilight into me and out of me. We are like risky parachutists, breaking open with compelling need. The one whose parachute has failed must link his arms into the other's straps. The arms linked through the straps will shatter since the force, the resistance of the opening chute will be too much with both the human weights together. But still, the parachutists must entwine and break. The need to fall is followed by the need to break and heal.

In the ionized air, Daddy is intoxicating. Daddy is getting me drunk on his speed and his leather and the lulling ocean noise. The waves scroll forward like the arms of swimmers doing the breaststroke to the shore. I think about the strength of arms, and Daddy's arms, which signify a thrilling kind of power. People do not realize that the arms are just a ruse. The power is beneath them. Power is the riptide. Power is what's ripped. The girl beneath the arms, the mermaid of the undertow, is who will steal the breath away. The girl who's torn and smooth as driftwood breathes in every place unseen.

When Daddy sputters to the side and kills the engine, on an overlook that has a slight climb down a brambly patch of incline and then a sharper drop, I hear the waves and feel a thrilling kind of power. Daddy takes my hand and leads me off the bike, his leather gloves still warm from gripping. Then he pulls me to him. When we kiss, it feels like we're inside a conch shell, something microcosmic that is moon and tides preserved in one small insular environment. I feel a sting of sand against my face, its tiny mirrors, the sting of self-reflection that can interfere when I am kissing people but this time, takes me further into both of us. "I'm going to punish you because you make me need to fuck you," Daddy says, and pulls away his swollen salty lips. He makes me touch the bulge he's packing. "Daddy's cock is hurting it's so hard for you," he says. He slaps my sand-stung cheek. "I hope you've figured out that nobody can hear you here." He slaps me hard again. He grabs my chin and turns my head to search the stretch of highway. "In just an hour or two," he says, "there will be no one. No one but a trucker who's been driving seven hundred miles, and he'll be filling up his cab with cum to see you sucking off your Daddy on the roadside."

Daddy grabs my tits. He pinches through my cotton bra

to feel my nipples. He takes his warm and seasoned leather-clad hands and pries the bra aside and takes the fullness in his hands and says, "I love your lovely tits." And then he gets up in my ear and says, "Now Daddy wants a show. He wants to watch you play beside the ocean."

"What do you mean?" I ask. I'm suddenly confused. Then Daddy walks back to his saddlebag and pulls out a small dick, and says, "I want to see you fuck yourself. I want you to be ready for your Daddy." We are somewhat hidden from the highway down the little wooden steps but still a car could pull up any time. He starts to stroke his cock. "I want your skin to feel the ocean air," he says. He turns me so I'm standing facing toward the waves and wraps his arm around my neck so if I move it stops my breath. I feel his cock against my ass, his exhalations on my ear. He takes his palm and shoves it down my pants and underneath my cotton panties. "You're always wet," he says into my ear. "You're lucky you got me and not the lonely trucker, little whore."

"Now strip," says Daddy, pushing me away. "Your Daddy wants to come."

I jerk off all the time at home. I think of Daddy and the way he talks to me. I tell myself I am a hungry, greedy whore and Daddy needs to fuck me all the time. I tell myself I am a nasty, piggish bitch and Daddy needs to fuck me all the time. I tell myself that Daddy needs to take me from behind as he can't stand my greed, my open mouth, the way I want him. I tell myself that Daddy needs to hold me back because I must not come till Daddy says so. I must not come till Daddy's got his fill, and filled me, taken me so long and hard. He's quite articulate. He uses words like *surfeit* when he says that there will never be too much of me for him. But when he fucks me nasty, gripping at my hair, he chokes on his own words. I like to see him gagging on his voice the way I gag on his cock.

The dick's too small. It's just a knickknack dick. It's just a break-her-in. Just riding on his bike can make me cavernously open. My hands unbutton all five buttons leading to my clit. I slip out of my shirt. I slide my jeans down, feel the ocean lashing at the shore. The waves are quarrelsome. They're pushing to the stage. They're framing the acoustic that will take me in, deflect my sound, and vibrate with me. Here, I am a rock star when I touch myself. I take the dick into my palms as if it is a microphone. I slide it down my front and ease the tip into my cunt. Behind me, Daddy's stroking himself off. Sometimes I wish he'd have the look of vacuous old Johns instead of gazing so intensely and intently at my hands. When I fuck myself he's fucking me. He's fucking me with visceral ventriloquism. I slide the surrogate inside of me and try, with all my imagery, to make it him.

I close my eyes. A lazy cat is batting at a skein of highway. The road uncoils a trail of light. The trail looks like the kind of pattern slugs leave on my doorway in early mornings, not the orderly and luminous crochet of spiders. I take an extra finger and I slide it in beside the dick. I take the finger out and ease it in my mouth. I trace the finger into patterns on my belly, on my legs. My other hand starts moving Daddy's extra dick inside of me. I think about my body as a map of mirrored highways, flashing bright with moisture from a sudden rain that only sticks a moment. I hear him groaning and I open up my eyes and watch him rubbing hard. His hips are pushing forward uncontrollably. He's dying to grope me, shove it in. He moans so helplessly. I want to lick his leather pants and help him come.

"So good for Daddy," Daddy says. His sentences are breaking up. He's breaking up like wood in water, how it splinters into pieces then waves keep gathering it back. The way he's breaking makes me blissfully on edge. I want to fall into a net of light. I want to fall into a raft of illusion, tumble through the wooden words of Daddy's broken speech and sink down to the broken undiscovered vessels on the bottom. "Come on my little girl," says Daddy, suddenly calm. "Come my little girl, for Daddy." The curio cock ripples through me like a maritime explosion, leagues below the surface. I barely moan but Daddy knows what's happening and he grunts.

"That's very good," says Daddy when I'm done. His lips are burrowed in my breezy hair. "It looks like you can handle practice dicks quite well." He pushes his bulge up against my ass again. I feel the rough edge of his zipper casing and the fabric of my panties pushed into my crack. "But now it's time to meet your fear."

He gives me cheese and crackers from his bag. He gives me grape juice like I'm only old enough for kiddie wine. He lets me stare off at the waves to think about their threats. I am afraid of falling so I am afraid of edges. I stand close to the precipice and look at all the disappearing darkness. Daddy grabs a few more items from his bag and leads me through some brush along a trail until the drop-off gets steeper. His flashlight glints. The darkness is consuming. The distant headlights pulse. Like novice pilots, I can't tell horizon from the sky. I feel like I am in an avalanche. A place where whiteness becomes darkness and vice versa. "What did you get?" I ask him when he comes back from his bag. I'm feeling shaky. My legs are wobbly like they get when I'm on bridges looking down.

"A harness," Daddy says. In the penumbral flashlight glow I see his lips curl up. He's plotting something but I don't know what. He's had his harness on the whole time, plus he never says that word, that word that makes a dick seem too detached. "That makes no sense," I mumble to myself. Then Daddy puts his hand over my mouth and he says, "Be quiet, mouse." I suddenly hear voices from the overlook. They're talking about whether we are dead. They must be looking at the empty bike. I see their flashlight breaking zigzags through the sky and then turn off. It seems forever once a motor starts again. It sounds so far away now, and I'm scared. My brain makes desperate distance computations. But Daddy puts his nasty voice against my ear. "If you're not quiet, bitch, you'll get a nightstick in your pussy. Want that?"

"No Daddy," I say softly. Daddy's told me many times I must behave in outdoor sex or cops will want to fondle me and do indecorous arrests.

"I didn't think so," Daddy says. "Now stand real still and close your eyes. Don't open them until I say." He slides my panties down my legs. He takes my feet and makes me step inside of something, pulls some scratchy straps around my legs. He fastens them around me tight. The edges of the straps are pulling tight against my legs and make my pussy go just slightly numb, but open. He pulls more straps around the rest of me. He yanks on something that seems to be hooked onto my chest and makes me lurch a little forward. "Figure eight and D-ring, check" he mumbles. "I just need to find a place to hook the carabiner. Don't you move." I've heard these words before—harness, D-ring, carabiner—but I'm not sure where. I think I read them in a mountaineering story where the characters all died. I have a sudden horrifying inkling of what's happening. He's going to make me fall.

"Don't open up your eyes," I hear him saying from a distance. The goose bumps and the prickly wind abrade my arms. The waves are roaring somberly. They're swallowing up sailors in an unforgiving night. The wind is hollow and loud. I keep my eyes clamped shut because I know how Daddy hates it when I'm bad. I do not have a compass in my head for where he's gone. I have the kind of night blindness that comes from being led and never noticing the landmarks. Then suddenly, I feel a rough hand on my chest, a shove against my breastbone, pushing back. I stumble and I start to lose my footing. I give a little scream and feel my eyes bolt open. Daddy's arms are crossed, not even trying to give aid. I grapple for him but he is too far. I'm falling back. I'm stumbling back. I hear the water rushing up to catch me, and the rocks. I scream a bloodcurdling "Help, Daddy!" as I feel myself fall backwards. My legs are braced against the rock. My back is dangling over the precipice. The nylon catches me. The D-ring pulls. The straps go taut against my back. And Daddy's watching, smiling all the time.

"Goddamn you, that's not funny!" I scream louder, and I feel my eyes get wet. My heart is racing and the nylon on my chest is suffocating me. The straps against my legs are pulling me. I'm hanging on the edge of night and day.

He lowers me beyond the jutting lip of rock, adjusts some straps so I am hanging parallel to sea, then shuttles down and leans back right alongside me. He's hooked into a harness too. I see the safety on my chest that leads into the darkness. The neon colors of the nylon barely glow. We're scaling slightly down an overhang that drops down to a shelf and then to nothing. Daddy has his lube in one hand and he's balancing himself. He takes my legs and spreads them wider, braced against the rock. "That's right, my little girl. I bet you're feeling vacant now. And Daddy's going to fill you."

"I can't believe you did this," I yell at his face. I want to spit it so he'll feel the words. I want to make him feel my helplessness. My heart is shot up with adrenaline. "I hate this, Daddy."

"I don't think you do." He shoves three fingers into me, so hard I suddenly feel weightless, lifting off away from rock and into space. "That's right," says Daddy, pushing in again. "You're Daddy's Supergirl and you can fly." He slides his fingers into me, all five of them. I moan and wriggle onto him. I feel the loosening of rocks around me and I hear the trail of tiny pebbles falling. Daddy's working his whole fist inside of me. He's concentrating on the way my pussy's taking him. I'm paranoid and thinking about rockslides starting and the pull of empty space. He starts to work his knuckles into me. He rams in hard, so every time he thrusts I'm pushed back into emptiness.

The sense of nothingness breeds somethingness. His fist begins to pulse. His rhythm gets more furious. The rocks and dust are little bits of shrapnel as he thrusts. I feel my body breaking into rocks. There is no echo here. I'm screaming, "Daddy," but the ocean is a void. My voice just seems to scatter out like particles of surf. He's got a magic trick inside his clenched and thrusting hand. One moment it is empty; the next it's full of doves. "Come on my little girl," he says. "Come on."

And then I'm lifted and I'm flying. Our warped sound falls off to the ocean. "Damn you," I say when I cannot resist the urge to soar, and come and yell into the waves. "This is too scary, Daddy." But I know that I'm invincible.

He brings me back to earth and holds me when it's over. It is almost time for night and day to merge. We rest and Daddy strokes my hair. He tells me about shipwrecks and the people who survived. The light flirts with arrival on the mountain side. The sky is filled with wispy strains of orange and pink. The moon is waiting for the sun. We kiss, then Daddy takes my hand and moves it to his bulge again. "Again?" I say. "You're hard again?" I grapple at his buttons and pull down his pants. His breath gets raspy, like a crackly old transistor. I work my pussy down onto his cock. His breath grows fractured, treading water near the sharpened rocks of coves. I tease him while the patient moon is hovering. I tease him while the eager sun is coming. I push on him when night and day join in a symbiotic union. I slide on him like someone falling.

Just a Girl

Shireen Deen

Did I have an orgasm that night? I think I did. It's so hard these days, my body just shuts down. The passion of making love to all the curves of her delicious body is like a freight train in my head. I think I'm going to explode.

The North Carolina night is warm, perfect. Molly unlocks the door to her white, one-story house and I follow, letting Sophie out of her kennel. We both know we are going to make love tonight as we walk past each other silently, attending to details: something to drink; a snack; music, something romantic yet passionate—a deep, sexy, female a capella. When I'm ready I sit on the couch. My white linen pants bunch around the crotch and ride up around my hips. My tight black T shows the curve of my flattened breasts, still flattering, not too feminine. Sophie jumps up to sprawl out beside me. Her reddish boxer head flops over my thigh. I bury my hands behind her ears, in the soft, puppy fur that remains, and give her a good kneading. Molly walks from the kitchen to the bathroom. Sophie's head picks up with a smile; her red tongue lies just over her bottom teeth.

If she's in the bathroom then she's almost ready. My heart starts to drum with both hands. I stand up to fix my pants and sit back down, trying to find the most inviting and sensual pose. I go through three or four, Sophie eyeing me, confused. I settle back into my Zen place with a few deep breaths.

Oh god, does she have any idea how much I want to touch her? To taste her on my lips? How I long to feel her fingers on my cheek, her other hand gripping what she can of my cropped black hair? To feel her nails rake across my back? Where is your tongue, my love? Your eyes, your earlobes, your sweet scent unlock my beast.

I am so in love with the woman in the bathroom. I could watch her forever, her bourbon-blonde hair, the incredibly sexy way she bites her lower lip, and those green butterfly eyes. I love her strength, her courage. I love her stories: beautiful tales with twists and turns and the smell of ferns growing by the edge of the forest, the awe of looming mountains, the smiles, the laughs, her beautiful lips as she spins and spins. My stories aren't like that. They are short and foreboding with thick swirling storm clouds.

I used to be proud of my stories as friends and I sat around comparing abusive mothers, fathers, brothers, uncles, grandfathers, Joe Schmoe on the beach with his penis rammed in hard. Now they embarrass me. I want to speak them out. The scenes play out in my head over and over, the light changing, the names, the dialogue, but the story is the same. I want to put them to rest. I want someone to hear them, but I am too ashamed.

Molly walks out of the bathroom, a mischievous smile on her face. She takes her time and with every step I inhale my own longing. Scooting Sophie over, she climbs into my open arms and the weight of her body against mine is like coming Home. I bury my hands in her hair, massaging her scalp gently. She sighs against my neck. My fingers trace designs along her arms, some Celtic, some chaos, some neither. I can feel my breath quicken. I lift her hand, the hand I had dreamt of before we even met, and kiss the palm. It was a beautiful dream really. I think of this as I slide my mouth over her fingers, one by one, tonguing the skin between them.

I feel her breath against my ear and her pelvis pushing against mine. She drives her tongue into my mouth and then backs away, looking at my begging eyes. She smiles slyly, knowing that every nerve and cell of my body is at her mercy. My hard-on packed in my trousers bucks for freedom and my body arches up in mad desire, as my moan becomes a low, deep, primal growl.

She smiles at her butch all riled up.

"Baby," she coos, as a whimper escapes from my beast.

I may be the butch, but she's the boss. She kisses me long and deep, sucking on my lower lip. With one hand, she leads me into the bedroom, to the small twin mattress that has become our nightly nest.

Sophie follows us into the bedroom, curling up at the foot of the bed. She doesn't like to be alone.

My kisses are full of stories I want to tell her, full of tears and screams and even laughter. I feel naked. Does she really want to make love to all of me? To the pain and hard pinches of the past, to the anger that wanders lost, to the ghosts who grip my balls tightly in clenched fists? She returns my kisses with such compassion I want to cry. Her tongue unfolds me like a flower. In this moment I want to give it all to her—my heart and my vulnerability and my sexual abandon. I want to give her my beast howling sweet freedom to the miracle that is our love.

Oh god please please let me be able to have one tonight. No ghosts tonight. Please let me be able to give her this one thing.

You see, I don't know how. I seem to have forgotten. I can't remember how to have an orgasm.

Molly smiles up at me. She trusts me completely.

I kiss the soft skin under her elbows, brushing past it with my wet lips. I kiss the pulse in her wrist, in her neck. My fingertips, like dancers, find their way to the bottom of her tank top and underneath. They skip lightly over the soft, white skin; one rib at a time they climb up until I can feel the curve of her breast. My thumb spans her rib cage to her sternum, lightly brushing the skin that delicately curves around her nipple. My breath quickens again as I sit up and help her off with her tank top. She lies back once more, naked to the waist this time. I cannot help but stare. Her soft breasts, her pink nipples, the flat of her torso so trusting under my long, brown hands. She is so beautiful I want to weep.

I make love to Molly the best I know how. Like it's the first time. Like it might be the last time. Take nothing for granted. Ever.

Her eyes close. Her hips come up to meet my tongue. Her fists grip the sheets tightly as her muscles tense.

"Don't stop," she pants, "Don't stop."

I tease her along for a few more minutes before I give her what she wants. I hear her screams and want so badly to look up, but I know not to stop. She screams again and again, until slowly, exhausted, she comes to rest. I move up to face her, hold her in my arms, kiss her.

"Was that okay?"

"Baby, that was so amazing! Couldn't you tell?"

I breathe a sigh of relief as I hold her against me.

I know what the next question will be. I want her to ask it. I want it, oh god, do I want it. Maybe she'll forget. She loves me too much to forget.

"Baby?"

"Yeah?"

"That felt so good."

"I'm glad."

"I want to make you feel that good." She waits for my reply but I don't know what to say. "Can I make love to you?"

"Yeah, but...what if I can't?" The embarrassment builds on my cheeks. I can't look her in the eyes.

"Baby," she sighs in my ear. "we don't have to if you don't want to—"

"It's not that. I want to! I want to! I...just...I..."

"Look at me. Baby, look at me!" She waits until my eyes slowly rise to meet hers. "Don't put so much pressure on yourself. If we can, great. If not, we've always got Clyde, right?" She picks up the vibrator we keep next to the bed. Her grin makes me smile.

A tear comes to my eye, but I blink it back. "Will you just kiss me first?"

"Of course," she says climbing back toward me with that smile on her face, her eyes alight. She knows just how to coax me out of my sheepish shell. She kisses me softly first, then more insistently. Her hands wander to my breasts, cupping them, tugging, pulling. "I want you so bad," she breathes into my ear. As she moves down my neck, she leaves sharp bite marks, on her way to my nipples. I cannot help but growl and arch my back in desire.

I am so turned-on. She is the most gorgeous woman I have ever made love to and now I am at her mercy and it is the ultimate turn-on.

"Promise me, one of these days you'll tie me up."

"I promise."

My hands are in her hair, on her back. I want to kiss her again but her mouth is kissing me wetly behind my knees, up one thigh and down the other. I am already so wet as she slides down to suck on my toes. I cry out, burying my head in the pillow to keep the noise down. Every nerve in my body is on, pulsing, vibrating. My legs spread wider. All that lies between us is a pair of black Fruit of the Loom briefs.

"These are getting in the way." She smiles as her hands slide down from around my hips, dragging the underwear off and dumping them next to the bed.

Sophie looks up for a minute, then goes back to sleep.

Molly is the first woman I've ever trusted this much. I want her to touch me, to kiss me. I want her inside of me. All the way inside. I want to be full of her. I want to feel her heartbeat echo inside my own.

My head drops, color rushing to my cheeks. Like a daylily at sunset, I curl into my self. She gently unfurls me.

"You're beautiful," she whispers, her fingers gently parting my beastly fur.

I feel one slick finger slide down the groove from my clit, almost entering me. Then two fingers.

I whimper like a dog caught in a bear trap.

I see her head go down as she shakes the hair out of her face. My brain is a blur of synapses firing. I can feel the tingles sparkle right behind my ears and at various constellation points around my skull.

Her tongue is wet and warm and gentle.

"OH GOD!" I moan deep into the gravel of my desire.

Waves crash with white foam caps and oily colors swirl throughout my body as I offer myself to this woman buried between my legs. Her tongue writes with deep, solid strokes on my quivering body. I am surfing through the biggest tidal tunnel ever to grace the beaches of my brain. I am racing towards the sunlight at the other end.

And then it happens. Just when I think I am a star about to be blown supernova, the surf settles. As my brain rages with the buildup of colors and lights and white electricity, the water becomes warm, calm, as it laps across and over my body. I can feel her tongue and it's solid and strangely comforting and my body wants to suck on it like a child would a thumb.

As my brain rips itself apart, my body becomes prepubescent with innocence as if I had never heard the word *sex* before. Every muscle goes limp. I am in so much pain I want to sob.

I reach a hand down, gently pulling her face up.

"What is it, baby? Do you want me to stop?"

A gorgeous woman is asking me if I want her to stop going down on me.

"I…I don't think I can…" One tear curves a salty arc into my ear. I hope she doesn't notice. She does. "I'm sorry, sweetie. It's not you. It's…it's just me."

Molly kisses the corner of my eye, catching the next one before it can get away.

"Do you want to use Clyde?" The smile never leaves her face. Somehow she manages to caress me with just her eyes.

I nod, trying to suck in my breath.

"Will you just hold me first?"

"Of course," she says as she gently takes me in her arms.

Molly holds on even though there's no leather jacket or big black boots. Even though there's no tight black T or sports bra to flatten me out. Even though my eyes have lost their swagger. Molly holds me, her right hand in my hair as I bury my head in her chest, even though I'm just a girl.

With the help of Clyde, Molly's fingers stroke my clit and slide into my depths, sending vibrations to every cell within my body. The ocean is boiling and I am flying higher and higher until I'm blown to billions of tiny particles, spread as wide and as far as the ends of the universe. I say, "I love you" in dying breaths, as if an orgasm is the end of the world. And it is, just as it is the birth of a new one.

We hold each other in the silent, thick, post-sex air.

In the stillness of the North Carolina night, voices clamor for attention. My stories come like cigarette smoke curling upward through my consciousness. I do not want to listen.

The basement was a favorite place in the summer months, keeping much cooler than the rest of the house. It offered some privacy and as everyone was upstairs getting ready for dinner, I had the room to myself, space to concentrate. I was working hard at a drawing that was looking to be better than any drawing I had ever drawn before. I had my crayons spread before me and I looked at each color carefully before choosing one with my tiny hand, gripping it tightly so as not to slip and color outside of the lines I had drawn. As I neared the picture's completion, I could feel my heart beating loudly. I had really done such a good job this time. Mom would be so proud of me. I looked at it. The way it curved up was just right. The color was as close as I could get with a Crayola 64 box of crayons. The size was even pretty close. My smile was almost too big to fit on my face.

When I was done, I carefully wrote my name on the bottom right-hand corner of the page, and, standing triumphantly, ran upstairs to show my mom. As I held the picture up for her inspection, I watched her brows furrow together and her eyes grow dark. I could hear her rage. I inhaled it and have never been able to breathe it out again.

"This is a disgusting picture! Don't you ever draw this again!"

My face fell.

"Do you understand me? You are never to draw such filth again!"

She was screaming. Other people, my brother, my dad, my cousin, were staring at me. I left my picture and ran downstairs. I sat in the corner, curled into the cold, slightly musty couch. I did not know then what I had drawn that had elicited such a response. I know now. My mom did not like my penis.

Lying on the bed next to Molly, I can feel my mother's rage course through me. I can see her eyes and the storms that hide within them. I can see her watching me as I lie on the black beach with a big dredlocked man on top of me. The man looks at me, laughing. I can hear his voice echo deep and full. His weight is suffocating.

"I knew you would end up pregnant," my mother whispers. I am twenty-two years old and backpacking in Costa Rica. The man on top of me laughs again. I'm embarrassed and ashamed.

"You'll probably get some filthy disease and be like those women on welfare" my mother's voice hisses.

He is pushing down on me. He is trying to get in. I am shaking. My head is turned away from him. I am pushing with all my might.

"No! Get off me! Get off!"

"It's okay, baby. It's okay." I feel Molly's arms around me, but the heaviness is still there. I am pushing, but he is very strong. I struggle on the bed with solid stories, real stories, my stories. I am telling the stories not with my mouth, but with my body.

"I love you I love you I love you..." Molly repeats the mantra over and over again in my ear. It is a beacon. It seeps through the pages and chapters of my life, writing its own story as it goes. I focus on her words, on the feeling of her love wrapped around me like a lighthouse and I am swimming towards it.

Who is this strong woman beside me? Who is this woman who is not afraid of my stories? Who is not afraid to let me take care of her, not afraid to take care of me? The voices stop. My shaking subsides. I look at Molly. She is beautiful, radiant.

Sometimes I'm a big, bad butch. Sometimes, I'm just a girl. Molly loves me through it all.

I look at Molly curled up next to me. For the first time, I have good stories.

Lessons Learned
AJ Miller-Bray

She looked up at him from her chair and leaned back, throwing an eyeful of cleavage in his general direction. He only paused in his tirade for a minute as he took in her lewd tableau.

"Are you listening to a word I'm saying?" he hollered, "Is everything just a game to you?"

"You're overreacting, as usual, dear. I was just talking to her. Just common *politesse*—nothing you'd know about." Her tongue darted out to lick her berry-glossed lips, and she finally lost the internal struggle, letting her eyes gleam with mirth. They seemed to have the same fight every two weeks, just before his shot. His testosterone-induced mood swings were worse than any PMS he'd ever had as a woman, and they were starting to wear on her nerves. In fact, it had reached the point of amusing her, and that's always a bad sign. Whether or not she'd been flirting with the salesgirl was totally irrelevant, anyway. Hadn't she gotten a hefty discount on those four-hundred-dollar shoes? He should be thanking her.

He seemed to read her thoughts. "Oh, you think I won't mind, because you flirted and teased your way to getting her to knock off a few bucks, is that it? Well, you're wrong! I do mind, and for that matter…"

Her mind strayed as she deliciously licked the wounds he sliced on her ego. A few bucks? One flash of the same cleavage he had brushed off a second ago had reduced that salesgirl to a puddle of blubbering mush. Without her shameless displays of skin and lashes, they would never have "found" that 80 percent off "sale". Her reverie was interrupted as one of his words cut like an icy dagger.

"…whore!"

She leapt to her feet, all humor and pouting forgotten. He seemed to realize his mistake, because he took two steps back, and raised his hands in defense, but it was too late. Her open palm connected with his face with such force, her entire arm stung from the slap. He stumbled backwards into the wall, his visage a mask of shock and pain, his hand pressed to his injured jaw. She stood her ground, arms akimbo, her tiny hands drawn up into tight fists. Her eyes burned with pure scorn.

"You fucking bitch! You hit me! What the fuck do you think you're doing?"

His shock was wearing off, with rage close on its heels. She knew she should apologize, but the words wouldn't get past her burning throat. Instead, she drew herself to her full height, which was only a few inches shorter than his six feet, her body pulsing with indignation. "How dare you!" she shouted, "You have no fucking right to call me a whore, you prick! Or should I say no-prick, because we all know you'll never be a *real* man!" The instant the words fell from her mouth, she cursed herself for saying them. She only wanted to hurt him as much as he'd hurt her, but she knew she couldn't take it back. She could never take it back. She closed her eyes in a silent prayer to long-forgotten gods, only to find herself alone in the room when she opened them again. "Shit," she thought, "now I've done it," and she headed straight for the bedroom.

Her guess was all too accurate. He was tearing clothes out of the closet and wadding them into a duffel bag. Just for a second, her mind left the situation, and she focused on his huge, muscular arms tensing and flexing with anger. She wanted to stroke them, stroke him, be safe in those arms, be safe from the pain she was feeling right now. She crashed back to reality with the realization that *she* had caused the anger pumping through those muscles. In a too-late attempt, she bowed her head. "I'm so sorry, baby. I didn't mean it. I was just trying to get you like you got me," she said softly.

She heard the flurry of activity cease, and she raised her eyes to his, but what she saw there made her choke. Where she'd expected to see rage, tears glistened like innocent rain. His shoulders slumped, his hands opened of their own accord, and his favorite shirt fell to the ground. They both looked down at the lump of soft material on the floor, minds clicking on the same memory.

When he first told her he wanted to become a man several years ago, she'd left him standing there, open and exposed. She returned that night to find him sitting in the dark, crying.

"I did some thinking," she'd said, "and I came to a realization."

"Yes?" he said, sounding small and afraid.

"I came to the realization that every man needs one nice shirt, and all you have are grungy old T-shirts. So I went and bought you this one. I thought you'd like it." They had made love all night after that, right there on the living room floor.

Now, in the bedroom, they had come to another juncture. Their eyes met once more, and locked with the same passion they had felt a moment before, but this time there were no angry words to throw. She bounded blindly to the strong arms she'd briefly thought lost, and they tumbled to the bed unceremoniously. He was kissing her wildly and ripping at the frail, filmy material that clung to her needy breasts. It tore easily, and she grabbed his hair, forcing his head down between them. He licked and sucked his way to her throbbing nipples, paying homage first to one, then the other. Her body thrashed wildly as adrenaline and lust concocted a powerful cocktail in her veins. He replaced his hot mouth with palms that thudded with his hammering pulse. His hands pawed and kneaded her elastic globes, and their mouths joined—he kissing tenderly, she ravenously. His hips moved between hers, still fully clothed, and pounded her with such authority, she squealed like the little brat she truly was. A smile spread over his soul, something secret, diabolical, and all too rare. He hid it with his ever-present compassion, and stroked her flushed cheeks.

"Ohhh, gorgeous," he purred. "Why don't we have a little fun?" He nuzzled her neck, his hot breath making her sigh and bite her lip to restrain her moans. "I think you'd look soooo pretty tied up and fucked senseless." Inwardly, he congratulated himself on a timely bow to her vanity. His gamble won the jackpot.

"Oh, please!" she breathed gloriously, her entire countenance a show of preened sexual perfection.

He regarded her with internal annoyance as she writhed perfectly for his inspection. *She never used to be so...so* perfect, he thought. With mission in hand, he set off to find instruments of her imminent imperfection.

All the regular equipment was resurrected from well-placed hiding spots. He secured his favorite dildo, and tucked the monstrous hard-on into his briefs. He opted for the leather, industrial-looking restraints in lieu of frivolous fuzzy cuffs and scarves. He chuckled as he returned to the bedside of his goddess, armaments at hand. He began to sprinkle soft, pretty words on her as his hands went to work securing her to the bed by wrists and ankles. His verbal finery did well to occupy her, and before she had time to pout, she was drawn, quartered, and completely nude.

He mounted the bed deftly, and quickly began his ministrations on her voluptuous body. He traced the curves of her full breasts with his tongue, his fingers creeping over the swells of her soft stomach toward her neatly trimmed and waxed mons. He stoked every inch of flesh in his path, inciting squirms and moans from his victim. As his kisses neared her throat, she stretched her neck as either an invitation or a command, he was not sure. His hand had reached her sculptured mound, and was sliding in and out of her slit, just touching her button enough to frustrate. Her pussy lips were just as pouty and glossed as the ones his mouth kissed with unsheltered passion. He ground his dick into her hip, only the thin, blue-ribbed material of his briefs keeping her from the sanity she craved.

He finally slid a solitary finger into her hungry pussy. He played her like a perfect flute, making her climb the scales of pleasure, only to bring her back down sans crescendo. She was losing all hopes of composure, tears pouring down her face, her mouth begging and blubbering incoherently. She pulled frantically at her restraints, her body arching off the bed. Finally, he climbed between her legs and unsheathed himself with tortuous grace. She eagerly pushed her hips at him and licked her lips anxiously. He reached inside her without ceremony, and stole her wetness. He slid his lubed hand over his shaft, making the base of it rub his smaller, testosterone-engorged dick. He stopped jerking his cock and looked into her eyes, his usual softness replaced with the anger of earlier.

"So, what do you have to say for yourself?"

She blinked up at him in confusion. "Wha-?"

"I said, you fucking little bitch, what do you have to say for yourself? How does it feel to be played? I'm sick of being the one who always feels stupid. I'm sick of..."

"What the fuck?!" she stammered, trying in vain to calm the throbbing frenzy in her sex. "You have no right! You... you...please!" she begged in exasperation.

"So that's all you can think about? Good. Now listen closely to me, and I may just give you what you want." He punctuated his words with strokes of his cock. "No more comments about my manhood. Period. I've had enough shit to deal with in regard to my gender, and I won't take any more from *you*. Next, T is not the reason I get so pissed at you. I get pissed because you're a conceited little bitch of questionable fidelity. No more flirting. Ever. Not with men or women. I don't care how old they are, or what they can offer in exchange for a glimpse of boobs. Grow up, and I mean fast, or else you'll have to go find some butch-dyke sugar daddy who'll put up with your ass. Now," he said, crawling up her body, his cock just bobbing out of her tongue's reach, "suck my dick, if you can, whore. Oh, yeah, that reminds me. I never called you a whore earlier, bitch. I said no one's gonna think they can offer my woman shoes for a glimpse of her tits like a whore. If you had been listening, you might not have behaved like an idiot. Now, *suck!*"

She craned her neck, tears freely flowing in humiliation, trying to lick the precious manhood of her lover. She begged for him, for forgiveness, for anything she could think of at that moment. She had fucked up, and she knew it, and despite the fact he could see her remorse, the lesson wasn't over. He laughed openly, and stroked his cock in her face. The pressure in his gland under the dildo was building rapidly, accelerated by the look of want still shining in his woman's eyes.. Suddenly, with a startled roar, he exploded in an unexpected orgasm that rocked through him. He came on her tear-stained face, depriving her of her noblest task.

When his heart slowed enough for him to think rationally, he looked down at his deeply disappointed lover. He now had two choices. He could reach down and caress her face, showing her that all was well. He could then remove the restraints and make love to her, bringing her to the same wondrous climax he had just experienced. He could even cum inside her, bringing them together as one perfect being. He could. He could do anything.

He got up off the bed without looking back, leaving her strapped down and stuttering a steady flow of shocked interrogations. He would take a nice hot shower, maybe catch the last period of the hockey game on TV.

This time, she would learn her lesson.

Boys
Ana Peril

"You think that one's cute?" said Mariano, pointing across the bar. I hung out with the boys every night then, watching boys, drinking and smoking and rolling and snorting and not looking for a girlfriend. Mariano got anyone he wanted, and not just on gay.com but in these sketch-ass places downtown with everyone so fucking hot and drunk, including, I hope, us. I looked where he was pointing.

I looked at you, dancing close, your hand on the guy's waist, your mouth next to his ear. Twenty-five or thirty? Maybe a grad student. Femme, but you were leading him. I felt rather than saw you press your cock against his thigh, and felt a sharp, unexpected pain between my breasts. The music was house, or something, something I was supposed to like, and just as I turned back to the boys, the cute bartender spilled a shot of dark booze across the counter. It dripped between us to the floor. "Sorry," she said, smiling at me from under blonde curls. She looked straight, but I'm not sure. I wasn't looking, but if I had been it would have been for a dyke. I looked back at you.

"I heard he fucks women," said Adam.

"I don't care. I'm not interested."

"Yeah, you are," said Mariano. "Yeah you so fucking are." But I knew that was an occupational risk of time with the boys, the continual projection of desire so intense that it seemed to spill over onto everyone. I watched him as he walked over to you.

The three of us lost Adam to some med student and somehow left the bar. You said your place was close, that we should all walk there together and smoke a little. But I was tired, almost tired enough to skip the weed and leave the two of you to it. When we got to your doorstep, you turned under the streetlight, your dark eyes serious. "Good night, Mariano. It was lovely meeting you." You kissed on the lips the way the boys do. He turned away from the house. With your strong arm, you opened the door for me, and let me, transfixed, walk in first.

Inside the house, you didn't bother to turn the lights on. You kissed me, your lips soft, sucking on my lower lip, biting. I was drunk enough to like it. You pushed me up against the wall and your knee came up between my legs. I put my hands up your shirt, stopped short for a confused moment, and in a moment of decision frantically unbound your breasts.

"Get on your knees, bitch," you said. With your hand in my hair, you jerked me around to face the wall. With the other you traced my naked spine. You licked your finger and circled my nipple with it, jerked my head back by the hair, bit my earlobe. Breathing raggedly on my neck, you moved your left hand down and stopped right above where I wanted it. You pinned me against the wall, with your whole body, your nipples hard. I arched against them. "I said get on your fucking knees." I slid down the wall, my tits and right cheek aching from the pressure. You knelt behind me. "Tell me what

I'm going to do to you."

"You're going to fuck me," I whispered.

You slapped my left cheek hard. My chin banged against the wall.

"Tell me louder."

I didn't know exactly what you had to do with the university and was afraid to ask, to uncover complications. A lot of people won't fuck undergrads, a lot more than I would have thought. A lot of people have kinks they won't show to someone they'll see again, especially someone who might know or be one of their students.

"You're going to fuck me."

"I'm going to fuck the shit out of you," you answered, letting go of my hair. You ran your arm down my shoulder to my tied hands, and in one swift motion grabbed my wrists and jerked them up behind my back. I arched and cried out from the sharp pain that ran up my arms to my shoulders. You laughed, bit my neck, and twisted my nipple, a little too hard, between thumbnail and forefinger. "Beg me."

"Please," I said softly.

You slapped me again, harder. I braced myself to avoid banging my face against the wall. You pulled my wrists higher up my back. "Again."

"Please, please," I said. "Put your dick in me."

"Shut up," you said, and hit me hard across the ass, licked two fingers and plunged them in my cunt. I squeezed them with my whole body and you thrust in and out, your hand slippery, adding a third. I cried out in surprise. "Shut up!" And then a fourth finger. For a while you rammed into and slid out of me, your fingers finding that spot and pulling out, thrusting in and pulling out, your body slamming my tits and shoulders against the wall. You hurt me again and again, and each time I almost came, till I was exhausted, leaning back against you. You banged my breasts and face into the wall one last time, your hips so hard and fingers so deep into me that I thought I would break, I thought I would come, and then you pulled out again.

"You want my dick, you little cunt? You want me to fuck you?"

"Yeah," I whispered. I had played this game before, but only at parties, with all those sex-positive riot grrls and their rulebooks. I was used to knowing what was going to happen. It was a good sign that you kept asking me if I wanted you, it meant you weren't an ax murderer. Not that I cared so much at that moment. No one had ever hit me so hard, or fucked me so mercilessly, and I knew you were going to do worse. My cunt and pulse pounded in fear and frenzy. Come *on*.

"Face me." You jerked my head around by the hair, and I whipped around, sat on my haunches in front of you. You knelt facing me, held my hands tight against my back, untied the rope, and in one motion pulled my wrists in front of me and tied them again.

"Show me. Touch yourself."

I couldn't get in deep enough, could just play around the opening, touch the engorged lips but not hard enough. You laughed at me with your red mouth, arching your back. Your breasts were tight against your sleeveless undershirt, and your chin jutting out in the dark between us, your dick bulging against your pants. You stood up. "Unzip my pants." I brought my wet fingers to your fly, unzipped it, unbuttoned your pants, and tugged at the waist of your boxers. A little black tattoo, a long, swirling 3-shape, shone on your right hipbone. You pushed your purple dick into my mouth and then pulled out, slapped my cheeks with it twice. "Suck it, you little slut." Your hand tightened in my hair. I licked the base, circled the head with my tongue. You pushed into my mouth and I swallowed as much as I could, sucking hard. I rubbed my thighs together, felt the pounding between my legs.

"I'm so fucking hard," you said. "I'm going to fuck you in the throat, in the cunt, in the ass. I'm going to make you beg, you little bitch, and you won't know whether you're begging for me to stop or never stop."

All of a sudden a wave of panic swept through me, and confusion, and something worse. I slumped on my haunches, rested my head on your strong hip, and started to cry. You stroked my face. "Do you want to talk about it?"

"No. I don't want to talk about it." If I let myself go in these moments, let myself have flashbacks, feel anger towards the person there with me, it can go on and on. Stopping is no solution. Or that's how it feels—that I'll never feel desire again, that I'll be flooded with unrelenting anger like pain, that I'll kill rather than feel pleasure. I can't stop. I sniffled, straightened up, wiped my face with the back of my hand, and played with the fallen waist of your sailor pants, touching the crease between them and your soft skin.

"How long have you been a boy?"

"I'm not. I pass."

I spent a long minute studying you.

"Well? Do you want me to fuck you or what?"

"Untie me," I said.

You didn't look that pissed off, just took the razor from your pocket, snapped it open, and cut the rope. It fell onto my knees, and you snapped the razor closed and threw it on the floor. "Now what?"

I jumped to my feet and pounced on you. You put your hand on my hip and I took it in mine, twisted it behind your back, and backed you up against your desk. "Oh," you gasped. Books, papers, your cell phone and pencils crashed onto the floor. I slid my hand into your fly, under the waist of your boxers, and touched you where your dick met your body. You shuddered a little, arched your breasts into me through the thin cotton. "I'm going to fuck you," I snarled into your cheek. "I'm going to put my whole hand in you. You fucking cunt."

"No," you whispered, smiling, and edged your ass back on the desk, opening your legs a little. I slapped you hard twice across your beautiful cheekbones. "Stop smiling." I licked your lips, your teeth. We kissed. "Open your legs wider," I said, and edged two fingers against the lips of your cunt. You sighed, pulled your arm out of my grasp, and rested your palms against my chest.

We kissed again, and in one motion you knocked me onto my back. I shuddered and gasped as my head hit the floor, dizzy from pain. "Fuck you."

"I'm going to fuck you. I'm going to fuck you." You knelt next to me, held my wrists above my head in your right fist, and with your right knee pinned my struggling left leg. "Come on, play nice," you coaxed. I kicked you away with my right leg, and you took hold of my knee and held it down bent, against the floor, my legs open. I was so hot from the force and the closeness of your body that I forgot what I had wanted to do. I wanted you to make me, force me, hurt me, show me your desire. I closed my legs again and you opened them, hard, with your knee, ran your hand up between them to my clit. "You want me to fuck you so bad," you said. "So play nice and I won't hurt you." You leaned over me, your shirt hiked up your belly, your breasts smooth and swaying, still pinning my wrists and knees to the ground. With your free hand you caressed your dick, sighed a little, played with my clit, laughed at my outrage, and spit on your hand. "What's the matter? You still a virgin? You afraid it's going to hurt?"

"Yeah," I said. I pulled my right hand free and shoved you, but you didn't fall. You smacked me hard in the face and then again, across my tits. "Don't worry. It's only going to hurt when I fuck you in the ass." My cheeks and nipples stung. You spat on your free hand, passed it across your dick and entered me, hard. Your cock was thick, and you moved in and out fast, each time making me wait a little too long and then, as I was about to cry in desire and frustration, penetrated me deep, deep. I couldn't believe you were fucking me with a dick lubed only with spit. You licked your fingers and swiftly put two in my ass, fucking me so that as your dick went in, your fingers came out. You swung your breasts over my face teasingly. "Please, please," I moaned, "please, anything you say, please. Ohhhhnnnnhh, oh, oh."

I don't know how long you fucked me, your breath coming hard, your face flushed. "Oh, god," I said, "Please, god, please, please." Your grip on my wrists tightened as you came, and you trembled and shook, thrusting harder and harder into me. I struggled against your hands, fucked your cock and fingers. I came hard, biting your neck, feeling my cunt contract over and over, fast. You knelt, panting, your face in my neck, rocking back on your haunches, sweat glistening on your auburn breasts and my come shiny on your erect dick, still making little coming noises. I held the back of your smooth neck, stroked your spine. "Shh, shh." You kissed me, tasting mysteriously of cunt. I felt a sudden, frightening wave of softness, of compassion, like my chest was open under your hand. When you finished shivering and rocking, you said in your boy's voice, "Mo? Will you make me a soft-boiled egg?"

"Sure." The dark still came in the windows. I went into the kitchen, put the water on, and turned on the radio.

About the Authors

SAMIYA A. BASHIR is a poet, writer and editor. She is coeditor, with Tony Medina and Quraysh Ali Lansana, of *Role Call: A Generational Anthology of Social & Political Black Literature & Art*. Winner of the 2002 Lesbian Writers Fund Poetry Award, Bashir is currently completing *Blood & Wine* (Third World Press), her debut collection of poetry, and editing *Best Black Women's Erotica 2* (Cleis Press) both due out in 2003. Bashir's work has most recently appeared in *Obsidian III*; *Kuumba: Journal of Black Lesbian & Gay Literature & Art #4*; *Contemporary American Women Poets*; *Arise*; and *Bum Rush the Page: A Def Poetry Jam*.

BETTY BLUE is a neurotic sex-kitten who burns down houses and stabs people with forks in the South of France...er, no, that's the movie. Betty Blue is a neurotic sex-kitten who writes trashy smut in San Francisco and only very occasionally stabs people with forks. Betty's fiction has appeared in *Best Women's Erotica 2003*, *Best Lesbian Love Stories*, *Best*

Lesbian Erotica 2002, *Best Bisexual Erotica*, and *Tough Girls: Down and Dirty Dyke Erotica.*

Under her real name, **CHEYENNE BLUE** writes back country travel guides for the western United States and Europe, and she often blends outdoor themes into her erotica. Her writing has appeared in *Best Women's Erotica 2002*, *Clean Sheets*, www.mindcaviar.com, and www.brilliantsmut.com. It is forthcoming in *Best Women's Erotica 2003*, *The Mammoth Book of Best New Erotica 2002*, and *Clean Sheets.*

SHIREEN DEEN was born in New York City and grew up in Connecticut. She graduated from college with a self-designed degree in writing and theater. She is an actor, playwright, and social activist. She currently writes for the *Valley Advocate* in Massachusetts. Her work has been published in the *Coe Review* and the *Peregrine Journal*. Her play, *Shut Up*, has won two awards, the Dennis Johnston Playwriting Prize and the James Baldwin Award.

KENYA DEVOREAUX is an always aroused and always flushed copper-colored femme whose alter ego Vivienne Page forever has her up at midnight touching herself to the hot and heavy fantasies which ultimately become published works. Currently, Kenya and Miss Page are "teasing out" a collection of lesbo-erotic stories in a book entitled *Crushing Cotton*. Kenya loves pussy and all things womanly, Vivienne hopes the stories she creates bring you bliss and many more orgasms to come.

MARÍA HELENA DOLAN is just your average lightnin'-eatin', thunder-drinkin', eye-quakin', Earth-shakin', pistol-packin', patriarchy-whackin' Latina living on the edge of Hotlanta with lush tropical plants, Feline Supremacists, and spousal unit. She has a collection of Southern-accented erotica and a Lesbian Vampire Mother novel that are both looking for a fearless publisher.

KATE DOMINIC is the author of *Any 2 People Kissing* (Down There Press). Her stories appear in the anthologies *Herotica 6 & 7*, *Best Lesbian Erotica 2000 & 2002*, *Best Women's Erotica 2000 & 2001*, *Tough Girls*, *Wicked Words I & IV*, *Strange Bedfellows*, and many other anthologies and magazines under a variety of pen names.

R. GAY is the fiction editor for *Scarlet Letters*. Her writing can also be found in *Love Shook My Heart 2*; *Best Lesbian Erotica 2002*; *Shameless: Women's Intimate Erotica*; *Herotica 7*; *Best Transgender Erotica*; *Best Bisexual Women's Erotica*; *Sweet Life*; and others.

SACCHI GREEN writes in western Massachusetts and the mountains of New Hampshire. She's contributed to a sizable stack of books with inspirational covers, including four volumes of *Best Lesbian Erotica* and two of *Best Women's Erotica*; *Best Transgender Erotica*; and most recently *Shameless: Women's Intimate Erotica*; *Wet: More Aqua Erotica*; and the June/July 2002 issue of *On Our Backs*. Coming soon is *Wild Flesh*, an e-book collection of her erotic science fiction and fantasy.

LAUREL HALBANY has managed, to her astonishment, to combine being a hopeless geek with having a sex life. Her writing for role-playing games has been published in amateur press publications and in the Ars Magica *Bestiary*. She lives in Silicon Valley, locally referred to as "Valley of the Dorks," and wishes they all could be California girls.

LYNNE JAMNECK is a twenty-six-year-old writer, photographer, and digital artist from Cape Town, South Africa. Her work has been published in *EOTU E-Zine*, *On Our Backs*, www.scarletletters.com, www.horrorfind.com, www.bloodlust-uk.com and *Diva* magazine. She is a regular contributor to *Womyn* magazine (South Africa). Her first mystery novel, *Down the Rabbit Hole* was published by Artemis Press. She spends her days creating fastidiously, kept fastened to the real world by her partner Heidi, and Maya the Cat.

TAMAI KOBAYASHI was born in Japan and raised in Canada. She is a screenwriter, songwriter, poet and author of *Exile and the Heart* (Women's Press). Her collection of erotic short stories *Quixotic Erotic* is forthcoming from Arsenal Pulp Press in the spring of 2003. Her work has appeared in *West Coast Line*, *Fireweed*, *Prairie Fire* and *absinthe*. She lives in Toronto.

ROSALIND CHRISTINE LLOYD'S work has appeared in many anthologies including *Best American Erotica 2001*, *Skin Deep*, *Set in Stone*, *Faster Pussycat*, *Pillowtalk II*, *Hot & Bothered II* & *III*, as well as on *Kuma* and *Amoret*, both erotic websites for literature. Currently working with a women's nonprofit organization, this womyn of color, native New Yorker and Harlem resident lives with two unruly felines, Suga and Nile, while obsessing over her first novel.

SKIAN MCGUIRE is a working-class, Quaker leatherdyke who lives in the wilds of western Massachusetts with her dog pack, a collection of motorcycles, and her partner of twenty years. Her work has appeared in *Best Bisexual Erotica 2*, *Best Lesbian Erotica 1999, 2001, & 2002*, *HLFQ*, and the webzines *Nest O' Vipers* and *Suspect Thoughts*, and will soon be in *On Our Backs*.

CATHERINE MILLER's erotic stories have appeared in *Dare Magazine*, *Biblio Eroticus*, *Australian Women's Forum*, and the Black Lace anthology *Wicked Words 5*. Other short fiction of hers has been published in *The Storyteller*, *Kids' Highway*, *Skipping Stones*, *Short Stories Bimonthly* and *Phoebe*. She is a mental health professional who believes in the power of erotic and emotional intimacy. Born and bred in New York City, Dr. Miller now lives in the heart of Northern California wine country, where she enjoys wide open spaces, horseback riding, and the all-too-occasional journey to the tropics for warm-water scuba diving.

AJ MILLER-BRAY is a devoted Washingtonian (as in the District, not the state) and a high femme with a notorious foot fetish. She lives with her husband of three years and hopes to attend culinary school with her best friend. AJ is an unwavering fan of all things Celtic. Her work has also appeared in *Best Lesbian Erotica 2002*.

MARY ANNE MOHANRAJ is the author of *Torn Shapes of Desire*; editor of *Aqua Erotica* and *Wet: More Aqua Erotica*; consulting editor for *Herotica 7*; and has been published widely. She founded the erotic webzine, www.cleansheets.com and serves as editor-in-chief for the Hugo-nominated SciFi webzine www.strangehorizons.com. Mohanraj has received the Scowcroft Prize for Fiction and holds a Steffenson-Canon fellowship in the Humanities. Her website is www.mamohanraj.com.

PEGGY MUNSON's recent work has appeared in *Tough Girls*; *Best Bisexual Erotica 2*; *On Our Backs: The Best Erotic Fiction*; and elsewhere. She has stories in the '98, '99 '00, '01, '02, and *Best of* editions of *Best Lesbian Erotica*. Her rappelling consultant says that the stunts performed in this story will cut off most circulation to the pelvis (erotic pelvic asphyxia-tion?). She is hoping the actual story will have the opposite effect. She is putting together a self-aggrandizing website, so dot-com her name in your browser soon.

MADELEINE OH is a transplanted Brit, retired LD teacher, and grandmother now living in Ohio with her husband of thirty years. She has erotic short stories in *Best Women's Erotica 2001*, *Wicked Words 6*, *Herotica 7* and several magazines including *For Women*, *Eroticus*, and *Blue Food*. Her erotic novel *Power Exchange* is available from www.ellorascave.com.

ANA PERIL is a BA candidate in Comparative Literature. She has produced for Dyke TV, and her fiction and nonfic-tion work has appeared in publications such as *Current*. She is currently a dyke and trans rights activist on campus, and is working on a documentary film about queer Jewish women in early twentieth-century New York.

ELSPETH POTTER lives in Philadelphia, where she reads and writes a lot of genre fiction. Her credits include *Best Lesbian Erotica 2001 & 2002*, *Best Women's Erotica 2002*, and *Tough Girls: Down and Dirty Dyke Erotica* which was nominated for a Lambda Literary Award. She was a big fan of Miss Baker as a child, and might consider going into space herself if paid one billion dollars up front.

CAROL ROSENFELD is a New York City-based writer and poet. Her work appears in *Best Lesbian Erotica 1999* (Cleis) and *Poetry Nation* (Vehicule). Carol also has stories in two anthologies that will be published in 2003: *Shadows of the Night: Unusual Queer Tales* (Haworth) and *Back to Basics: A Butch/Femme Erotic Journey* (Bella Books). She is working on a novel, *Fool's Mushroom*. Her favorite New York City museum is The Metropolitan Museum of Art.

JULIE LEVIN RUSSO is waiting to see what happens. She recently graduated from Swarthmore College, where she facilitated erotic writing workshops and collaboratively produced Swarthmore's first smut 'zine, *Unmentionables*, in which "Elizabeth" first appeared. She also writes dirty fan fiction, as well as academic articles about it. She currently lives a life of adventure in New York City, where you may spot her doing something naughty (if you know where to look). This is her first publication.

SHARON WACHSLER is a writer, humorist, and disability-rights activist who lives with her service dogs in Western Massachusetts. Sharon's work has appeared in *Ragged Edge*, *Moxie*, *Sojourner*, and *Bitch*. Previous anthology credits include *Restricted Access* and *Yentl's Revenge*. Sharon's disability-rights cartoons can be viewed at www.SickHumorPostcards.com. Her monthly humor column is at www.AbilityMaine.org. Sharon can't throw, catch, or bat to save her life.

KYLE WALKER's work has appeared under many names and in many forms: onstage (the 2002 HomoGENIUS Festival), on the page (*Gargoyle*, *The Catholic Review*, *Writer's Digest*), and on the Internet ("Sticks and Balls" was winner of *Hottlead*'s Erotic Fiction contest). During the day, Kyle edits nonfiction books on a completely different topic.

About the Editors

CHERYL CLARKE is an African-American, lesbian-feminist poet and author of four books of poetry: *Narratives: Poems in the Tradition of Black Women, Living as a Lesbian, Humid Pitch,* and *Experimental Love.* Her poems, essays, and book reviews have appeared in numerous publications, including *This Bridge Called My Back, Home Girls, Inversions, The Persistent Desire, Feminist Studies,* and *The Black Scholar.* She is the Director of Diverse Community Affairs and Lesbian-Gay Concerns at Rutgers University.

TRISTAN TAORMINO is the award-winning author of three books: *True Lust: Adventures in Sex, Porn and Perversion; Pucker Up: A Hands-on Guide to Ecstatic Sex;* and *The Ultimate Guide to Anal Sex for Women.* She is director, producer and star of two videos based on her book, *Tristan Taormino's Ultimate Guide to Anal Sex for Women 1 & 2,* which are distributed by Evil Angel Video. She is a columnist for *The Village Voice* and *Taboo* and series editor of *Best Lesbian Erotica,* for which she has edited nine volumes. She

has been featured in over three hundred publications includ-
ing *The New York Times, Redbook, Glamour, Cosmopolitan,
Playboy, Penthouse, Entertainment Weekly, Vibe,* and *Men's
Health.* She has appeared on NBC's *The Other Half,* MTV,
HBO's *Real Sex, The Howard Stern Show, The Discovery
Channel, Oxygen,* and *Loveline.* She teaches sexuality
workshops around the country and her official website is
www.puckerup.com.